DEATH BY BEER

A SUDS FERGUSON MYSTERY

WADE FOWLER

MILFORD
HOUSE
an imprint of Sunbury Press, Inc.
Mechanicsburg, PA USA

MILFORD HOUSE

an imprint of Sunbury Press, Inc.
Mechanicsburg, PA USA

Copyright © 2020 by Wade Fowler.
Cover Copyright © 2020 by Sunbury Press, Inc.

For information about special discounts for bulk purchases, please contact Sunbury Press Orders Dept. at (855) 338-8359 or orders@sunburypress.com.

To request one of our authors for speaking engagements or book signings, please contact Sunbury Press Publicity Dept. at publicity@sunburypress.com.

FIRST MILFORD HOUSE PRESS EDITION: November 2020

Set in Adobe Garamond | Interior design by Crystal Devine | Cover by Jose Rosado | Edited by Lawrence Knorr.

Publisher's Cataloging-in-Publication Data
Names: Fowler, Wade, author.
Title: Death by beer / Wade Fowler.
Description: First trade paperback edition. | Mechanicsburg, PA : Milford House Press, 2020.
Summary: Ex-cop Suds Ferguson and his estranged wife, Chief of Police Evie Pinson, join forces to solve a series of murders embroiling the staff of Hop Central Craft Brewery.
Identifiers: ISBN : 978-1-62006-331-6 (softcover).
Subjects: FICTION / Humorous / General | FICTION / Mystery & Detective / General | FICTION / Crime.

Product of the United States of America
0 1 1 2 3 5 8 13 21 34 55

Continue the Enlightenment!

MISTER BIG BEER

Franklin Ames loved to watch his brewery employees scurrying about below him. During the remodeling of 2012, he had designed a one-way glass citadel of an office on the brewery's third floor. It gave him a bird's-eye view of the bottling operation on one side of the factory and of the tanks and tasting room on the other. The workers knew that no secrets could be kept from the man upstairs.

Franklin's attention was not on the production line but on the folder that lay open on his desk. Porter Detective Agency confirmed that his no-account stepson had transgressed once again. The girl was 17, giggly, pimply, and pregnant. It was irrefutable. His 16-year-old stepson, Richard "Dickie" Cox, was the father. The little bastard had fathered a little bastard.

"I wonder how much this one is going to cost me?" Franklin mused.

To make matters worse, the girl was the daughter of an assistant brewer who loved tattoos, piercings, and Harley Davidson motorcycles. He was of the sort to exploit the advantage of a daughter impregnated by the boss's stepson.

1

Dickie's Mom, the former Jasmine Cox, represented the one big mistake of Franklin's life. She was a knockout. Drop-dead beautiful and cunning enough to conceal her card-carrying bitchiness behind a facade of expensive clothes, expert makeup, subtle perfume, and coy demeanor.

Jasmine showed up three years after the tortuous cancer death of Franklin's first wife, Emma, just as his libido, dampened by grief and confused as it always had been by conflicting desires, had finally emerged from hibernation. Petite, brunette, and buxom, she broadcast that she was available and willing.

Franklin shouted down his brain and followed his penis to the altar. His second marriage was a statement of his masculinity for the entire world to see. Jasmine was a trophy he wore on his arm. But his ardor for her soon fled like a teenager distancing himself from a furtive fart in the high school cafeteria.

His desk phone buzzed. "Your wife is on the line," Jan Murphy said. His secretary's distaste for Jasmine oozed through the telephone. Jan's devotion to her boss was common knowledge on the brewery floor.

"Speak of the devil," Franklin said.

He sighed, picked up the phone.

"Yes, dear." He imbued the word DEAR with all the disdain four letters could contain.

The sarcasm sailed over Jasmine's head, circling like a vulture over the battlefield of their relationship.

"I don't care what anybody says. Dickie is not the father. He's far too discriminating to stick his Richard into that trailer park trash."

The thought occurred to him that Jasmine was living in a trailer—a doublewide, mind you—when they first met. But that was ammunition to be expended on another day when it would have more effect. Jasmine was in a rage, and that made her, for the moment, bulletproof.

"The DNA evidence is irrefutable," Franklin said. "I have it right here in front of me."

"Well then, that little hussy must have got him drunk and seduced him. You're just going to have to fix this."

"Like I've fixed one under-age DUI and one possession for personal use? I'm into the lawyers for $20,000 so far to clean up Dickie's messes. And this one's going to cost a lot more. You can forget about that Cadillac."

Jasmine climbed down from her high horse. "What do you mean? Abortions are cheap."

"And Catholics will not abide them, or so say the Dubbels. We're talking at least $12,000 a year in child support for the next 18 years. You do the math. Poof. No Cadillac."

"This would be so much simpler if you'd go ahead and adopt Dickie. He's the closest thing to a son you'll ever have."

The low blow made his testicles clinch up. Emma had wanted nothing more than to give him children, but severe endometriosis made that impossible and sometimes led him to seek sexual release elsewhere.

Adopting Dickie was out of the question. He wanted out of his marriage to Jasmine. Unfortunately, there wasn't much he could do about the 200 shares of brewery stock he had given her as a wedding gift . . . unless he could prove she had violated the morals clause of their prenuptial agreement.

For now, he was stuck with her. Bitchiness was not grounds for divorce. Besides, it would be humiliating to tell the world that the canny beer baron wasn't so shrewd after all.

Jasmine's voice jolted him from his reverie. "Well. What do you have to say to that, Mister Big Beer?"

He said what he always said when she raised the issue of his adopting Dickie. "I'll think about it."

"You're a real slow thinker," Jasmine rejoined.

"Measure twice. Cut once," Franklin said. It was advice he wished he had followed.

His laptop dinged, indicating an incoming email had cleared his filters.

"Jasmine! Got to go. Beer business." He hung up on her sputter.

Franklin willed his blood pressure to recede. He launched his email and opened a notice tagged *23andme*. He skimmed the header and then buried himself in the body. He scrolled through the electronic address book on his iPhone and punched the number for his attorney, Ernest Flowers, Esq. Franklin's call circumvented the law office's protective layers of underlings. The man himself answered on the third ring.

"Attorney Ernie," Franklin said because he liked the rhyme of it. "I have another task for you and our gumshoe."

"What may that be?"

Franklin told him.

HOPPY BEER THE BREW FOR YOU

Boyd Porter's first and last encounters with forklifts were disastrous. The first had occurred during a brief stint as a lumberyard jockey twenty years earlier.

On his first day, with no instruction from his supervisor, he removed a skid of 4-by-12-foot drywall from a ceiling-high stack in the warehouse. Shrugging off his inexperience with the I-got-this confidence of youth, he centered the blades and worked the levers, raising the skid off the stack.

He backed away, shifted into forward gear, and headed for the big doors leading to the loading dock, having accomplished all of the tasks on the checklist . . . save one.

Alas, it was the most important of all—lower the blades to clear the doorway.

The collision snapped the fragile wallboard in half. Debris rained down on the forklift as a startled contractor retreated from a cloud of gypsum onto the bed of his half-ton pickup truck, which was backed up to the loading dock.

Reflecting on this, Porter studied the brewery loading dock and its array of five tractor-trailer slips. The overhead doors were open, and Porter could hear the clinking of beer bottles. Sounded like the bottling line was in full production. He iPhoned his employer from the parking lot.

"Be there in five," Franklin Ames said.

Porter climbed the steps to the loading dock and turned his back on the factory, studying the rolling hills of Derry Township, where industrious Mennonite farmers had planted fields of barley and kept pastures for their herds of dairy cows. The barley fed the brewery, and Milton Hershey's candy factory fed the cows and vice versa. The scene was bucolic, a pastoral of 19th-century vintage.

Porter heard the whine of a forklift. Turning, he saw the blades lower as the machine approached the doorway. The forklift rumbled onto the loading dock, boxy and orange. The blades rose again to their fullest extension, trembling under the weight of case upon case of Hoppy Beer, The Brew For You.

Porter didn't have time to be startled. The blades tipped forward, and a tsunami of 16-ounce Hoppy IPA cascaded down on him. Froth from exploding cans turned crimson with his blood as the forklift blades under full pneumatic power crushed him to the concrete floor. The forklift operator, alit, poked gingerly through the debris, picked up Porter's briefcase, and walked away, whistling *Ninety-Nine Bottles of Beer on the Wall*.

TROUBLE BREWING

At age 38, Suds Ferguson had found a job he loved more than being a cop. He was the brand-new head of security at Hop Central Craft Brewery, where employees were encouraged to drink good beer.

If there was one thing Suds was good at, it was drinking beer. He came by his nickname honestly and welcomed it. Sidney is a ridiculous name for a six-foot-seven-inch behemoth. Suds's working-class moniker belied an elitist's palate. A gourmet rather than a gourmand, he disdained the puny pilsners and frothy lagers of mass production and mass consumption.

Suds was no buds of Anheuser Bush.

He reveled in the bitter bite of an IPA. He savored the fruity spiciness of a saison and the heavy coffee oiliness of a double bock. Occasionally when convention required, such as the ritual of watching Sunday afternoon football with friends, he could be found with a pounder can of Pabst Blue Ribbon in hand. But he hated himself on these occasions—for the football and the feckless beer.

Any sport that reveled in pedestrian beer was bad sport as far as Suds was concerned. But awkward adolescence had taught him that kowtowing to social norms was far less painful than swimming upstream against them. He was a geek in the body of an athlete.

No amount of stooping could obscure the fact that he towered above his classmates. He was so big that he was always among the first called when picking sides for flag football or basketball in PE classes. And he accounted well for himself and his teammates in those situations because he was quick and coordinated. But he despised competition, and his teams occasionally lost because he lacked the killer instinct of his smaller classmates.

His internal litany went something like this: *I am six inches taller and thirty pounds heavier than their biggest guy. What does my winning prove, other than I am bigger and stronger than they are, and what virtue is there in that?*

A stint with the military police and keeping the peace with the Harrisburg, Pennsylvania, Police Department had toughened Suds up considerably, but he still was a gentle giant. Oh, he could be mean when the situation demanded. But more often than not, he reverted to his default—conciliation vs. confrontation. His size lent menace to compromise. A heavy hand on the shoulder of an alcohol-sodden pugilist often was enough to turn beer muscles to jelly.

A discriminating palate goes hand in hand with a sensitive sense of smell. As a cop, he seldom went wrong if he followed his nose. The lingering smell of bacon grease on the cash register drawer meant the short-order cook had his hand in the till. The scent of KY Jelly mixed with cinnamon led him to a dilettante who favored an obscure brand of prophylactic, left behind at a sex crime scene.

As he crouched over the pile of beer cans and the crash-dummy awkwardness of the body buried beneath them, Suds caught a whiff of perfume (or was it aftershave?) competing with the essence of barley, hops, and yeast. He had encountered that smell somewhere before. But where?

The forklift was still running. Bloody footprints led to the overhead-door entrance to the factory where a pair of rubber brewers' boots had been abandoned, ending a bloody trail pointed toward the interior of the brewery. Suds didn't recognize the man who lay buried in beer, blood, and froth.

It didn't take a genius to figure out what had happened, but he would leave the sorting out to the police. The active-duty ones. He had taken this cushy job at least in part to avoid scenes such as this. He arose, stepped carefully away from the immediate crime scene, and dug his cell phone from his back pocket.

"Mr. Ames," he said when his boss picked up. "We have a problem. There's a dead man on our loading dock, and it doesn't look like an accident."

"I'll be right down," Franklin Ames said, clicking off the phone.

Something was jarring about the boss's reaction. No surprise. No shock. What was it . . . resignation?

Suds shrugged it off. Did his civic duty. Dialed 911.

CRIME SCENE

Derry Township Police Chief Evie Pinson crouched beside the corpse. "You disturb the crime scene?" she asked.

"Come on, Evie. There's no audience to play to here and no reason to bust my balls," Suds replied.

"If anybody has balls worthy of busting, it's you."

"Show some respect for the dead guy. There no need to air our personal laundry here and now."

Evie wasn't feeling contrite, but she pretended to be. "I hate it when you're right. Do we know who this guy is?"

"Franklin Ames recognized him from the cheap suit. Says he's a private investigator named Boyd Porter."

"Who's Franklin Ames?"

"President of Hop Central Craft Brewery. My big boss."

"Ames have any idea why a PI would wind up dead on the brewery loading dock?"

"Nope, but apparently, Porter was working for Franklin . . ." Suds held up his right hand. "And before you ask, he says it's none of our business."

"What's none of our business?"

"Why Franklin hired Porter. Says it's a personal matter that couldn't possibly have anything to do with Porter's murder."

"Murder? I'll be the judge of that," Evie said.

"I'm sure you will be, but I know Franklin. Won't say shit even if his mouth is full of it."

'Taciturn?"

"More like imperial. He asks questions. He doesn't answer them."

The forklift sputtered to a stop having run out of gas. A black panel van pulled up alongside the loading dock, and the forensic unit for the Pennsylvania State Police piled out. Two men and a woman already suited up with gloves on their hands and baggies on their shoes.

"Who called them in?" Suds asked.

"I did. We don't have the forensic expertise to work this crime scene."

"So you do think it's a murder?"

"Duh!"

"Then we best get out of their way. You'll want to talk to Franklin. He's in his office. He is expecting us. I'll show you the way."

They negotiated the back stairs to the boss's third-floor office suite in silence. Suds's knees were acting up, so he let Evie go first. Gave him a chance to enjoy the view from behind as she climbed the stairs.

"No ogling my ass," she said over her shoulder.

"You used to like it when I ogled."

"Not anymore."

Suds unclipped his ID badge from his belt and waved it in front of the security lock on the second-floor door. A click, a push, and they were inside. Suds nodded at the woman behind the reception desk. It was her job to work the phone and buzz in strangers. "Hey, Suds. Everybody's talking. What's happening on the loading dock?"

Suds punted. "Can't say, Jessie, without Franklin's OK." He waggled a thumb at Evie. "Township police chief needs to talk to Mr. Big Beer."

The camaraderie implicit in Suds's use of the boss's nickname made Jessie giggle. Jessie was cute and flirty, further souring Evie's mood.

Evie followed Suds down a corridor flanked on the left by a row of spacious offices for the white collars. Boxy cubicles were stacked four deep on the right, where the pencil pushers pushed. The cubicle row ended. They passed across the edge of a big common room dominated by ping-pong and foosball tables and a corn hole setup.

Evie cast a disapproving look Suds's way. "Franklin fosters a loose workplace vibe. Says beer is supposed to be fun," he explained.

Evie snarked: "How imperial of him. I suppose you feel right at home."

Suds toreadored the sarcasm. "Best job I've ever had. Hell. They've made me an official beer taster. Biologist says I've got a discriminating palate."

"Biologist?"

"Yep. Good beer is good science. It's all about the proper selection of malt, hops, water, and yeast."

"Yeah. Yeah. You wax poetic with all that home-brewing shit. Always have."

Franklin's office door was open. He was ensconced behind his big desk, drumming his fingers on the desktop.

Suds knocked on the doorframe, and Franklin beckoned them forward. Suds took care of the introductions. "This is township police chief Evie Pinson. She wants to ask you some questions."

Franklin waved them into two office chairs facing his desk. Evie picked up the gauntlet. "Might as well clear the air. We used to be married."

"To each other," Suds added, helpfully.

"I know. I read the papers," Franklin said.

Evie started over. "Suds tells me that the deceased was a private detective in your employ. What exactly was he investigating?"

"A personal matter. I'm sure it had nothing to do with Porter's accident."

"Accident? How does a skid full of 16-ounce beer cans accidentally drop on someone's head from a great height? From the looks of it, someone used the forklift's blades to crush the poor guy's skull."

"So, you're treating this as a murder?" Franklin asked.

"It's certainly not a suicide," Evie said. "The trail of bloody footprints leading from the murder scene belies that. Not to mention the bloody rubber boots just inside the doorway. Now I'll ask you again. What was Boyd Porter investigating?"

Franklin sighed. "You are determined to air my dirty laundry." He opened a drawer, pulled out a folder, and slid it across his desk.

Suds was surprised that his boss caved so easily. He cocked his head, and Franklin nodded. "I've reconsidered stonewalling the police chief, Suds. This isn't a time to stand on propriety."

To Evie, Franklin added: "You can keep the folder. I know what it contains. To summarize, Porter investigated a claim by Chuck Dubbel, an assistant brewer, that my stepson, Richard Cox, impregnated his daughter, Lisa. Dickie is 16, and Lisa, 17. Both Lisa and Dickie work for me part-time. DNA results from amniotic fluid prove my stepson is the father. The Dubbels are Catholic. So abortion is off the table. I'll be paying child support until Dickie's old enough to pick up the tab."

Evie looked up from the folder. "I would have thought this sort of thing is more a matter for your attorney."

Franklin nodded. "Actually, I hired Porter at my attorney's suggestion."

"Who he?" Evie asked.

"Ernest Flowers. Has an office on Front Street in the burg. But he will trip you up over attorney-client privilege 'cause that's what I pay him to do."

"That begs the question, why hire a PI?" Evie said.

"Lisa Dubbel has a reputation. There were other candidates for fatherhood among the staff here at the brewery. I wanted to rule them out before I paid up."

"So, there's no question your step-son is the father?"

"That's right."

"What was Porter doing on your loading dock?"

"I have no idea. Some sort of follow-up, maybe?"

Evie arose. "Do you have a business card? Something with your private number on it?"

Franklin slid open his top drawer. Pulled out a business card, turned it over and wrote on the back of it. He handed the card to Evie.

She nodded, slid Ames's card into the folder, which she secured under her arm.

Suds stood up, too, ready to escort her from the office. Evie waved a hand dismissively. "I can find my own way out. I need to check in with the forensic team, and I don't want you blundering about my crime scene."

"Have a seat Suds. There's another matter I need to discuss with you," Franklin said.

The two men watched as she left the office.

"Pretty woman," Franklin observed. "Big. Just like you."

"Determined woman," Suds added. "Now, about that other matter?"

"They tell me you were a good investigator in your day."

"Who's they?"

"Porter for one."

"Never met the man."

"Porter was aware of your reputation."

Suds shrugged. "And?"

"I was less than candid with your ex-wife. Porter was working on something else for me. He was on his way to deliver his report when . . ."

Suds winced. "That was something you probably should have told the police chief."

"You're not going to tell her, are you?"

Suds shook his head. "I may have to. But I work for you. I'll be discreet until I can't be."

Franklin relaxed.

"OK, here it is. Porter called me from the parking lot about 8 A.M. I told him to meet me on the loading dock."

"Why there?"

"Didn't want the office staff to know he was working for me . . . again."

"What was he investigating?" Suds asked.

"That's a sensitive matter. Not ready to tell anyone yet. Until I know what was in his report. By the time I got to the loading dock, he was dead, and I couldn't find the silly little briefcase he always carried with him."

"The bloody brewer's boots?" Suds asked.

"They are mine."

"And will Evie be able to determine that?"

"Probably. If she dusts them. I'm in the Navy reserve. My fingerprints are in the system."

"Shit."

"Yep. Shit. I wasn't thinking clearly. The shock and all, but I didn't want to go clomping around the office in bloody boots."

"So, what do you want me to do?"

"Run your own investigation. I need to offer other suspects in the event the police show up to arrest me."

"Where do you suggest I start?"

"I need Porter's report. There must be a copy in his office somewhere."

"You're asking me to break and enter?"

"I'm asking you to do whatever it takes."

Suds made a tent of his fingertips. Studied his boss over the top of it. "I appreciate what you've done for me. This is the best job I've ever had. But I won't be party to a cover-up if the evidence convinces me that you did it."

"Nor would I want you to," Franklin said. "You have impeccable taste in beer. That's an attribute worthy of my trust."

BREAKING AND ENTERING

Tuesday, July 10, 2018

The late Boyd Porter had a dog, a pug named Sally. Suds knew this because Franklin had told him that the PI was perpetually covered in dog hair. So much so that Porter's mere presence elicited an allergic reaction in people like Franklin, afflicted by a sensitive immune system.

"I always sneezed when that man entered the room," Franklin said. "Porter apologized. Said it was his pug. Said 'Sally is a shedder.'"

Thank god Sally wasn't a Rottweiler. Suds could handle a pug, if it came down to it.

Porter's ranch house lay behind a thicket of landscaping. This made Suds's current enterprise of breaking and entering easier than it might otherwise have been. Prying eyes would not see even a big man kneeling before the front door lock because the porch was obscured by tall shrubbery.

Suds circled the block twice casing the joint. The development was otherwise so well-kept that the neighbors would immediately recognize the approach of a stranger. Suds parked his nondescript dark blue Ford Crown Vic four blocks away next to a convenience store Dumpster. He hoofed it to 421 Sharon Street, Porter's address.

Suds's burglar kit included a credit card to foil a deadbolt and a series of picks he had recovered from criminals and crime scenes over the years. He was prepared to beat a hasty retreat if he couldn't foil Porter's security system. An ADT decal on the edge of the driveway portended trouble.

The credit card slipped the deadbolt. And there was no beeping as Suds pushed open the front door. The ADT decal was either a decoy or Porter was behind in his payments. The house smelled like stale farts and cheap aftershave. Suds asked himself if it was the same aroma he had divined at the crime scene and decided it was not. Essence of Porter was of the Aqua Velva ilk. The smell that permeated the hops and barley of the crime scene was more Channel-ish.

A quick run-through of Porter's three-bedroom ranch told much about its late occupant. Sally was not evident, but a wispy layer of dog hair lay on the hardwood of the living room and intertwined the comforter on Porter's bed. Suds wondered what had become of the dog. There was an empty water bowl on the kitchen floor but no barking and no stench of a dead dog. A friend, or relative, must have rescued Sally.

Bureau and nightstand drawers in the master bedroom revealed women's panties, a nightgown, a vibrator, condoms and KY jelly. The DVD player disgorged a disc labeled "Asian Titty Fest."

Apparently Porter entertained.

The kitchen was neat. A layer of dust on flat surfaces bespoke short-term neglect, but there were no dirty dishes in the sink nor crumbs on the countertops. The larder was well stocked with cereals, canned goods, snacks, and pasta. The Mr. Coffee carafe had the patina of regular use and the refrigerator contained half-and-half, iceberg lettuce, milk, butter and Modela Negra, a pretty damn good beer, in Suds' estimation. Two sirloins marinated in what he guessed was Burgundy wine. Or maybe a Sauvignon. Looked like Porter's murder had forestalled a romantic dinner for two.

He found a laptop situated precisely in the middle of the desk in Porter's home office, which occupied what once had been the dining room. The desk faced a window mostly obscured by a rhododendron bush that had grown unchecked for decades from the look of it.

The Toshiba Satellite, still plugged into an outlet, awoke when Suds drew his finger over the touchpad and he was encouraged to input a password.

Suds shrugged, guessed, and tapped out s-a-l-l-y. That didn't work, so he tried S-a-l-l-y. Bingo! Case sensitive. Porter didn't have much of an imagination. The desktop materialized, and Suds sat down behind the dead man's desk to see what secrets the laptop might reveal.

He was so engrossed in that enterprise that he failed to recognize the approach outside of a tricked-out Ford Escape bearing a door decal reading "Derry Township Police Department." He didn't hear the whisper of polyestered thighs as a pretty cop emerged from the driver's side and slammed the door.

Among the folders on the computer desktop was a file marked "Franklin Ames." Suds pulled a memory stick from his pocket, inserted it in the USB port and dragged the Ames's folder onto the memory stick's icon. The files copied. When the progress bar stopped. He dragged the memory stick icon into the trash. After a moment's thought, he deleted the original files. Now he had the only copy of what the private detective had been up to in Ames's employ.

By the time the squeak of rubber soles on hardwood alerted him to the ominous possibility he was no longer alone, it was too late to do anything but yank the memory stick, pocket it and close the lid of the laptop. A password would be required to reactivate the computer and Suds intended to keep that secret to himself, at least for the time being.

"I've dreamed about this moment for months," a woman voice said.

"What moment is that?" Suds asked.

"The one where I get to haul your ass to jail."

"You can put away the gun. I am not armed." Suds' ex-wife re-holstered her sidearm.

"Find anything interesting on the computer?" Evie asked.

Suds didn't lie, but he dodged the question. "It's password protected. And the password is not his birthday."

"How would you know that?"

"Facebook."

"So the old dog has learned some new tricks. Have you figured out how to beat a breaking-and-entering rap?"

"Yeah. How bout I show you mine."

"Already seen it. And I wasn't impressed."

"Ha. Ha. You know what I mean. I know some stuff that might help with the Boyd Porter murder investigation. I'm willing to share for a get-out-of-jail-free card."

"So give it up," Evie said.

Suds arose, stepped toward his ex-wife and gestured toward the kitchen. "There's a table in there. Let's sit down at it and talk."

"So," Evie said when they were settled at Boyd Porter's kitchen table.

"Porter was investigating something else for Franklin Ames."

"What?"

"Not sure yet. Franklin won't say. I was hoping the answer lay in Porter's computer."

"I'll turn his computer over to the geek squad, but you haven't told me anything to persuade me not to file burglary charges," Evie said.

"My gut just tells me there is another layer to Franklin's relationship with Porter. I'm not sure what that is, but I'm almost certain Franklin didn't kill Porter."

"Why is that?"

"Franklin is an aggressive businessman but he isn't a killer, and even if he were he's far too smart to commit a murder where he would be the prime suspect."

"What makes you think he's a suspect?"

"The bloody brewer's boots are his."

"How do you know?"

"He told me so, right before he asked me to run a parallel investigation. Said Porter called him from the parking lot. By the time Franklin arrived on the loading dock Porter was dead. I told him I would work the murder but that I wouldn't hesitate to implicate him if my investigation indicated he was guilty."

"What did he say to that?"

"He said he wouldn't expect anything less of me."

"And that persuaded you he was innocent?"

"Persuaded me to withhold judgment."

Evie circled back. "So why is Franklin being so coy about what Porter was working on?"

"My guess is that he was trying to get some dirt on his wife, the former Jasmine Cox. She's a real bitch and it wouldn't surprise me if Franklin was looking for grounds for a no-fault divorce."

"Wouldn't he have had her sign a pre-nup?" Evie asked.

"That is a question for his lawyer."

Evie nodded. "I'll ask."

"So that makes his wife a prime suspect. Or maybe her son, Richard Cox," Suds said.

"The little prick?"

"The little prick," Suds agreed.

"If Franklin shoots so straight, why wouldn't he just come out and tell you he thought his wife was screwing around?"

"Yeah. That bugs me, too. So how about it Evie? You willing to look the other way on the breaking-and-entering?"

"Only if you tell me why you fucked Linda Fontaine."

"Because she was willing and for some time you hadn't been."

Evie's eyes teared. "Rufus died and you weren't there for me."

"Rufus. I still can't forgive you for giving our son that name."

"It was Dad's name . . ."

Suds held up his hand like a traffic cop. "I know. I know. Grief is a royal bitch. She compels you to do stuff you never would do had she not darkened your door."

"Our door," Evie said.

"That's right. Our door. But you changed the lock and wouldn't give me the key. After awhile I got tired of knocking."

"So you fucked Detective Sergeant Linda Fontaine in the evidence room and lost your job for fraternization."

"And you filed for divorce and then wouldn't let me explain," Suds said.

"I miss Rufus."

"I miss Rufus, too."

"God damn leukemia."

"God damn leukemia," Suds agreed.

BACKTRACKING THE TRAIL

Suds plugged the memory stick into his laptop. When the icon flashed on his desktop, he opened it and studied the file menu, which contained names such as: Fetal DNA, Richard Cox DNA, Jasmine Cox DNA, Lisa Dubbel DNA, Julie Dubbel DNA, Charles Dubbel DNA, Cloyd Jackson DNA, Jasmine Cox Surveillance, DNA Analysis, Franklin Ames, DNA, Sample Key, and Charleston Travel Itinerary.

The DNA files made sense. He didn't bother opening them, at least not right away. He wondered most about the Charleston itinerary. So he opened it first. It was an expense report of a trip Porter had taken to Charleston, South Carolina, two weeks ago. He had flown first class and stayed at a Hilton property. There was a receipt for four meals, a breakfast, lunch, and two dinners. Also expensed were Uber fare receipts for trips to and from the airport and to and from the hotel to an address in Charleston.

Perplexed, Suds easter-egged through the other files and found what he expected. DNA reports on the principals in Lisa Dubbel's pregnancy. The file marked Sample Key assigned a letter that corresponded with the name of each person sampled. Diller, apparently, had devised a blind testing of the samples. Cloyd Jackson, Suds surmised, was another plausible suspect in the pregnancy of Lisa Dubbel, but the DNA analysis clearly fingered Dickie Cox as the father of the unborn child, which incidentally was a girl, according to the sampling key.

The Jasmine Cox Surveillance file documented Porter's shadowing of Franklin's wife. It gave times dates, destinations, and remarks on what his surveillance had revealed, which was, basically, nothing. Jasmine Cox went to the grocery store, beauty salon, gym, her Bunko group, and church. Nowhere else.

"Church," Suds thought. "This woman is way too squeaky clean." Porter's report certainly didn't jibe with Jasmine's rep around the brewery. Jan Murphy had once confided that Jasmine was so bitchy she made other bitches look lame. Suds thought about it for a while and concluded that even churchgoers could be bitches.

The Charleston trip had to relate to Porter's other and mysterious assignment on Franklin's behalf. Suds reopened the Charleston file and made note of the address Porter had visited via Uber. It turned out to be the residence of Graham and Geraldine Smith. Google Earth revealed the Smiths' house to be a brick, two-story colonial. An impressive edifice in just about any community. Suds had no idea of its value in the Charleston suburbs. Trulia had the answer. The Smiths had purchased their home six years ago for $1.3 million. Whitepages.com and Google couldn't discern a specific phone number for a Geraldine Smith at that address.

Was it worth a trip to Charleston on the company's dime? Suds decided to put the question to Franklin Ames.

He called him. The boss didn't hesitate.

"Charleston. Haven't seen that expense report. Go there and tell me what you find out."

Suds's next call was to an old friend. Harrison Ford. Not the actor. His old partner as a rookie on the Harrisburg PD. Harry had moved to Charleston with his second wife, joined the local police force, and segued into a job as a security consultant. Suds got him on the phone and consulted.

"What can you tell me about Graham and Geraldine Smith?" he asked.

"Jesus Suds. There have to be a thousand Smiths in Charleston."

"Thirteen-thousand, four hundred and seventy-eight, according to white pages dot com. These Smiths live at 2323 Spanish Moss Drive."

"Spanish Moss, huh? That's an exclusive address."

"I wouldn't know."

"I would. They pay me to know that sort of thing."

"Which is why I called you in the first place."

"I thought it was because you missed your old partner."

"Like a case of the hemorrhoids," Suds said.

"You were the pain in the ass," Harry rejoined.

"That's what Evie says."

"How is Evie?"

"Fine. She divorced me."

"Which is why she's fine."

"I could always count on your support."

"That's what I'm here for," Harry said.

"That and to find out who the hell are Graham and Geraldine Smith. You can tell me when I get there."

"You're coming down?"

"Yeah. I arrive tomorrow at 1:30 P.M. Meet me at the airport?"

"You can count on it buddy. And I'm sorry about Evie."

"Rufus died. Leukemia."

"Shit."

"Shit," Suds agreed.

"You can tell me all about it over a couple of beers . . . I always thought Evie was a keeper."

"She is. I wasn't."

THE PLOT THICKENS

Evie regarded Chuck Dubbel from across the Formica-topped folding table in the break room at Hop Central Craft Brewing Company. Franklin Ames had made the space available to interview potential witnesses to the demise of Boyd Porter.

"When is the baby due?" she asked.

"What baby?"

"Don't be disingenuous, Mr. Dubbel.

Dubbel scratched his right elbow, which was coiled with tattooed serpents. "What's disingenuous mean?"

"Pretending you don't know something you know I know you know."

"Huh?"

"It means you know that your daughter is pregnant and that Dickie Cox is the father."

"The little fucker."

"Apparently so," Evie agreed.

"The baby's due in August, the 12th. I think. Julie keeps track of that sort of stuff."

"Julie's your wife?"

Dubbel nodded. "That's right."

"What sort of accommodation have you reached with Dickie?"

"Accommodation?"

"How much is he going to pay in child support?"

"My lawyer is negotiating that with the boss's lawyer."

Evie went fishing. "I heard that maybe Dickie isn't the father."

Dubbel slammed his hand down on the Formica. "Whoever said that is a God damn liar. My little Lisa is a good girl. Dickie was her first. I'd make him marry her if he was old enough."

Dubbel was her third interview of the afternoon. The others had confirmed what Franklin had said. Precious Lisa was the company pump.

Evie changed tacks. "Did you know Boyd Porter?"

"The dead guy?"

She nodded.

"I may have seen him around."

"Around where?"

"In the parking lot. Talking to Mrs. Ames."

The revelation startled Evie. "When?"

"Couple weeks ago."

"How did you know it was Porter?"

"I asked Jan Murphy. We arrived at the same time for our shift. I saw the two of them—Porter and Jasmine, that is—arguing and asked Jan, 'Who's the dude?' She says 'Boyd Porter, a private detective who works for the boss.'"

"How did you know they were arguing?"

Dubbel stabbed the air between them with his right index finger. "Mrs. Ames jabbed him in the chest like this."

"Could you hear what they were saying?"

"Nope. Too far away."

"What did Jan Murphy say about that?"

"She said 'looks like a falling out between thieves.'"

"What does that mean?"

"Dunno. You'd have to ask Jan."

"You like Jan?"

"Sure. She's a looker. Lot of the single guys have made a run at her but she's got the hots for the boss."

"Mr. Ames?"

Dubbel nodded.

Evie took another path. "I'll be interviewing Lisa, too. You know that, right?"

Dubbel nodded. "Be gentle with my little girl. She's been through a lot."

— —

Lisa Dubbel's complexion was not enhanced by impending motherhood. Angry eruptions pitted her cheeks, chin, and forehead. Acne for some reason spared her generous nose. She had the look of a proboscis monkey with bad skin.

Fleshy with a chest big enough to stir the prurient interests of teenage males, Lisa exuded a lack of self-esteem. Evie speculated that Lisa would be eager for the self-serving attention of the opposite gender. Lisa's blouse rode up as she sat down and Evie noticed a multi-colored, fuck-me tattoo encircled her navel, straining against the shiny skin of her growing belly. She should have embraced maternity clothes months ago.

"When's the baby due," Evie asked, just to break the ice.

"August 14th."

"Do you know the gender?"

"Doctor says it's a little girl."

"Have you picked out a name?"

"I'd like to call her Julie, after my mom. But Dickie wants to call her Jasmine, after his mom."

"How are you going to settle that?"

"Dad says that if Mr. Ames pays up we'll call the baby whatever Dickie wants to call it."

"You OK with that?"

Lisa shrugged. "Whatever."

"You were working when the man was killed on the loading dock, right?"

Lisa nodded. "I was on the bottling line."

"Where is that in relation to the loading dock?"

"Just inside and to the right, facing the building."

"Can you see the loading dock from there?"

"U huh when the big doors are open."

"And were they that morning?"

"Yep."

"You notice anything unusual?"

"Nope. Just forklifts driving around beeping their horns to warn people."

"Did you see Boyd Porter?"

"He's the dead guy, right?"

"That's right."

"Wouldn't have known him if I saw him. But I did see a forklift with pounder cans drive through the door right before I heard a big crash."

"Could you see the driver."

"Just from the back."

"Could you tell who it was?"

Lisa shook her head. "But I did see Mr. Ames run back inside from the dock. He kicked off his boots just inside the door and headed toward the stairs to his office in his stocking feet."

"Was he carrying anything? Like a briefcase?"

"Nope."

———

Jan Murphy fiddled with her skirt before she sat down, perching on the edge of a folding chair like a bird wary of a cat. She crossed her ankles primly and considered Evie apprehensively.

"What sort of fellow is Franklin Ames?" Evie asked.

Murphy blinked rapidly before deigning to respond. "He's a great boss. Treats his employees like family."

"A father figure?"

Murphy cocked her head to one side. "A stern father figure. He's not shy about discipline when it's called for. And he won't truck with a union. I'll tell you that."

"What's his relationship like with his wife?" Evie asked.

Murphy sucked her teeth. "I don't feel comfortable answering that question."

"Why?"

"I feel like I would be breaking a confidence. A good secretary is discreet."

"Other employees have told me you've been anything but discreet. Your disdain for Jasmine is well-known."

"People talk. But not me. Honest."

"We'll circle back to that. But here's something to think about. Would you consider breaking confidence if you thought it would keep your boss out of jail?"

"Jail?" Murphy's voice was shrill. "Why would you put Franklin in jail?"

"A witness puts him on the loading dock at the time of the murder."

"Impossible."

"How so?"

"Franklin was in his office until Suds called to say there was a dead guy on the loading dock."

"Lisa Dubbel says she heard a crash and saw Mr. Ames hurrying from the loading dock that morning."

"That lying little hussy," Murphy hissed. "That little tramp and her no-count father are trying to extort money from Franklin. I wouldn't trust anything they say."

"Why should I trust anything you say?"

"What do you mean?"

"I hear that you are in love with your boss."

Murphy bolted from her chair. "I won't put up with this . . . this inquisition any longer."

She stormed from the employee lounge, leaving a slime trail of indignation.

SOUTHERN EXPOSURE

Suds Ferguson arrived in Charleston in fine fettle, thanks to the first-class accommodations Franklin Ames had graciously afforded. Tourist-class travel was agony for someone of Suds's size. He had packed in an overhead bag, so there was no need to visit the baggage carousels.

Harrison Ford was waiting for him just beyond the arrival concourse. Harry was a big guy, six feet four. When the two old partners embraced and back slapped, oblivious to the amused glances of spectators, they looked like dancing bears.

"Harry. How the hell are you. It's been too long," Suds said as the two men disengaged.

"Living the dream. Janice is pregnant with our second. Imagine that. Me, a father, two times over so well into my 40s."

It hurt Suds to ask it. But he did. "How's your boy, Seth, isn't it?"

Harry swam through the emotional undertow. "Seth is fine," he said. And let it at that.

"That's good. Will child number two be a boy or a girl?"

"Dunno know yet. Too early. And I'm not sure we'll want to find out."

Harry clapped Suds on the back. "Follow me big guy. I know the duty cop at arrivals. He let me park at the curb."

Harry waved at the duty cop and the two big men piled into Harry's big boxy Ford Flex. "Figures you'd drive a Ford," Suds said.

Harry pulled away from the curb. "Yeah. Janice is amused by that, too. But it's a big car with lots of head room."

Suds couldn't wait any longer. "Graham and Geraldine Smith?"

"Geraldine has a notorious nome de plume."

"Huh?"

"I'll get to that when we get settled on the expressway. Tell me about your brewery gig. It sounds . . . serendipitous."

"Hah. A good adjective that. A guy named Suds working at a brewery is a happy accident."

"Or a hoppy one?"

"Punny. Actually Franklin Ames, the company president, sought me out. My departure from the PD was spectacular. Made the papers. Franklin is a vet, a reserve navy officer. He likes to give other vets a fair shake. Called me up. Saved my ass."

"And Evie?"

"Bitter. With every right to be. I fucked up."

"I'd give you a pass on that one."

"Yeah but you're not my wife."

"There's no dishonor in a relationship blowing up with the explosive stuff you two were dealing with."

"Don't want to go there. I'll need to wallow in self-pity for a while longer before I accept a hand up."

Harry nodded. "No worries partner. But if you ever need to talk . . ."

Harry accelerated on the ramp and merged with heavy traffic.

"Geraldine Smith? What's with the nome de plume?" Suds asked.

"Girty's Snatch. She was a stripper and a whore. A notorious one, according to the vice guys. Before she got religion and got married. To a preacher of all things."

"Graham, a preacher? You're kidding."

Harry nodded. "Jury's out on whether the Rev. Graham Smith is aware of his wife's illustrious past. Some say he was a customer. Others say that Gertie got religion before she got religion. If you know what I mean."

"What sort of preacher is the good reverend?"

"An evangelical of some ilk. Runs a fancy megachurch where rich people go to seek absolution for being rich by paying lip service to the poor."

"Aren't you the cynic?"

"Cop and cynic are synonymous. Or is it vice versa? Everybody's got an angle even if they don't know they have one."

"How long have they been married?"

"Six years, according to the church website. She's the director of music. He's the lead pastor. They got a six-year-old son. Alex is his name."

Harry paused. "There's no way to sugar coat this. Their kid? He's sick. Leukemia. There's a big effort to find a bone marrow match. So far no go."

"Fuck!"

"Fuck," Harry agreed.

MADAM MADAME

The Google Earth pictures didn't do the Smiths' home justice. The two-story colonial sat at the apex of a semicircular drive protected by brick pillars and a gate, which at the moment was open.

Harry snugged the Ford Flex against the curb, shifted to park, and shut off the engine. "You ready?"

"You called ahead?"

"That's right. Told her I knew her past, but we'd be cool if she agreed to met you. No mention of prostitution when others are within earshot."

"Others?"

"Her husband, apparently, works from home, mostly. And they have a nanny."

"Being a mega-minister must have its unjust desserts," said Suds.

"Cynic," said Harry.

"Cop," said Suds.

They got out of the car and ascended four steps to the front door, which opened before they had a chance to knock. A beautiful, slender blonde in her mid-30s greeted them. Her eyes were dark amber, her hair expertly coiffed, and her sheath dress exquisitely tailored in Carolina blue. The ensemble was complete with a strand of pearls. Open-toed Prada pumps framed a perfect pedicure. More unjust desserts.

She was gracious. "Gentlemen, please come in. My friends call me Gerry."

Harry took care of the introductions.

"We'll talk in the living room, but please keep your voices down. My husband is preparing Sunday's sermon, and Mary is reading to Alex in the playroom," Gerry said.

The living room was dappled by sunlight filtered through a copse of live oaks. A Steinway grand piano dominated one corner of the room. A sofa, love seat, and two wing chairs, situated in front of a fireplace, created a comfortable conversation nook in the center of the large living room where the three of them soon perched, she on the love seat and they in the wing chairs.

She leaned forward and whispered. "I will admit to a colorful past, but God and my husband have forgiven me. Alex is an inquisitive child, and his condition has made him restless. He might well escape the attention of Mary. So please be circumspect."

"You have quite the vocabulary for . . ."

"A whore? I have a brain and Charleston has a fine community college at which I matriculated. Music and theatre. Graham insisted. Polished this pretty penny."

Harrison took his lumps while Suds struggled to find his voice. Finally, Suds said:

"This is difficult for me. I don't want to cause you anymore pain, but I recently lost my son . . ." his voice broke . . . "to leukemia." Suds bought some time. Half rose to pull a handkerchief from his back pocket. Dabbed his eyes with it and plopped back down in his seat with rather more impact than he had anticipated. The cushion made a farting noise, which they all ignored, although a smile curled the corner of Ford's upper lip.

Gerry's eyes softened. "I'm so sorry. But it's good to know that you will be empathetic. What's was your son's name and how long ago did he pass?"

Suds blew his nose. Harry averted his eyes unwilling to come to grips with his friend's grief.

"Two years ago. We had just found a solid match for a bone marrow transplant but Rufus caught an infection with his immune system suppressed. He didn't survive long enough to get the transplant."

"I'm so sorry," Gerry said one more time. "Alex is doing as well as can be expected. His stomach is distended; his lymph nodes swollen and joint pain keeps him awake a night. His physicians are maintaining, but he has a rare blood type, so finding a bone marrow donor is next to impossible."

"What's his blood type?" Harry asked.

"Rh-null. We've put his DNA sample in an on-line database. We've got a hit, but . . ."

They were interrupted by a disturbance in the hallway outside the living room. And a little boy burst into the room followed closely by a young woman.

Alex, slight and white with startling Siamese-cat blue eyes, wore a red do-rag bandana about his head, green shorts and a white T-shirt emblazoned with the slogan "I'm Tougher than Cancer." He was barefooted.

The nanny, 20ish and pudgy, wore scrubs, rubber-soled shoes, and an RN nametag. "I'm sorry Mrs. Smith. Alex got away from me while I was in the bathroom. Are you almost done here? I'm due for my hospital shift in . . . " she checked her wristwatch . . . "an hour-and-a-half and the traffic will be bad this time of day."

"I'll need a few more minutes, but I'll ask Graham to watch her so you can get going," Gerry said.

As Gerry arose from the love seat, a slim man in country-club golfing attire walked into the room. His navy slacks had razor-sharp creases and his UnderArmor polo was form fitting, revealing no belly at all. His hair parted on the right was dirty blond and hair-sprayed into place. His eyes were black as coal in stark contrast to fair skin and light-colored hair.

"It's OK, Gerry. I'll take over," Graham Smith said, his voice a rich baritone of the sort cultivated by people who speak for a living. "I've got a solid handle on Sunday's sermon. Come on little man. We'll play a game of spit."

Alex pouted. "I wanted to see who Mommy is talking too."

Graham's voice took on an imperial tone. "Alex!"

"OK. I'll play."

They filed out of the room.

Suds heard the nanny's rubber-soled shoes squeaking on the foyer hardwood. The front door opened and closed. And the voices of Alex and his father faded as they moved farther from the living room.

"Now, where were we?" Gerry asked, resuming her seat.

"You were saying that you'd identified a potential donor," Suds reminded her.

"That's right. But the database is blind. The site generated an email to the donor, but we didn't hear anything . . . until that horrid little man showed up. Said he represented someone who could help."

"What horrid little man?" Harry asked.

"A private detective. Boyd Porter, according to his business card. He said he might be able to broker a meeting with a donor . . . if I ponied up some cash."

"How much did he want?" Suds asked.

Gerry spat the words through tight lips. "Fifty-thousand dollars."

"That slimy bastard!" Suds said.

"You know him?"

"I know of him. Unfortunately . . ."

Gerry interrupted. "We are well off. But our money's tied up. Had to sell some stocks to raise the cash. Graham says there will be hell to pay at tax time. But now that son of a bitch isn't returning my calls. I'm at my wits end. Alex just keeps getting sicker. And there's someone somewhere out there who just might be able to help."

"I take it neither you nor your husband are Rh-null?" Harry said.

Gerry studied her toes, raised her head to look him in the eyes. "That's right."

Suds cleared his throat. "You and your husband have dark eyes . . . Alex's are light blue . . ."

Gerry took a deep breath. "That's right, Mr. Ferguson. Graham is not Alex's father."

Harry picked up the gauntlet. "Does your husband know that?"

"Of course he does. He's not a stupid man."

"And apparently he's a forgiving one," Suds said.

"That is the lesson Christ teaches us," Gerry said.

"If your husband isn't the father. Who is?" Harry asked.

Gerry wiped her brow with the back of her left hand. "I have no idea. I was a high-priced . . . escort. I rarely got their real names."

She arose, plucked a handful of tissues from a box on the end table and returned to her seat, worrying a tissue between the thumb and index finger of her right hand.

"This is painful. When I look back on that period of my life . . . it's like I'm holding onto someone else's memories. Like I was a witness to those events rather than a participant. My shrink says the detachment is a defense mechanism. And believe me I have a lot of memories I need to defend myself against."

She wiped the corners of her eyes with the tissues, smearing expertly applied eye shadow. "Poor. Poor. Alex. His mother was a whore. If only that asshole Boyd Porter would return my calls."

Suds took a deep breath. "He can't. He's dead."

And the whore once known as Girty's Snatch sobbed in her million-dollar living room.

CONSOLATION PRIZE

Suds arose from his wing chair. Sat beside Gerry on the love seat. Put his arm around her.

"I can't make you any promises, but I may be able to help you. Porter expensed his trip to Charleston to my employer's account. I'm not sure why, but I intend to find out."

"Do you know if your employer had any reason to register his, or her, DNA into the 23andme data base?"

"What's 23andme?" Harry wanted to know.

Gerry explained. "It's a service that analyzes a DNA sample. You spit in a tube, and they tell you your ethnic heritage. As the data base has grown it's also become a way to find relatives you may have lost touch with and to identify a predisposition to disease."

Harry snapped his fingers. "Or to ID criminals like that serial rapist in California they tracked down by finding one of his relatives in a DNA data base."

Suds nodded. "That's right. My employer recently paid for a series of DNA samples that showed his stepson had fathered a son."

"You think that's the information Porter was going to sell me for $50,000? Maybe the stepson is a match for my Alex. Wouldn't that be wonderful?" Gerry said.

"Yes and no. Dickie's a little shit. Not the sort of guy who would willingly submit himself to being a bone marrow donor."

"Dickie. That's the stepson?" Gerry asked.

"Yeah. Probably shouldn't have named him. Just slipped out."

"Will you reach out to him for me?"

"Yes. But I can't reveal his last name. If he's unwilling, I'll do what I can. But I can't push it too far. Understand?"

"I'll give you the $50,000, if you can persuade Dickie."

"Whoa! Slow down. It's a leap Dickie's a match. Could be Porter was expensing another client to my employer's account. Wouldn't put that past him. In any event. I don't want your money. Let's circle back a bit. You say you have no idea who Alex's father might be?"

"That's right. Why does that matter?"

"Dickie would have been 10 years old at the time of Alex's conception. Maybe Porter was shielding another client by falsely expensing the trip to my employer."

Gerry nodded. "The thought that I could ID Alex's father had occurred to me as well."

"When was Alex's birthday?" Suds asked.

"June 15, 2013."

"And when did you hook up with Graham for the first time?"

"Late October of 2012."

"So you would have conceived Alex sometime in September of 2012," Harry interjected. "Who were . . ." Harry cleared his throat. "Your clients back then?"

"Don't patronize me. Most of my Johns were military officers, O-5 and better because they had to be big wigs to afford me. Navy officers mostly, commanders and captains, maybe the odd admiral visiting Joint Base Charleston. Of course Alex's father could be a salesman, a lawyer a doctor or a truck driver feeling flush at the time. There's no way of knowing, really."

"There is one thing we know for sure," Suds said.

"What's that?" Harry asked.

"We know the father has blue eyes. I wonder if the military keeps a DNA data base of some sort," Suds said. "I'll back-track Porter's trail. See what I can find."

"And you'll let me know?" Gerry asked.

"As long as it doesn't violate privilege," Suds said.

BUSTED

Ernest Flowers, Esq. considered his client over the top of 2x reading glasses. He dropped the criminal indictment onto the table in the visitors' room at Dauphin County Prison. "I can see why they arrested you. The affidavit of probable cause is pretty compelling," he said.

Franklin Ames didn't look good in orange. His skin looked pasty under the florescent lights, which buzzed like a bottle fly. "How soon can you get me out?"

"It will be awhile."

"Why?"

"You should never have put Jasmine's name on the deed. I told you that when you married her. She's refusing to release the equity on her share of the house. You'll need to come up with another two hundred and fifty thousand surety."

"I thought my broker was working on that."

"He is, but these things take time. Best-case scenario. I'll have you out by noon tomorrow."

Franklin scratched both forearms from elbow to wrist. "I'm not cut out to be a convict. Didn't realize how claustrophobic it is living in such a small space."

"Getting you out on bail isn't even half the battle. The affidavit for probable cause shows we have a lot to worry about. Your fingerprints on bloody brewer boots and on the levers to the forklift. Eyewitness testimony that puts you on the loading dock at the time of the murder. We've got to come up with some ways to rebut this."

"Lisa Dubbel is not exactly a reliable witness. We've been playing hardball in the child support negotiations. You know that. I didn't arrive until after the murder. Lisa is lying."

"How do we impeach her testimony?"

"Jan Murphy will testify that I was in my office at the time. I think a jury would give more weight to her testimony than to Lisa's."

"I hope so," Ernie said. He paused, considering.

"What?"

"How do we explain your fingerprints on the forklift and your bloody boots inside the loading dock door?"

"I often drive the company forklifts," Franklin said. "Ask around. Anyone will tell you. I like for employees to see the boss isn't too high-and-mighty to do some grunt work."

"And the boots."

"I put on brewers boots when I go to the factory floor. It's an affectation for the benefit of the peons."

Flowers winced. "I wouldn't use that term on the witness stand," he said.

Franklin waved a hand in acknowledgment and picked up his story. "I went over to check on Porter. He was obviously dead. I kicked off the brewers boots, grabbed my loafers, and ran back to my office to call 911. Before I could call, Suds rang me from the loading dock. He took care of the 911 call."

"Will Suds back you up on that?"

"Can't imagine he won't."

"You told Suds to run a parallel investigation."

Franklin nodded. "That's right. He accessed Porter's computer and decided to fly to Charleston to follow up on a lead."

"That explains why I haven't been able to get in touch with him," Ernie said. "Why Charleston?"

Franklin looked uncomfortable.

"I sent him there to investigate whether it's possible I fathered a son, but Suds doesn't know that. Not yet, anyway."

"Right. The DNA thing we discussed earlier. What did Suds find out?"

"Dunno. I'm sort of out of the loop right now."

DID DICKIE REALLY DO IT?

Jasmine stretched on the chaise in her luxurious master bedroom and considered her options now that Boyd Porter was dead and her husband was in jail, charged with Porter's murder. Sunlight streamed through the eastern exposure windows and birds chirped in the dogwood trees that bookended the front walk. How her circumstances had changed since she married Franklin Ames and moved from the doublewide! Her husband's incarceration was fortuitous. A murder rap would distract him from another fight in the offing, the hostile takeover of Hop Central Craft Brewery that she and her lover-attorney Zach Dunkel were plotting.

Zach had reviewed her pre-nup and assured her that she would not have to surrender the 200 shares of Hop Central Craft Brewery should she divorce Franklin Ames. Those 200 shares were the wedge that would effect the takeover and secure a nest egg Franklin couldn't touch. She took some solace in the realization that her husband would profit from the deal, too, lessening the bite on the hand that had fed her.

Many a conspiracy has been plotted abed. Jasmine hadn't counted on her husband siccing Boyd Porter on her. The weasel had captured compromising photos of her in erotic embrace with Zach. Jasmine did what she had to do to silence Porter. She fucked him. Repeatedly, while studying how to squash the fly who had settled upon her ointment.

Her son knocked on the doorframe and by her leave entered the boudoir, interrupting her reverie. He smelled of eggs, bacon, and Clearasil. "Did Franklin do it? Kill Boyd Porter?"

"Probably not."

"Then who did?"

"I wish I knew. I'd shake his hand."

"What?"

"Nothing. But Porter's death does solve some of our problems."

"You mean the paternity thing? I don't care what the DNA report says. Lisa and I didn't do it."

Jasmine sighed and straightened her robe about her legs. "Do you even know what 'do it' means?"

"I don't want to talk about that. But yes I know what it means."

"Tell me."

"Come on Mom. They cover this stuff in health class. Show us diagrams of penises and vaginas. Show how one is poked into the other and what happens after that happens."

"So you didn't have sex with Lisa?"

Dickie studied his toes. Jasmine concluded he was lying. "Come on out with it!"

"She gave me a blowjob. That's all. There's no way I could be the father. But I can think of a half-dozen guys on the bottling line who could be."

Jasmine studied her son's face, which had flushed scarlet. Like all teenagers he was deceitful but she could usually tell when he was lying. "OK. So why did DNA finger you as the father."

The double entendre was unintentional.

Dickie snickered.

Jasmine couldn't help but smile. "You dirty little boy."

Dickie didn't even try to look contrite.

"Wild guess. If you aren't the father, who is?" Jasmine asked.

"Cloyd Jackson, probably. Maybe Chad Petry. But Cloyd's more likely. They were hot-and-heavy back then. Cloyd said they took a cheek swab from him, too. Maybe the lab messed up the samples."

"Maybe it's more nefarious than that," Jasmine said.

"What's nefarious mean?"

41

"Maybe that little shit Boyd Porter back-stabbed me."

"Huh?"

"Go away honey. Get ready for school. Mommy has some work to do."

As the sound of Dickie's footsteps receded in the hall, Jasmine arose from her chaise, crossed the room, and took a seat before the secretary tucked away in a far corner. Her cell phone, still plugged into its charger, and a laptop were arrayed before her.

She disconnected the phone, awakened it with her passcode, and scrolled to her phone book. The call to Zach Dunkel went straight to voice mail. "God damn. He better not be blocking my call."

She opened her laptop and tapped in the security code, navigated to her email program, and began to type:

"I need to talk to you pronto. Boyd Porter's death solves one problem but creates another one. I'm pretty sure Porter switched out the DNA swabs he collected for my husband to implicate Dickie, but why? And if those photos show up, our whole deal is cooked. You told me to shut up and fuck Porter. As I recall you enjoyed fucking him, too. Now it looks like he may be fucking us still . . . from the grave!"

CHUCK DUBBEL SMELLS A RAT

Chuck Dubbel peered through a window into the wheat-beer room and spied a dead rat at the base of one of two 800-barrel, open-top fermentation tanks, which bubbled away, spewing carbon dioxide into the air. Protocol demanded that the room be vented before anyone entered, but job one was to remove that damn rat. If he did so quickly, without anyone noticing, Dubbel could avoid an arduous cleaning regimen.

Dubbel decided not to wait. He could hold his breath long enough to pick up the rat. He punched the brewers' code into the keypad, took a deep breath, and opened the door, which closed behind him with an ominous click. Crossing the room in a hurry, he bent and picked up the rat by the end of its long tail.

Returning to the door, he punched in the code, but the door refused to budge. Shit! He punched the code in again. Again! Again! With the same result. Nothing! Finally, he surrendered to the inevitable. He drew in a deep lungful of the carbon-dioxide infused air. Then another. His chest heaved; his vision tunneled; he pitched forward, banging his head on the concrete floor as collapsed. Blood gushed from the scalp wound and pooled about him.

By the time assistant brewer Dexter Lager found Dubbel and pulled him from the room, no amount of CPR or bottled oxygen could save Dubbel.

———

Lager was studying his shoes when Evie Pinson entered the interrogation room at the Derry Township Police Department to question him about the death of his good friend Chuck Dubbel.

"How long have you worked at Hop Central Craft Brewery?" she asked.

"Five years."

"And for how many of those years have you been . . ." Evie rifled through the pages on a clipboard she had carried into the room . . . "a qualified tank attendant."

"The last two years."

"So, what went wrong."

"Dunno. Chuck knew better than to go into an unvented fermantion room. Musta thought he could hold his breath long enough to remove the rat."

"Rat?"

"Yeah. The dead one I found lying right beside Chuck."

"Why would Chuck have done that?"

Lager studied his shoes. "Probably to avoid the cleanup. A lot of work just because of a dead rat."

"So what went wrong?"

"Dunno."

"Could Chuck have locked himself in the room by mistake, or maybe on purpose?" Evie asked.

"Chuck was too smart to kill himself by accident and wouldn't have done it on purpose," Lager said.

"What do you mean by that?"

"Chuck had a lot to live for."

"Such as."

"Such as a big payday, seeing as how Dickie knocked up Chuck's daughter," Lager said.

"How likely is it that Chuck just made a mistake?"

"Chuck was a pro. Way too careful for that."

"So you think maybe someone locked him in?"

"Dunno."

"He have any enemies?"

"None that I know of."

"Notice anything unusual about Chuck's behavior before the . . . accident, if it was that?" Evie asked.

"Well, I saw him arguing with his daughter on the bottling line about a half hour before I found him dead in the fermentation room."

"What were they arguing about?"

"Dunno. It's noisey on the bottling line and I wasn't close enough to hear. But they way they were acting, I could tell it was heated."

KILL THE INFIDELS

Thursday, July 12, 2018

Suds Ferguson felt like an interloper in his own house. Or at least it used to be his house. The one he had shared with Evie before she threw him out.

By her leave, he was perched on the edge of his former recliner in his former living room. Evie's demeanor indicated his visa could expire at any moment. He studied the bookcases that flanked the fireplace. "What happened to my bowling trophies?"

"I donated them to the Special Olympics."

"That was nice of me," Suds said. "So when are you going to let my boss out of jail? I discovered some things in Charleston that I need to bounce off of him."

Evie said: "That's not up to me, but he's posted bail. My guess is this afternoon. Charleston?"

"Is this the part where I show you mine?"

Evie's smile was vintage Cruella Di Vil.

What Suds had to say would wipe that smile off her face. He didn't look forward to doing that.

"Boyd Porter went to Charleston to interview a former prostitute about her sick kid." The words stuck in his throat. They came out all phlegmy like a coffin cough. "Leukemia, just like Rufus."

Tears pooled in Evie's eyes. "God damn it Suds! Will you never tire of wounding me?"

Suds snarled: "That's so like you! Never considering that I have feelings, too."

Evie retreated. "Didn't we have this same conversation, a year ago?"

"Right before you kicked me out. This isn't a contest to determine which of us is hurting more."

"I had just come to embrace that when you fucked Detective Sergeant Linda Fontaine."

"So that's why we broke up? My infidelity? If it's any consolation, she cut things off soon as you kicked me out. Seems she fancied a fuck more than a commitment."

"I know. Office scuttlebutt."

"And for the past year . . . I've been celibate."

"Penitence?"

"Nope."

"What then?"

Suds squirmed. "Impotence. Not that there have been that many attempts. My therapist said it was a guilt reaction and suggested Viagra. It's an experiment that I haven't tried . . . yet."

Evie laughed. "Poetic justice."

"Think so?"

"You betcha."

"Do you think for old time's sake maybe we . . . ?

Evie cut him off. "Not a chance, cowboy."

Suds snapped his fingers. Shook his head. "Nuts!"

"Now about this prostitute," Evie said.

"You ready to talk about that now?"

"I think so."

"Her name's Geraldine Smith. Her friends call her Gerry. Her former Johns called her Girty's Snatch."

"Ouch! Go on."

"Then she got religion. Married a minister. But not before a nameless John knocked her up. Her son, Alex, has stage four leukemia. He's Rh-null, a super rare blood type, but a potential bone marrow donor cropped up in an anonymous DNA data base."

"Don't tell me. Boyd Porter knew the potential donor's identity and he went to Charleston to sell that information to a desperate woman."

"Wow! You know Porter pretty well."

"I've been backtracking his trail for two days now. He was a slime ball. A voyeur who enjoyed peeping on cheating spouses a little too much. Some whispers about his accepting sexual favors to suppress the evidence of sexual favors."

"Fits with Gerry's impression of him."

"How did you know that Porter had gone to Charlestown?"

This was dangerous territory. Evie didn't know he had cracked Porter's computer. So he lied. "Franklin combed through the paperwork. Found Porter had expensed a trip to Charleston to his account and had visited an address belonging to Geraldine Smith."

"How did you know that?"

"An Uber receipt. But Franklin won't discuss Porter's trip to Charleston. That's why I need to talk to him."

"I guess this is the part where I show you mine," Evie said. "We have a strong case. Your boss's fingerprints on the forklift levers and on his bloody boots. And an eyewitness puts him on the loading dock at the time of the murder. I'd start looking for another job if I were you."

"Damn! I had no idea it was that bad. How about motive?"

"I'm still working on that," Evie admitted. "So far nothing has cropped up. State police's computer geeks have cracked the password on his laptop and are combing through his documents file. Funny thing, someone logged in using his password on the morning after his death, copied some files and then deleted them. Have any idea who might have done that?"

"No. But I'm sure you'll get to the bottom of it."

"Already have."

Suds tried to look innocent and failed. "My best guess is his dog, Sally."

Evie laughed. "Sally is his password. But you're the dog who deleted the files."

Suds held out both hands. "Want to slap the cuffs on me now?"

"Nah. I'm already guilty of obstruction for letting you skate on the breaking and entering. Makes me an accomplice after the fact on the computer crime. So I guess it will be our secret, as long as you tell me what was in those files. The state police will be able to retrieve them soon enough."

Suds hesitated while he considered whether that knowledge would supply the missing piece of motive for the state's case against his boss.

"Come on, Suds. Out with it. Miller backed up his files to the cloud. His cloud password is not the same as his computer password. Soon as we crack that we'll know anyway. That's why I'm not busting your balls on this one."

"They were records of DNA analysis of the people Porter tested to determine the paternity of Lisa Dubbel's impending child."

"Who was tested?"

"Lisa, her parents, Dickie Cox, Franklin himself, and a guy named Cloyd Jackson, who apparently was the prime alternate suspect in Lisa's pregnancy."

"What else was in the files?"

Suds paused.

"Come on. Out with it!"

"OK. OK. Porter had been following Jasmine Ames, apparently to determine whether she was having an affair."

"Aha. The plot thickens."

"But she wasn't. At least, according to Boyd Porter, Jasmine was squeaky clean. So squeaky clean that it set off my bullshit detector. Porter paints her as a saint. Brewery scuttlebutt is that she's a conniving bitch."

Evie pulled at her earlobe, a habit when she was in deep thought. "I don't see a motive there, do you?"

"Maybe Franklin found out that Porter had cooked the books on his surveil of Jasmine and . . ."

"Killed Porter in a rage?" Evie said.

"Yeah. Unlikely."

"What else did you find?" Evie asked.

Suds tried not to look guilty . . . and failed. "The expense report of Porter's trip to Charleston. That's how I sniffed out Geraldine Smith."

"So the bit about Franklin finding the expense report and sharing it with you?"

"Never happened. Just covering my tracks. The trip was news to Franklin, but he let me expense my trip first class. Was eager for my report. Six missed calls from him while my phone was in airplane mode. My return calls went straight to voice mail because, as it turned out, you had put him in jail."

"So Porter's trip to Charleston might provide the motive for his murder?"

"Or it might prove that Franklin had no reason to murder him at all."

"How so?"

"Dunno. Just my gut talking."

"Your gut was pretty reliable right up to the time you fucked Detective Sergeant Linda Fontaine."

"Back to her again, are we? You giving her anything to do in this investigation?"

"After I found out about you two, I thought about putting her on permanent pervert patrol, but people would have called me vindictive. And she's too good a cop for that."

"Why do you think she stuck around? She could have moved on to more pleasant pastures."

"To fuck with me because I got the promotion to chief and she didn't. I've been stepping around landmines she's been planting for the past year. But she is a good detective. I've got her sniffing around the life and times of Chuck Dubbel to see if she can find out why someone would have wanted to murder him."

"You think he was murdered?"

"Suicide just doesn't seem to fit his MO."

"An accident, perhaps?"

"He was meticulously careful by all accounts."

"Too bad. He was a capable brewer," Suds said.

"You might say beer was the death of him."

"Not a bad way to go," Suds said. "Death by beer."

"Lot of that going around," Evie said.

SERGEANT FONTAINE IS A REAL PAIN

Cigarette skinny with the sharp angularity of a jackknife, Julie Dubbel didn't look like the grieving widow, as she perched on the edge of a threadbare sofa in the living room of her shotgun two-story duplex.

Detective Sergeant Linda Fontaine had decided to interview the new widow on Dubbel's home turf on North Second Street in Harrisburg. The house was close enough to downtown to avoid suburban gentrification. It smelled like an ashtray. Linda would have to change into her spare uniform when she got back to the station. She could not abide the stench of cigarette smoke, which was ironic because she had consumed two packs of Merits a day for the first 10 years of her police career. Then she got religion and quit, which explained 15 pounds of extra padding on her once svelte frame. Men more poetic than Suds Ferguson had told her she resembled Sophia Loren, olive-skinned and voluptuous. Suds had been more succinct. He settled for hubba-hubba.

She had taken Suds to her bed shortly after Rufus died. As much out of pity as of desire. The poor man obviously wasn't getting any at home. And she could tell that Suds needed the consolation of good sex.

"Can you think of anyone who'd want to hurt your husband?" Linda asked.

Julie took a deep last drag on her cigarette and stubbed it out in an overflowing ashtray. She blew a cloud of smoke Fontaine's way. "My husband was a saint. Ask anyone," she said.

"Then how did you come by that black eye?" Fontaine asked.

"I punched myself in the face. Used to do that a lot, but I won't be doing it anymore. Enough said?"

"So your husband abused you?"

"You didn't hear me say that. The kid might be eavesdropping from the other room. I'd hate for him to think less of his old man."

"You realize your telling me that makes you a suspect in his murder," Fontaine said.

"Murder? The way I hear it he forgot to vent the CO2 from the open-tank fermentation room and Dexter botched the extraction."

"His coworkers say your husband was a careful man and a slave to protocol."

"Musta had a bad day."

"Where were you at the time of the accident, if that's what it was?"

"Here at home with the baby."

"The baby?"

"We've got a seven-year-old. Chucky junior. Didn't want any more kids but senior came home drunk and was in too big a hurry to use a condom. I've got a good lawyer. The brewery will be paying me for my loss . . . big time. Junior needs a college education. Wouldn't want him to turn out stupid like his father."

"Actually you'll be double-dipping," Fontaine observed.

"How's that?"

"You still expect child support from Richard Cox, right?"

"Who's Richard Cox? Oh. Right. Dickie. Yes."

"You intimated that your husband was physically abusive . . ."

"What's intimated mean?"

"Hinted."

"I didn't say that. You did."

"If I were to check police and court records, would I discover that you filed a PFA against your husband, say, three or four years ago?"

Julie glared. "Sounds like you already have."

"PFA request says he punched you in the face and broke your nose. Is that true?"

"Lying to the police is a crime. They told me that. So, yeah. It's true."

"Why did you go back to him if things were so bad."

"Believe it or not. Things would have been worse without him. I've got no family, no skills, and no looks, at least not any more. Living without him would have been a lot tougher than living with him."

"He have life insurance?"

Julie fumbled a cigarette from a pack on the coffee table, lit up, sucked in as much smoke as her lungs would hold and let it trickle out through her nose long and slow. "He's got a $50,000 term policy through work."

"And you'll probably get some wrongful death money from the brewery."

Julie brightened. "Yeah. Lawyers say I could get a million, maybe more."

"How did you land a lawyer so quickly?"

"Weren't hard at all. Three or four of them called me up right away. All I had to do is choose between them."

"So it's fair to say that your husband is worth more to you dead than alive?"

"What are you trying to do? Set me up for his murder? I'm telling you I was right here at home with little Chucky when big Chuck bought it at the brewery. You can ask my neighbor, Susan, she always comes over at two for *Days of Our Lives*. I was here when it happened. Susan will swear to that."

"I'll be sure to do that."

"Know what, Sgt. Fontaine?"

"What?"

"You're a real pain."

THE BEER BARON ESCAPES
THE HOOSEGOW

Friday, July 13, 2018

Ernest Flowers, Esq.'s office occupied the 19th century mansion of a long-dead railroad titan. The edifice to excess overlooked the Susquehanna River on North Front Street in Harrisburg not too far from the Pennsylvania Governor's Mansion at Front and McClay. Suds snugged his Crown Vic into a parking space between a Jaguar and Lexus. His car door screeched as he opened it, being careful not to ding the door of the Jag.

The big doors facing Front Street were for show. An arrow-sign marked, "Law Office Entrance," directed him down a patterned brick sidewalk to a single door that opened into a vestibule guarded by a desk in the center and gates on either side. A middle-aged woman sat behind the desk. She was wearing a blue blazer that exposed the wide lapels of a white-silk blouse. Coiffed silver hair, diamond-stud earrings, and a pearl necklace completed her Girl Friday ensemble. The nameplate on the desk read Eleanor Rider.

Suds slouched over the desk to be less imposing. Eleanor must have mistaken the gesture. She rolled back in her chair, hand poised over the telephone to summon help. Suds backed up. Smiled. "I'm here to see Ernie," he said.

"Do you have an appointment?"

"Don't think I need one. He asked me to come."

"Your name."

Suds blushed reverting to Catholic schoolboy form. "Sidney Ferguson."

"That's funny. You don't look like a Sidney," she said, covering her smile with her left hand as she picked up the phone with her right. "Sidney Ferguson is here to see you."

She nodded and reached under her desk. The gate lock buzzed. "Just push right through. They're in the conference room. Second door on your right."

Three people already occupied the conference room. Franklin waved Suds to a chair across the table. "This is attorney Ernie, and his legal secretary, Amy Lantz."

The attorney wore his lawyer suit with an aplomb tacked down by a Windsored tie in power red. He half rose to shake Suds's hand, exposing a belly that strained at the bottom three buttons of his silk shirt. The jacket of his gray two-piece suit was unbuttoned, unfurling the fabric around him like a magician's cape. Despite his current girth, it appeared he had lost weight recently. Flowers straightened the jacket behind him before he plopped back into a big swivel conference room chair.

The lawyer was bald and mustached. His hands were manicured and soft. "Pleased to met you," he said, shoving a document across the table at Suds. "Read this."

Suds pulled his readers from his shirt pocket and perched them on the end of his nose. "What's this?" he asked.

"A standard employment contract. I'm hiring you to be my investigative consultant."

"Why's that?"

"Another layer of protection. If you work for me anything you hear in this room is covered by attorney-client privilege. Anything Franklin says in our presence from here on out will be protected. Understand?"

Suds scanned the document and patted his pockets. "Anyone have a pen?"

Lantz picked up the conference room telephone and punched the keypad. "Eleanor could you come in here for a moment, I'd like you to witness a document signing."

Flowers slid an expensive ballpoint across the table. Suds waited for Eleanor to join them before signing the document. "What's the job pay?" he asked.

"Seventy-five dollars an hour for anything you do for Franklin that's off the clock with your brewery job," Flowers said.

Suds returned the document, which was intercepted by Lantz who paused to allow Eleanor to witness it. Lantz busied herself with her notary seal. When she was done, she collected her papers and both women filed out of the room.

"OK gentlemen," Flowers said. "Now that the formalities are finished, let's get down to business. We'll want to hear a report on your trip to Charleston, Suds, but before you get started, Franklin wants to bring you up to speed on what precipitated it, the trip, I mean."

Ames pushed back in his chair and crossed his legs ankle on thigh. "Boyd Porter was a double agent," he began, and paused to collect his thoughts. "By that I mean he was working for my wife at the same time he was working for me. I hired him to see if my wife was faithful. He reported that she was. His report was a lie."

"How do you know that?"

"I rented a truck. Staked out his house and wasn't all that surprised when my wife arrived for a weekend rendezvous. I couldn't believe she was visiting a sick aunt. She wasn't. Showed up on Porter's doorstep carrying an overnight bag. And he let her in."

"Ouch!"

"Actually, the revelation wasn't painful at all. I was relieved."

"Why?"

Ernie took over. "Jasmine's indiscretion may give Franklin the legal authority to seize 200 shares of common stock he gave her as a wedding present."

"Why's that important?"

"Those 200 shares in the wrong hands could empower a hostile takeover of the brewery."

"Who would want to do that?"

"A lawyer name of Zach Dunkel. He's fucking my wife, too. I followed Porter, who was following Jasmine," Ames said. "We all ended up at the Starstream Motel."

"The place on Jonestown Road that rents rooms by the hour?" Suds asked.

"That's right."

"So if you knew Porter had filed a false report on Jasmine, why did you ask him to go Charleston," Suds asked.

"Who says I asked him to go to Charleston?"

"Well you did. Didn't you?"

"No."

"Who did?"

"Porter went on his own and expensed the trip to me, the bastard. Guess he figured he had me by the short hairs."

"Why?" Suds asked.

Franklin sighed "Here's the part where things get dicey."

"How so?"

Franklin took a deep breath. "For a long time, I've wondered about my ethnic heritage," he said. "One of the services offered by the company I hired to confirm Dickie's paternity, was an evaluation of heritage. I sent in my sample along with the samples for Dickie, Lisa and her parents to take advantage of a discount."

"So?"

"My test triggered an anonymous email telling me that I had a sick relative living in Charleston, S.C. and would I please get in touch."

"So Porter went off to Charleston . . ."

"To twist the arm of a desperate mother, I presume. The little shit. Funny thing is . . .

"What?"

"I'm sterile, or the next thing to it. So few swimmers that Emma never had a chance to get pregnant given her endometriosis. Poor woman."

"Emma?"

"My late first wife."

"So what happened?" Suds asked.

"Our best guess is the DNA samples got mixed up at the lab," Ernie interjected.

"That also would call into question Dickie's paternity of Lisa's child, wouldn't it?" Suds asked. "What a mess."

SUDS JUST ISN'T WORTH FIGHTING FOR

"So what did Julie Dubbel have to say?" Evie Pinson asked.

Linda Fontaine occupied Evie's visitor's chair. She ignored the question because the room needed clearing of an elephant named Suds. The two women had done their best to avoid each other over the last year. But Linda sensed a thawing. Office scuttlebutt is endemic. Talk had it that Evie's mood had lightened. Perhaps she had re-knitted some of the tatters of her fondness for Suds.

But which of them would mention Suds first?

Linda took up the gauntlet. "I know that Suds is all tangled up in this case, too," she began. "I owe you an explanation. For our tryst."

Evie's silence offered her adversary no harbor.

Linda filled the silence. "True confessions. I have a character flaw, an affinity for lost souls and lost causes," she said. "I've bedded all sorts of losers and the walking wounded because of it."

"In what category would you put Suds?"

"Definitely the walking wounded . . . with a little lost soul thrown in for good measure."

"I agree. Rufus's death wounded the both of us."

Linda winced. "I can only imagine what you went through . . . what you're still going through. I regret adding to your pain by sleeping with your husband."

Evie's half-smile surprised her. "Actually, it wasn't altogether a bad thing."

"How's that?"

"It re-channeled my grief. Gave me something else to be pissed off about."

"And to thank me you've assigned me every shit job that came down the pike?"

Evie laughed outright. "Yeah, I took a lot of pleasure in that. I also cut the crotches out of all of Suds's pants before I threw them out on the sidewalk. Made me feel a whole lot better."

It was Linda's time to laugh. "I heard about that. So we're OK now?"

"I wouldn't say we're OK. But we are a lot better than we used to be."

"Good. Suds Ferguson is just not worth fighting over," Linda said.

"Now about Julie Dubbel?"

"She's a battered woman. Left her husband a coupla years ago, filed a PFA then went back to him because she had no other prospects. His death didn't exactly fill her with grief. Why do you have me sniffing around this?"

"I'll get to that in a minute," Evie said. "Where was she when Chuck died?"

"At home taking care of Chucky junior."

"Not a very compelling alibi."

"Says her next door neighbor came over to watch the soaps. I checked. The neighbor confirms that."

"So the wife didn't do it."

"You think it wasn't an accident?" Linda asked, rephrasing her question.

"Let's just say I'm suspicious. So is the coroner. He may convene an inquest. I think maybe someone locked Chuck Dubbel in that room on purpose."

"Who discovered the body?"

"The tank watcher, Dexter Lager."

"Is he a suspect?"

"He's pointing fingers elsewhere."

"In what direction?"

"Chuck's daughter. Lager says he witnessed a heated argument between the two of them not 30 minutes before he found Chuck dead."

"You buying it?"

"Enough to ask the coroner to convene an inquest. He's tripping over the coincidence of two deaths at the same brewery in such a short period of time.

Gregg Taylor isn't a man who likes coincidences. He wants to call Dexter, Julie Dubbel and her daughter, Lisa, and the plant's safety supervisor to testify."

"I think we should have another chat with Lisa, don't you?" Linda asked.

"I have re-interviewing Lisa on my list of things to do."

"I could do that. Might be good to get another perspective."

"Job's yours."

"Anything else?"

"Nope. Meeting adjourned. And Linda."

"What?"

"In the future, I'd stay away from married men if I were you."

SUDS EXERCISES HIS TASTE BUDS

A drunk staggered up to Evie and Suds outside Harry's Tavern, known for its steaks and fishbowls of beer. The neighborhood bar sat on the fringes of Allison Hill, Harrisburg's ghetto. So it was no surprise when the drunk offered to sell them cocaine. Evie tensed and then relaxed. She was off duty. No need to intercede and spoil their date.

Inside, the hostess showed them to a dark booth in the back. A faux candle flickered on the tabletop. Suds watched as Evie slid onto the bench seat. He was glad she had worn a skirt. It showed off her legs, which in his opinion were the best among her many good features.

As Suds settled onto his bench opposite her, Evie asked: "So how goes your parallel investigation?"

Suds held up a finger. "We'll get to that in a moment. Here comes our waitress and I'm thirsty."

The waitress, a generation X'er with sleeve tattoos, lisped around her tongue piercing: "I'm Jenny. I'll be your server. Whadda ya drinking?"

Suds decided to eschew the Hop Central brand in favor of another prominent local brewery. "I'll have a Nimble Giant," he said, eager to wrap his palate around Troegs Independent Brewery's summertime double IPA.

Even sitting down Suds was as tall as their server. "Nimble Giant suits you," she lisped. "And for the lady?"

"I'll have an old-fashioned Manhattan, Makers Mark. Up, with an extra dash of bitters, and a cherry," she said.

"I'll be back with your drinks in a few minutes to give you some time to study the menu," Jenny said. She flip-flopped toward the bar, demonstrating poor judgment for waitressing footwear.

"A Manhattan? Your taste certainly has changed. You used to be a champagne cocktail sort of gal," Suds observed.

"Lately I've needed a higher octane. Boyd Porter?" Evie reminded, steering the conversation back on her intended path.

"Is this a date or an inquisition?"

"A little of both."

"Not much I can say. Not any more."

"I thought we agreed to cooperate."

"We did. And I will. But I'm handcuffed by attorney/client privilege."

"You go off and get a law degree in the last year?"

"No. But I have accepted a job as investigator with Ernest Flowers, Esq. My employment contract is signed and notarized."

Jenny showed up with their drinks. She could tell neither of them had picked up their menus. "Bar's not very busy. I'll give you a few more minutes," she said, and flip-flopped off again.

Evie rode through the interruption. "Wish I had negotiated a better deal."

"Whadda ya mean? You got the house and my bowling trophies," Suds said.

"And the mortgage. Should have clapped you in irons when I had the chance."

"I did mention our side agreement to Flowers and Ames," Suds said. "We kicked around how much I should tell you."

"So you're going to spoon feed me tidbits until the DA gets all you got in discovery? Not sure I can live with that."

Suds sighed. "It's the best I can do. Do you want to hear me out or not?"

"Go."

"OK. Here it is. Boyd Porter was playing both sides against the middle. We will present a variety of plausible suspects with much stronger motives for murder."

Evie swirled her Manhattan took a sip, smacked her lips. "So who's on the suspect list?"

"The late Chuck Dubbel, for one; Jasmine, for another. And how about Zach Dunkel?"

"Who's Zach Dunkel?"

"Jasmine's personal attorney and the legal representation for a group of investors angling to wrest control of Hop Central Brewery from Franklin Ames. Be easier to do that with Franklin in jail."

Evie was startled. "Hadn't heard about a hostile takeover."

"Franklin gave Jasmine 200 shares of common stock as a wedding gift. Just enough to unbalance his majority interest if those 200 shares vote in lockstep with those held by other investors."

"A big blunder for a buttoned-down businessman like your boss."

"He calls it an accounting error. Says the account doesn't work for him anymore."

"What else can you tell me?"

"I'm vetted to say that and nothing more."

"But there is more."

"Obviously."

"Will it come out at trial?"

"If it goes that far."

"What do you mean?"

"Ernie's angling to have the charges dismissed. Once they make their big reveal."

"And you can't tell me what that is?"

"Absolutely not."

"So where does that leave us?" Evie asked.

"With nothing else to do—other than enjoy a good meal. I'm having the 16-ounce New York strip, medium, with baked potato, and green beans. Maybe a cup of the seafood bisque for starters. How bout you?"

Evie picked up the menu. Scanned it for a moment. "Who's buying?" she asked.

"Dutch?"

"You owe me for letting you walk on breaking and entering. You haven't repaid that debt yet, not by a long shot."

"I was hoping to work that off later, between the sheets."

Evie patted Suds's right hand. "I like your optimism, big guy."

Bolstered by what was probably false hope, Suds said: "OK. Dinner is on me."

"In that case, I'll have the surf and turf."

"Big appetite."

"Big woman," Evie said.

"But in all the right places."

Jenny picked that time to show up for their orders. Suds ordered for both of them and waited until the sound of Jenny's flips had flopped.

"About Linda?" Suds said.

"Wow. Buzz kill."

"She was a mistake. An error in judgment. An expression of grief."

"To bad you expressed it on a desk in the evidence room with the cameras rolling."

"I didn't know about the security camera. I'd still like to know who uploaded the video to Youtube."

Suds heard a clunk. The sort of noise a woman's shoe makes when it hits the floor. A bare foot toed its way up his left pant's leg and settled in his crotch. "I did," Evie said, pumping her foot up and down gently.

Suds's response was predictable and immediate. Evie smiled.

"Son of a bitch," Suds said.

"Yes it was bitchy of me, but you deserved it."

"That's not what I'm talking about."

"What is?"

"Things are stirring and there's no Viagra involved."

"I noticed."

"What are we going to do about it?"

"Eat our dinners and see what develops," Evie said.

"You know that videotape cost me my job as police chief," Suds said.

"And created an employment opportunity for me."

"You stole my job," Suds said.

"You broke my heart."

Suds provided counter pressure to Evie's foot. "I think I can make it up to you."

Her eyes widened. "I think I know what I want for dessert," she said.

PILLOW TALK

Suds inserted the key in the lock of his former front door. Evie stood behind him, wobbling a bit with the effects of a second Manhattan.

"You sure about this? Suds asked over his shoulder as he turned the key.

"Don't read too much into it," Evie said. "I'm horny."

Suds withdrew the key, pushed open the door and stood back so Evie could enter. She dropped her purse on the vestibule highboy, kicked off her shoes and headed for the stairs. She paused on the first step. "There's a Mark West Pino Noir in the wine rack. Corkscrew lives in the same drawer as always. Give me a few minutes and bring me some wine."

Suds used the first-floor powder room to pee. His pocketing a Viagra tab before he picked Evie up was prescient. Just to be sure, he washed it down with a mouthful of tap water. He wondered if it would work. He was about to find out.

He made a production of opening the wine bottle, banging counter drawers as if he couldn't find the corkscrew. Anything to buy a bit of time for the Viagra to kick in. His face flushed with the effort. Or was it the meds? He prayed for the latter.

He poured two glasses of wine. Swirled the Mark West in his glass and took a tentative sip. Wine wasn't his thing. He preferred barley to grape. But the Pinot Noir wasn't bad. It lacked the heaviness of a Burgundy or Merlot. Much subtler, but the aftertaste lingered on his tongue long enough to overload his taste buds. An IPA was more his style.

Suds picked up both glasses and made his way down the hall pausing at the foot of the stairs to bump on the foyer light switch with his left elbow. He climbed the stairs on creaky knees, congratulating himself for not spilling a drop of wine.

Ardor shouted down remorse as he hurried past the closed door of Rufus's bedroom. Evie was waiting for him under the sheets on her side of his former king-sized bed. She was fast asleep.

Amusement fought with raging hormones and won. He laughed out loud. But not loud enough to wake Evie. He retreated to her dressing area just off the master bath and placed the wine glasses far enough back on her vanity to preclude an accidental spilling.

Evie had dialed back the rheostat but not enough to obscure his reflection in her big mirror which faithfully reproduced every bulge and blemish with no regard to vanity. He was carrying a few extra pounds. He had to admit it. Time to get back to the gym.

What to do? Wake her and hope her ardor would rekindle? Or let her sleep and chose a better time? Shrugging, he stripped to his undershorts, folded his clothes and stacked them in a neat pile on the floor.

Reentering the bedroom, he sat gingerly on the edge of the bed and swung his legs up and laid his head on the pillow, moving carefully so as not to awaken Evie. Despite his care, she stirred and rolled onto her side, facing away from him.

Suds inched his way toward her. Sensing his presence Evie snuggled backward until they spooned. Sexy underwear was part of their mating ritual. Her nakedness surprised him.

Contact established, Evie began to snore. Suds ignored his hard on and let her sleep. He was home again. He was content. Detente in the war between the sexes is a fragile thing. As he lay in his own bed again, Suds resolved to do everything he could to win Evie back. She was a big woman, just six inches shorter than he. The two of them fit. That's what she said the first time they made love. "When I'm with you, I don't have to slouch. I don't feel like a freak," she had said. "You feel pretty good to me," Suds had rejoined.

She still did.

Suds fell asleep to the rhythm of Evie's snoring.

At some point in the night, Suds became aware of movement. He had rolled onto his back. A naked leg, silky and warm, flopped over his thighs. The fingers of one hand teased his left nipple while the other hand explored the tip of his penis. He saluted the effort and squared his body underneath hers as she settled onto him.

The rhythms of her movement accelerated. He rose to meet her as she descended in ever-faster syncopation. He grabbed handfuls of breasts, squeezing then releasing to tease nipples between thumb and forefinger. She groaned pushed his hands away and offered her breasts to his mouth. He complied and her movements became more frantic. She pushed away far enough to find his mouth with hers. Their tongues dueled as climax overcame the two of them. She collapsed on top of him. And he held her tight to him wondering anew at the contentment a man could find in a woman.

"I love you."

Suds wondered who had said that. Was it he or she?

Evie settled that question. "And I forgive you," she said.

She rolled off him, arose from the bed, and headed for the bathroom, leaving Suds to bask in the afterglow of absolution.

She returned with a hand towel slung over her shoulder, bearing the wine he had left on her vanity. She set the wine glasses down on the nightstand and tossed him the hand towel. Clean yourself up she said. "I don't want pecker tracks on my clean sheets."

Suds laughed. "You always had a way with words."

He cleaned himself off and settled back, propping himself up on the headboard. The wine glass was within reach, so he picked it up, took a sip and winced.

Evie laughed. Disappeared into the walk-in closet and returned wearing a light robe and carrying Suds's wine glass. She settled in beside him. "Now that's over with, I'm taking sex off the table until we re-evaluate our relationship."

"We have a relationship?"

"Don't be flip with me Sidney Ferguson. I might be willing to take you back with some pre-conditions."

"Such as?"

"Such as you go with me to counseling so we can deal with our grief over losing Rufus."

"Aw Evie. You know how much I hate shrinks."

"I don't want either of us to shrink. I want us to expand . . . to realize that we can cope with our grief more effectively by leaning on each other."

"You're asking me to be vulnerable. I'm not sure I can do that. I cope by being strong, not by being weak."

"I get that and I love you for it. But I need you to admit that you're not bulletproof. That you need me as much as I need you."

"Didn't I just prove that to you?"

"I'm not talking sex. You know that."

"Sorry sex is my default. Now that I think about it, sex is a statement of vulnerability."

"How so?"

"I caught a glimpse of myself naked into your vanity mirror. If this isn't an expression of vulnerability, I don't know what is."

Evie laughed. "You have put on a few pounds," she said. "But I want you to be vulnerable with your clothes on."

"Give me a minute. I'll get dressed."

"I wish you would. I'm getting tired of staring at the naked fat guy."

"Ouch. I suppose I deserved that."

"You did. Now about counseling?"

Suds sighed. "OK. OK. I'm on board. Got anyone in mind?"

"As a matter of fact, I do. We have an appointment on at 3 P.M. on Wednesday, August 1, with Dr. Sharon Tillis. She's a Phd. A psychologist, not a psychiatrist. She specialized in grief and marriage counseling."

"Grief and marriage in the same sentence. Apropos that."

Evie set down her wine glass so she could punch him in the arm.

Rev set down his wine glass so he could take her in his arms. "Care for a rematch?"

She did.

FRANKLIN AMES GETS RELIGION

Franklin Ames slumped on his barstool, bellied up to the granite-topped island adrift in the center of his modern kitchen. He was surrounded by stainless steel, cold tile, and stark white cabinetry. The kitchen had the ambiance of a surgical suite. Jasmine's design, not his. He lived with it because it was easier that way.

On his first night of freedom, having been released on bail from Dauphin County Prison, he slept in a spare bedroom, mostly to avoid Jasmine's company. Of one thing he was certain. He was finished with her, no matter the consequence. That thought had awakened him at 5:30 A.M. He arose, peed and stumbled downstairs to brew a pot of coffee and think.

He sprinkled salt on the coffee grounds before he activated the Cuisinart, a trick he had learned from a master chief bosun's mate aboard the USS Compass Island, his first ship as brand-new ensign. The salt knocked down the bitterness.

Ames smacked his lips in appreciation as the coffee slid across his tongue, flavored with the perfect amount of half and half and honey. Clarity built with each sip. He reflected again about the colossal mistake of his second marriage.

His first marriage to Emma was a happy one. They were simpatico. They both liked James Taylor, home-brewed beer, island vacations, and supported conservative causes. Their sexual chemistry was low-key. Emma was the more eager.

Franklin was not entirely disappointed when endometriosis made sexual intercourse painful for her. Foreplay and oral sex became their mainstays but with increasing infrequency. The doctors recommended a hysterectomy. Emma resisted, cleaving to the false hope that one day she would be able to conceive.

Franklin met her at a mixer in Annapolis when he was a firstie at the academy. He left with her on his arm and married her over her father's objections right before he shipped out on the Compass Island. He abandoned ship after his second hitch in the Navy and they settled into domesticity in Harrisburg where he worked in a variety of management positions for insurance companies and banks before taking a flyer and launching his own brewery.

Through it all, he continued to serve in the Naval Reserve, in which he rose to the rank of captain. He figured if the brewery went bust, at least he would have a Navy pension to fall back on. Service in the Navy Reserve meant two weeks of active duty every summer. And on one such stint, to Charleston's Naval Weapons Center, his faithfulness faltered.

The details were unclear because alcohol had been involved. Way to much alcohol, consumed upon the occasion of his promotion to commander. The party was consummated by a trip to a whorehouse. He went along, reluctantly, eager to be just one of the boys.

What he had confessed to Suds and Ernie was true. His sperm count was well below average. So low that it was unlikely Emma could have conceived, even if she hadn't been afflicted with female problems. She knew that but still held out hope.

Was it possible that a prostitute had conceived his child? Was it possible that he had a sick son living in Charleston? If he could save his son's life. He had to do it. He had to be retested. Immediately.

Franklin pushed back from the countertop, collected his coffee mug and crossed the kitchen to the Cuisinart. He was pouring a refill when Jasmine swept into the room like Cleopatra arriving to take her place on the royal barge. Fitting because Jasmine was a real pain in the asp.

"Good morning. Why are you up so early?" he asked, wearily.

"We have to talk," Jasmine said.

"About what?"

"I want a divorce."

"Thank God."

"I want the house and $2,000 a month living expenses and $2,000 a month in child support."

"I never adopted Dickie so child support is off the table as far as I'm concerned. I won't fight you on the rest of it."

"Zach Dunkel says he can make a good case for child support."

"Who he?" Ames asked, feigning ignorance.

"My lawyer. He'll be filing the papers tomorrow. I'd like you to pack up and leave."

"Sooner the better as far as I'm concerned. But there is one unresolved issue."

"What's that?"

"The matter of your wedding gift. I'm exercising the moral's clause of our pre-nup. You haven't been cleaving to me and none other."

"Zach Dunkel says those 200 shares are mine free and clear."

"Not if you've been fucking other men. You have been and I can prove it."

"You bastard. Don't you get all high and mighty with me. Cause I can prove you have wandered, too. With men and prostitutes, no less."

Ames's face flushed. "That's preposterous," he sputtered.

"Not so much as you'd think. Before he died, Boyd Porter showed me the DNA results and the email from the whore who says you knocked her up."

"But the part about the men . . ."

"Oh come on Franklin. Anyone who's spent any amount of time with you can tell you are light in the loafers."

His head was reeling. Anger suffused his arteries and his heart pounded.

"Fatherhood is unlikely for medical reasons you are well aware of," Franklin said, shouting down the impulse to defend his masculinity.

"But you don't deny having sex with a prostitute, do you? Come on Franklin. I know you. The guilt is written all over your face."

Franklin had to choke out the words: "You are not the aggrieved party here. Emma was."

"Maybe so. But you still wouldn't want that to come out in court. And neither would the prostitute or her husband, whom I understand is a la-de-dah religious big shot in Charleston. Things could get real messy."

"How could you know all of this?"

Jasmine laughed. "I have my sources. You should be more careful about who you trust."

His mind ran over the possibilities. Suds? Ernie? Porter, obviously. Or maybe the walls had ears in Ernie's office. He had to get to the bottom of it.

"Now about your sick son? You're not thinking about writing him into the will, are you?" Jasmine asked.

"Whether he's my son remains to be seen, but he'll be sick, no matter what I do regarding you. Those shares are mine by contract and I intend to keep them."

"You might want to take a second look at our pre-nup," Jasmine said.

"Why?"

"It might not be as ironclad as you think." Jasmine switched to another tack, lowering yet another boom. "And then there's the matter of your arrest for murder. The prosecution has subpoenaed me. And let's just say that my testimony is negotiable."

"So you're willing to throw me under the bus on a murder rap as well as steal my company?"

"I'd say it's an either or proposition. Either I tell the court what a great man you are, and you don't contest my shares in the divorce. Or you fight me on the Hop Central shares and maybe go to jail for murder."

"My god woman. What did I do to deserve you?"

Jasmine's smile oozed evil. She grabbed her boobs. Squeezed them. "You're an odd man, queer, you might say. But typical of your gender, you think with your dick."

"Fuck you Jasmine!"

"No sweetie. It is you who are fucked."

SUDS AIMS TO REPAIR HIS RELATIONSHIP

Suds returned to his apartment the next morning to shower, shave, and dress in fresh clothing. Still aglow from last night's love making, he picked Evie up precisely at 10 just as they had planned. Evie admired punctuality. He snugged his Crown Vic next to the curb, hopped out and opened the door for Evie who had been watching for him from the front window.

She shouldered past his attempt at a smooch. Buyers regret? He hoped not. But then, again, she had never been a morning person. Her first words confirmed that. "Coffee!"

Suds nodded. "There's a Starbucks along the way."

They rode in convivial silence until Starbucks loomed. They were first up in the drive-through. A disembodied voice said: "How may I help you?"

Suds knew what to do. "Two large coffees. One with milk. One with cream and sugar."

"Love a guy who takes charge," Evie said, uttering her second through seventh words of the morning.

The window slid open. Cash was exchanged and Suds settled the two coffees into the cup holders on his console. "Yours is in front."

Evie claimed her coffee. Took a sip. "Now we can talk."

"About what?"

"About how I'm going to kick your ass on the shooting range. Got your piece?"

Suds grinned and grabbed his crotch. "Right here. Like always."

"Pervert."

"We re-established that last night, didn't we?"

"Yes we did," Evie agreed. "Whadda shooting?"

"I brought my .380 Walther PPK. Makes me feel like James Bond."

"A prissy gun for a prissy guy. I'll take my Glock 9 any day. More rounds. More stopping power."

"If you hit what you're aiming at the first time you don't need the extra rounds or the stopping power. Dead is dead whether you're run over by a VW or a locomotive."

Their marksmanship rivalry was legendary. Suds hit what he aimed at always. Evie hit what she aimed at mostly. She had never beaten Suds but she kept trying and trash talking.

"When was the last time you shot?"

"Been a couple of months."

"Good. Gives me a chance. I've been practicing."

They soon arrived at Boyer's Gun Shop, which boasted a modern shooting range with all the bells and whistles. The parking lot was full but Suds wasn't concerned, he'd reserved side-by-side booths for 10:30.

Evie collected her purse. As they alit from the car, she asked: "Where's your Walther?"

Suds patted his hip. "Inside-the-pants holster. Right here. That's why I like it. Can't tell I'm armed, can you?"

"Has nothing to do with the gun. More to do with the belly."

"Ouch."

Inside the shop, Suds turned right and headed toward the main counter. "Check us in at the range. I need to pick up some gun oil, cleaning patches and a couple boxes of practice rounds. Don't want to waste my hollow points on the range."

As he made his choices he glanced over at the counter where a salesman was showing a woman a handgun. She was short, brunette and well-endowed. Her ample chest rested on the countertop.

"The Ruger is a solid piece. Not expensive but good bang for the buck," the salesman said.

"That's the part I'm interested in. The bang," the woman said. "Can you show me how to work it?"

The salesman was young and handsome. The shopper was middle aged, sexy and flirtatious.

"Sure. I give lessons."

"How do I sign up?"

"They keep my appointment book back on the range."

The woman put the gun back on the countertop, contriving to brush hands with the salesman as she did. "I'll keep that in mind. I'll take it. The Ruger, I mean."

"OK. I'll need your driver's license to get the paperwork started. You'll have to pass a state police background check."

Suds had heard enough. Eager to avoid an encounter with the woman, he took his supplies to the back register. He paid and joined Evie in the queue, waiting for their range reservation.

"What took you so long?" Evie asked.

Suds cocked his head. "Why do you suppose Jasmine Ames would be buying a handgun?"

"I think that might be a clue," said Evie.

The clerk at the gun range said: "Next up Ferguson!"

"Come on Babe. It's time to make some noise."

"I thought we did that last night," Evie said.

They donned ear and eye protection in the anteroom before buzzing through the final door to the range. They had two booths on the far end where they set up their targets, the classic silhouette of a man pointing a gun at them. The bull's eye was in the center of the silhouette's chest.

"What distance do you want to start at?" Suds asked.

"Five yards. Ten rounds?"

"Only got eight. One in the chamber and seven in the clip."

"That's what you get for buying a wussy gun. Eight it is."

They punched five yards into the computer and the targets slid into place.

"Fire when ready!" Suds shouted.

Suds emptied his weapon. Evie stopped at eight.

They retrieved their targets to tally the scores. They both put all eight rounds in the center ring of the bull's-eye.

"Ten yards? This time, Annie Oakley?"

"You're on."

Suds ejected the spent clip. Inserted a new one and jacked a round into the chamber. He ejected the clip and inserted an extra round. Slamming the clip back in place, he said. "Ready when you are."

They sent their targets out 10 yards and steadied themselves on the firing line.

"Go!" Evie shouted.

Eight rounds for the both of them. Same result. Bull's-eyes all around.

The pause to reload gave Evie the opportunity to trash talk. "Got ya rattled now don't I?"

"I can tell you've been practicing," Suds said. "Want to take it all the way back?"

"Let's do it."

Eight rounds. Two just outside the inner circle. One each. Another tie.

"How about a tie-breaker?" Suds said.

"Shoot."

Suds retrieved his target and pulled a playing card from his shirt pocket. He masking-taped the playing card to the target so that the edge of it would face the shooter and sent the target out eight yards.

"You shoot first and we keep alternating til one of us splits the card."

Suds split the card on his third shot. Evie didn't hold serve.

"Game, set, match to Suds Ferguson," Suds exulted.

"Remember what happened last night?" Evie asked. "It won't be happening again for a long, long time."

"Can I have a mulligan?"

Evie nodded and Suds replaced the card. Sent it out again, shot and missed. "Shall we call it a draw?"

"You bet."

Suds holstered his Walther and collected his unspent rounds and cleaning supplies while Evie stowed her piece and ammo in her big purse.

"Let's get out of here," Evie said.

As they left the range, Jasmine Ames was banging away with her new Ruger 9mm in the first booth. Suds noticed that she was shooting left-handed. He glanced at her target, which was set out 10 yards and saw that she had grouped three shots in the bull's eye and three in the second ring. Not bad shooting for the first time out with a new handgun. Jasmine had some shooting skills.

FRANKLIN AMES TAKES A FLYER

While Jasmine Ames was banging away with her new handgun, Franklin Ames was ensconced in his office staring through the one-way glass as workers scurried about their tasks on the brewery floor. The clothes that mattered the most to him occupied a big suitcase he had dragged from the basement. "Give the rest to Goodwill or burn em for all I care," he said before he slammed the front door of his former house behind him.

Franklin traveled light. The possessions he cared about most already occupied his spacious office at the brewery, along with all of his personal and business files. He had treated his Country Club Hills house like a Hilton. It was a space that he passed through but never really lived in. Like Jasmine that big house was a big mistake. He took some solace in sequestering his two big booboos in one place where he could keep an eye on the both of them.

Furniture from the home he had shared with Emma was in storage because Jasmine would have none of it in her new house and Ames couldn't stand to part with the vestiges of Emma. He could easily refurnish a modest space for himself without buying anything new. There was some poetic justice there, the memories of Emma were far less painful than those of Jasmine. The math of it was simple Emma=wistful regret. Jasmine=excruciating pain.

The results of the DNA test he had submitted that very morning wouldn't be known for a couple of days. He'd arranged to expedite the test through his personal physician who had drawn the requisite blood sample.

Suds had supplied the address and name of the woman who may have borne Franklin's child. He intended to fly to Charleston as soon as he had the results in hand, confront Geraldine Smith with the results of the DNA test and arrange for a bone marrow donation on the spot if the test confirmed that he was indeed the father of Alex Smith. It was the right thing to do. In a perverse sort of way the thought that he may have fathered a child with a prostitute gave him some validation as a man. Maybe he wasn't a sterile vessel with no biological future. Maybe something of him would live on beyond his own inevitable death.

Franklin tried to picture Geraldine Smith in his mind's eye. But his recollections of her were addled by the alcohol he had consumed that night and by the sort of forgetfulness one embraces when a memory is shameful as this one certainly was.

He must not have worn a condom. He was thinking with his dick, which was incapable of foretelling bad outcomes. Given the level of his virility, pregnancy was an unlikely outcome he would soon put to the test. But thank God an STD hadn't happened. The thought that he might have carted a venereal disease home to subsequent lovers made him shiver. And, of course, AIDS was a constant specter.

The whore was short-skirted lithe, willing and skillful. He recalled that much. She had sidled up to him at the bar as he ordered his third, or was it his fourth vodka martini? Her hand on his arm as he turned to rejoin his shipmates at their table was encouragement enough.

Two empty barstools beckoned and he and the woman soon occupied them, knees bumping, her short skirt riding up on silken thigh, her breath hot on his face as she leaned in to make her pitch. "You seem to be celebrating something. Your 35th birthday perhaps? I could be the icing on your birthday cake."

Alcohol had reduced his inhibitions. He was in a celebratory mood having just been promoted to Commander in the Navy Reserve. It was a feather in his cap that would pay big dividends down the road when it came time to retire.

Her hyperbolic flattery tipped the scales. He was well into his 40s, but it felt good to be flattered—even by a pro. And so, Franklin bought her a drink, finished his own, and negotiated the terms for her to put icing on his birthday suit. Never mind the cake.

The deal was consummated in a Hilton. Franklin remembered that much because he had to explain the Visa bill to Emma. "I celebrated my promotion a bit too hard and had to rent a hotel room because I was too drunk to drive back to the base," he had explained. And Emma had bought it, because she trusted him.

How he hated that her trust was misplaced, just as his virtue had been that steamy night in Charleston.

It had cost him all the cash he had on hand to persuade the whore to sleep over. He recalled returning to the well at least twice for deeper draughts of sex before unconsciousness claimed him. He recalled that light was peeking through the curtains as she kissed him on the forehead and walked out of his life . . . until now?

His thoughts returned to his current dilemmas, a murder rap, and the possibility he had fathered a son, unlikely though that might be. Franklin sucked his teeth. Something about Jasmine's calm demeanor as she facilitated his exit from her life bothered him. He had escaped too easily. No dishes had been broken, and Jasmine was of the dish-breaking sort. She was promising a fight on the stock option issue, but Ernest Flowers was certain they would prevail in court given the evidence of Jasmine's infidelity. So the company would remain under his control, despite the disquiet of minority stockholders eager to cash in on their long-ago investment.

But what of the fate of the company after he died or became senile? Who would move it forward? It was long past time to begin that conversation with the experts. Jasmine was the sole beneficiary of his life insurance policy and would inherit all of his personal property in the event of his demise. That was something he would have to change with alacrity now that the two of them were parting ways.

Franklin picked up the phone, dialed Ernest Flowers's number. "Attorney Ernie. I need to talk to you about changing my will."

His lawyer was startled. "Don't you think we should be devoting most of our efforts to your defense?"

"Jasmine is divorcing me and has intimated that she will be a willing witness for the prosecution. It's time to cut her ass out of the will."

"I know it's a Saturday, but why don't you come in this afternoon. Say 2 P.M.?"

"Works for me." Hanging up, Franklin logged onto his computer and booked a 10 A.M. direct flight from Baltimore to Charleston, South Carolina, two days hence. It was a violation of the terms of his bail, but Franklin didn't care. It was long past time to visit the whore Girty's Snatch. He wondered what his reception would be.

HARRISON FORD IS A SUPERSTAR

Wednesday, July 18, 2018

The land-line phone was ringing on his desktop as Suds Ferguson arrived in his office at Hops Central. Suds sat down. Picked up the phone.

"Where the hell have you been?" Ernie Flowers bellowed. "I've been trying to reach you since six o'clock yesterday. Why haven't you answered your cell?"

Suds blushed. He'd turned off the ringer because he and Evie were like newlyweds, so preoccupied with their renewed carnal knowledge of each other that the rest of the world had slipped away.

Suds lied. "Sorry about that. My cell died. What's up?"

"Franklin has disappeared."

Suds didn't mean to be frivolous. But sex with Evie had made him giddy. "You mean like a magician. Poof he's gone?"

"Asshole. We were supposed to meet yesterday to prepare for his prelimi- nary hearing tomorrow afternoon and he was a no show. If I don't hear from him soon, I might have to waive his hearing, even though we have an outside shot at getting the charges dismissed at the DJ level. Thanks to you, I can make a pretty good case that Lisa Dubbel is an unreliable witness and she's the only one who puts Franklin at the murder scene."

"What do you want me to do about it?"

"Find him. You're the detective."

"Ex-detective."

"Whatever. Go detect!"

Suds wished he had lingered with Evie long enough for a second cup of coffee. His synapses weren't firing on all cylinders. "Got any clues. To detect, I need clues."

"Franklin was maudlin when we met on Saturday afternoon. Instead of preparing for his defense, we reworked his will to secure his legacy and to make sure Jasmine doesn't get a dime. He was expecting the results of a second round of DNA testing. If I had to guess, I'd say he absconded to Charleston, even though leaving the state is a violation of his bail. If he doesn't show up in time for the preliminary hearing, he could end up back in jail."

"I know a guy in Charleston," Suds said. "I'll give him a call and get back to you."

"How will we get in touch if your cell is dead?"

Suds paused, decided to come clean. "I lied. I turned off the phone because I was having carnal knowledge of a beautiful woman."

The attorney laughed. "A worthy excuse. She must be a special lady."

"She sure is," Suds said and hung up.

He extracted Gerry Smith's cell from his electronic phone book. His call went straight to her voice mail. He left a message and dialed up Harrison Ford.

———

Harrison Ford had just collected his coffee from a Starbucks barista when his cell phone went off. According to caller ID, Suds was on the line. Ford took his coffee to a table, sat down and answered his phone.

"What up my bud Suds?"

"I hate it when you say that."

"Which is why I say it. To what do I owe the pleasure?"

"My boss has taken a powder."

"Aren't you being all Micky Spillaneish?"

Suds ignored the interruption. "We can't find him and he's got a 3:30 preliminary hearing before the DJ tomorrow. If he doesn't show, he may end up back in jail."

82

"What's that got to do with me?"

"I'm hoping you can make some calls. See if he showed up at Gerry Smith house."

"Why don't you call her?"

"I did. Several times. No answer. Straight to voice mail. I was hoping you could stop by her place. Maybe run down the hubby at church."

"Wait one."

Ford put Suds on hold while he navigated to his electronic calendar. Picking up again, he said. "My morning's free. I'll see what I can do."

"Thanks buds."

"You're welcome Suds."

"We've got to take this act on the road," Suds said.

Harry Ford activated the Google Maps ap on his smart phone. Gerry Smith's address was in memory. He punched navigate and headed outside to his car. When he arrived at the Smith mansion, the gates to the circular drive were open. He cut the wheels to the curb, parked and headed up the steps to Gerry's front door. He rang the doorbell and waited.

And waited.

And waited.

He checked his watch. Punched the doorbell again. Just then he heard a car turn into the drive behind him. Gerry Smith alighted from a red Mercedes convertible with the top down. She paused and took a deep breath when she saw Harry on her doorstep. She squared her shoulders and walked toward him. "Mr. Ford, isn't it?"

"That's right. I'm wondering if you've seen anything of Franklin Ames. A little bird told me he might be headed your way."

Gerry cocked her head to one side. "Franklin is a saint."

"High praise. Do you know where he is?"

"At the hospital."

"Shit! What happened?"

"Nothing bad. Franklin's a match. He's agreed to be a bone marrow donor for Alex." She paused. And blushed. "Actually. Our son. Franklin's and mine."

"So he was the one?"

"That's right. Rh-null is as rare as hen teeth and he has it, too. Passed it onto our son."

"A John with a heart of gold."

Gerry stomped her foot. "Don't you be snide. We have a lot of baggage between the two of us. But I'm carrying far more than he. Franklin's a good man, willing to stand up behind a one-night stand."

"A saint. By all accounts."

Gerry let the gibe pass. "Anyway. I've got to get back to the hospital. We forgot Alex's Pooh Bear. He wants a cuddle."

Ford touched his forehead. A tacit salute to the generosity of Franklin Ames and the good fortune of Alex. "I'll be going then. Thanks, Gerry."

He returned to his car and called Suds to report on the whereabouts of Franklin Ames.

"Harrison Ford is a superstar," Suds Ferguson said when he heard the news.

ZACH DUNKEL GETS SCREWED

Zach Dunkel paused in mid thrust and leaned forward to grab double hands-full of breasts. Jasmine Ames was on all fours in front of him. She didn't pardon the interruption. "Whatsa matter? You miss Porter's dick up your ass?"

Dunkel thrust forward, hard. Aiming to inflict pain rather than pleasure, which for Jasmine often amounted to the same thing. "About as much as you miss his balls in your face," he said.

Jasmine gasped. "I love it when you talk dirty. But I do miss our ménage a trios'."

Dunkel groaned. "So do I. Porter was a good fuck. Shame the son of a bitch got himself killed." He squeezed harder and she slammed her rear into reverse with enough force to hurt them both.

They were thus engaged when the bedroom door flew open, banging into the doorstop with enough force to startle Zach to orgasm. He fell forward onto Jasmine's back and she collapsed under him.

"Talk about your simultaneous orgasms," a whiskey voice growled.

Zach Dunkel didn't need much of an imagination to conclude that the cold tube pressing on his anus was the barrel of a gun. A glance over his shoulder confirmed it. A revolver. A .38 police special nicely blued. The man wielding it pulled the trigger. Click. No bang. Dunkel clinched his ass cheeks on a shart.

The pressure relented as the man stepped back. "Cover that shit up. I've seen more than I want to."

Zach rolled off Jasmine. Both of them flopped to their backs and propped up on the headboard. Zach covered them with the bedspread.

The newcomer sat down in an armchair facing the bed, crossed one leg over the other and aimed the handgun first at Jasmine. Click. Click. And then at Dunkel. Click. Click.

He was a short man. Muscular and crew cut. A scar split his left cheekbone nose high to chin. There was more hair on his upper lip than his head. "It would seem that I have your attention."

"How did you get in?" Dunkel asked.

"You'll need to call a carpenter to fix your front door," the man said. "Unless you're handy with tools other than the limp one between your legs."

"What do you want, Zeke?" Dunkel asked, hating himself for the tremor in his voice.

"You are in some deep shit."

"How's that?" Dunkel asked.

"I hear the brewery deal is in the crapper. Mr. Lewis is not a happy man. He was counting on you."

"It's just a bump in the road, Zeke. Tell Johnny I've got things under control. We're going to execute Plan B."

"What's Plan B?" Zeke asked.

"You don't want to know. Johnny will want deniability."

Zeke brought the .38 to shoulder level. Squeezed the trigger. The chamber wasn't empty this time. The gun roared. The bullet splintered the headboard between their noggins.

Zeke arose in fluid motion. "I'd say you'd better get busy with Plan B."

He turned and left, banging the door closed behind him.

Dunkel's heart was pounding in his ears, which still rang from the gunshot.

"What's Plan B?" Jasmine asked.

"Huh?"

"I said: 'What's Plan B!" Jasmine screamed.

"I wish I knew," Dunkel said.

"What have you gotten us into?" Jasmine shouted.

"I wish I knew," Dunkel repeated.

"I think you do. I think you're screwed."

"Then so are you."

"No I'm not. Cause I'm not a ball-less weanie. You want a Plan B. I'll give you one!"

FRANKLIN AMES MISSES A COURT DATE

Thursday, July 19, 2018

Consciousness built like a tsunami in deep water and moved toward the shoreline of awareness. Sensation returned to his extremities first. He became aware of his fingers and toes, then his lips and nose. They tingled.

A woman's voice tickled his ossicles. "He's waking up."

"He's awake," Franklin Ames said, startling himself with his own voice.

Franklin opened his eyes. The recovery room, blurry at first, gradually took on definition as his eyes adjusted to the light. A nurse bent over him. Stared into his eyes. Checked the gauges and stepped back.

"How are you feeling?" She asked.

"How is Alex?"

"Don't worry about that. How are you?"

"Groggy."

"Alex is fine. He won't receive your donation for a while yet. They have to prepare him to receive it."

Franklin's synapses began firing. "I knew that. Must be addled by the anesthesia."

"Would you like something to drink? I can offer you Coke or ginger ale. Maybe some graham crackers?"

"Ginger ale and crackers sound just fine."

"I'll be back."

The nurse squeaked away on rubber-soled shoes.

His mind wandered. He felt tingly. Out of sorts.

The nurse squeaked back. Popped the tab on a tiny can of ginger ale and poured it over ice in a plastic cup. She plopped cellophaned crackers in front of him, glanced one more time at his monitors and said: "I'll check back with you in a few minutes."

Off she went, leaving Franklin to his reverie.

The harvesting site on his pelvis itched a bit and there was some residual soreness. Overall he felt pretty good, satisfied with himself for stepping beyond his own needs to help someone else. Emma would have been proud of him. Jasmine would be furious. Particularly when she found out that not only had he cut her and Dickie out of his will but he'd also established a bona fide heir. A blood relative, for Christ's sake. Fuck Dickie Cox. He felt sorry for Lisa Dubbel's unborn child, a little girl as he recalled. But he owed Lisa's daughter nothing. You can't save the world. Best you can do is secure a little piece of it. In helping Alex Smith . . . his son . . . he had done just that.

Alex's physicians were confident of the match, delighted with the aligning of blood type. Rh-null is practically one of a kind, they told him. It also pinned down his paternity convincingly. So his instructions to Ernest Flowers were spot on. Alex was his child. His heir as soon as he signed the new will and had it notarized. Tasks he intended to accomplish as soon as he returned to Harrisburg.

Thoughts of attorney Ernie reminded him. He had a court date he wasn't going to make. His attorney would be furious. Ernie intended to impugn the testimony of Lisa Dubbel at the preliminary hearing. Ernie thought they had a better than an even chance of getting the charges dismissed with prejudice at the DJ level. That would allow him to get on with his life.

Franklin knew that he had not committed murder, but the thought that someone close to him probably had troubled him. He was patriarchal in his dealings with staff. Porter's murderer almost had to be an employee of Hop Central. So who had killed him and why?

Franklin could not conceive of someone with more motive than himself. The son of a bitch had lied to him about Jasmine. Worse than that, Porter had fucked Jasmine. Everyone knew that Franklin Ames was not a man to be trifled with, which is probably why he had been the primary suspect from the very beginning.

Despite that, the Derry Twp. Police chief had seemed reluctant to settle on Franklin as a suspect, even in the face of the evidence of his fingerprints on the forklift levers and brewers' boots. He had Suds to thank for that. The love-hate needle on the meter chronicling the stormy relationship of Evie and Suds was trending to the love side of things. Franklin could sense that in their brief confab in his office. Suds had a reputation as a skillful investigator. His wife was no slouch either, by all accounts. Between the two of them, they just might come up with an alternate suspect that would complete the vindication of Franklin Ames.

He needed to make some phone calls. That much was clear. Ernie, Suds, Jasmine and her attorney, Zach Dunkel, were all on his call list. Time to get busy. He needed to figure out who had ratted him out to Jasmine. Where the hell was his cell phone?

He fumbled with his bedclothes. Found the buzzer drooped over his shoulder and summoned the nurse. She showed up five minutes later, harassed and harried like all RNs in hospitals, which are almost universally understaffed.

"You in pain?" the nurse asked.

"No. I need my phone."

The nurse sighed. "It's in the bag under your bed. I'll get it for you."

She dug the bag from beneath the bed, loosened the drawstring and handed it to him, tapping her foot as he dug through his possession and found the phone. She collected the bag, returned it to its spot under his bed. "Anything else."

"Nope."

For appearance's sake, the nurse glanced at his monitors and took his pulse. Satisfied, she sashayed away, polyester swishing on trousered thighs.

"Remind me not to spend any more time than necessary in hospitals," Franklin thought to himself as he punched the button connecting him to attorney Ernie.

LINDA FONTAINE SWEATS LISA DUBBEL

"How are you feeling?" Linda Fontaine asked.

"Pregnant," Lisa Dubbel replied.

"Couple of things I want to follow up on with you."

Lisa said nothing.

They were sitting on opposite ends of Julie Dubbel's threadbare couch. Julie wasn't home. Linda had planned it that way. She wanted unfettered access to the truculent teen.

"What?" Lisa said, finally breaking her silence.

Linda tried on her opening gambit. "Sorry about your father."

Lisa studied her toes. She was wearing lime green flip-flops and the orange polish was wearing off her toenails. She had ugly feet. But then Linda thought all feet were ugly. She wished Lisa would cover hers up.

"Uh. Thanks."

"It must be awful losing your father. I wouldn't know. Mine's still alive. He lives in Seattle. I talk to him every week."

Lisa studied her fingernails. Same chipped orange polish. "That's nice."

"You get along with your Dad? I used to fight a lot with mine."

Lisa made eye contact and broke it. "Dad was OK, I guess. He and Mom fought some."

"Physical fights or just mouth battles?"

"Both."

"That must have been tough on you."

Lisa shook her head, agreeing or disagreeing? Linda couldn't tell.

"Do you like boys?" Linda asked, ratcheting up the pressure.

"Whadaya mean?"

"You know. Young men."

Lisa shrugged. Linda tried again. "Boys are the enemy," she said. "All they are after, when they see a pretty girl, is one thing."

"Older men are like that, too," Lisa said, making eye contact and holding it.

"You know some older men?"

"Sure they are all around me . . . at the brewery. Their eyes follow me everywhere. They stare at my legs, my butt, my chest."

"How does that make you feel?"

"Sorry for them, mostly. So driven by that one thing."

"What thing is that?"

Lisa dropped the pretense of innocence. "The thing between their legs."

"Was Dickie Cox like that?"

Lisa's eyes softened. "Dickie is just a kid. He didn't know how to do it."

"So you showed him."

"Things never got that far. We fooled around. That's all. By the time Dickie got around to me, I was feeling sick. We necked mostly. Once I . . ."

"Yes?"

"You know. Went down on him."

"That's it? No intercourse?"

"He spurted. That's about all he had in him."

"So how do you figure he's the father?"

"He's not."

"Then who is?"

"I don't know. Could be a coupla guys."

"Then why was your father pressuring Franklin Ames for child support?"

"Because he could pay. And none of the other guys could."

"Is that what you and your father were arguing about on the day he died?"

"Who says we were arguing?"

"Cloyd Jackson for one," Linda said. "Dexter Lager for another."

"That weasel. Seems he's figured out another way to fuck me."

"Which weasel."

"Cloyd."

"You denying that you and your father argued?"

"Nah. Cloyd's a dick. That's all. Dexter? He's OK."

"So what were you fighting about?"

"You know. Just family stuff. No big deal, really."

"Tell me."

Lisa sighed. "I was feeling sorry for Dickie. I wanted to tell him he wasn't the father. Dad said if I did he'd bitch slap me to Sunday."

"Cloyd says your Dad pushed you and that you pushed back. Cloyd says that your Dad raised his hand to slap you and then thought better of it because other people were watching. That's sounds like a pretty heated dispute to me."

"Nothing unusual for our family," Lisa said, making no attempt to hide the bitterness in her voice.

Linda went fishing. "You sure you weren't arguing about Franklin Ames?"

"Why would we argue about him?"

"You sure you saw the big boss on the loading dock the morning Boyd Miller got killed?"

They were interrupted by Julie Dubbel's arrival. The front door banged open, butted by Julie's hip as she staggered into the room under the weight of three shopping bags full of groceries.

Lisa jumped to her feet. "Let me help you with those, Mom."

Julie sniffed. "Be the first time you helped me," she said. "Who's our visitor?"

"I dunno. Some cop, asking me stuff about Dad and Mr. Ames."

Julie stiffened. "Whoever you are. This interview is over. Lisa's a minor. You should never have talked to her alone."

Linda stood, straightened the creases on her uniform pants, pulled a business card from her pocket and dropped it on the end table nearest her. "I'm sorry Mrs. Dubbel. My name is Linda Fontaine. I'm a sergeant with the Derry Township police. Just a couple things I needed to clear up with your daughter. If you've got any questions for me, my number's on the card."

Linda left Julie and Lisa Dubbel glaring at each other in the living room. Julie's arrival had been unfortunate. Linda left feeling that she had been on the cusp of prying some important information from Lisa.

The interview by any measure was a success. No matter what the DNA test said, Dickie Cox was not the father of Lisa Dubbel's child. But who was? And how would she find out, if even Lisa did not know? She needed to ask state police to take another look at those DNA results. ASAP.

FRANKLIN AMES DODGES
A BULLET

Friday, July 20, 2018

Franklin's iPhone intoned *you're a bitch rich girl* by Hall and Oates. The ring tone told him Jasmine was on the line. It was childish, but it amused him.

"What do you want?"

"To meet. This evening at our house."

"You mean my former house?"

"Whatever."

"Why?"

"I've been talking with Zach about how we can handle those 200 shares of brewery stock in a way that will satisfy us both."

"Can't imagine how that might happen, but go ahead. I'm listening."

"Not now. Tonight at 9."

"Why then?"

"Ducks need to line up in a row. That's the earliest I can do it."

"Your lawyer going to be there?"

"No. This is just between the two of us."

"I might ask Ernie to join us."

"Ernie's a peach. I'm sure he'd show up for me, if not for you."

Franklin was nonplussed. "What do you mean by that?"

"Ernie's a horn dog. Likes to stare at my tits and ass. If he knows I'll be there, he'll be there."

"You flatter yourself woman."

"Ain't flattery if it's the truth. Don't forget, T and A is what got you to the altar which is why I think we should keep this between the two of us. I intend to put my ass-ets on the line."

Franklin snorted. He caught a glimpse of the Jasmine he had fallen for.

"So just the two of us. No seconds?"

She caught the allusion. "Ha. But I get to choose the weapons. Tits at 10 paces."

Franklin laughed. Picked up the gauntlet. "See you at 9."

Hanging up, he shouted down the prurience supercharging his synapses. This was not a matter to be settled between the sheets. Sex, after all, lay at the root of his current dilemma. He pushed his chair away from his desk. Stood and stretched the kinks out of his spine. He cracked his knuckles, rolled his shoulders, returned to his seat, and picked up his iPhone. He scrolled through his favorites' list, selected a number, and punched send.

"Hello."

"She wants to meet tonight."

"Yeah. I know. She told me."

"Got any idea what she's planning?"

"Dunno. But I've reviewed the pre-nup."

"And?"

"And no matter who she has been fucking, it is you who are fucked."

"That snake."

"What are you going to do?"

"Best you not know."

———

Franklin showed up at 9. Right on time. He pulled his Subaru Forester into the three-bay garage, which was below grade to the rear of the monstrosity of a house Jasmine had designed. He killed the headlights and was startled to see Jasmine silhouetted in the meager light of the garage door opener. She was waiting for him at the foot of a flight of three steps that led from the garage to the house.

She was holding something in her left hand next to her hip. He couldn't make out what it was in the gloom of the garage. She raised her left hand and it registered. Gun!

The shot sounded like someone clapping their hands. It shattered the windshield of his Subaru Forester. Fight/flight impulses competed. Fight recognized that the gun was silenced and the extra weight probably was affecting Jasmine's aim. Maybe there was an opportunity to disarm her. Flight urged him to get the hell out of there.

Another handclap. And the shot went God knows where. Flight won the fight. His car door was still open and he dove face first across the console banging his chest painfully on the gearshift. The Subaru had a push button start. He depressed the brake pedal with his left hand and jabbed the start button with his right index finger. The car turned over. Came to life.

He turned his hips, came to a seating position, slumping as low as possible as Jasmine fired a third and a fourth time. It was clear she was trying to kill him. Thank God the garage door was still up. He jammed the car into reverse. His steering was erratic and he lost the passenger side mirror on the garage doorframe.

As he sped away, the wind slamming him in the face, he wondered what Jasmine was thinking. Best guess? She would spin his murder as self-defense. Claim they had fought about her brewery stock and he had attacked her in a rage. She had no choice. Self defense. But four shots? *"Shit. She must hate me as muh as I hate her."* Should he call the police? No. He had more than enough of police of late. This was war. It was time to declare DEFCON 1 and empty the missile silos.

MATILDA DOES HER DOODY

Saturday, July 21, 2018

Simone Maxwell walked her miniature Yorkie, Matilda, past the beer baron's palace at 10 P.M. on a moonless night. The streetlight on the corner cast ominous shadows through sweet gum branches onto the side of the box-on-box contemporary. The Ames's had deposited their nouveau riche monstrosity on the last available lot in an otherwise exclusive neighborhood.

How Simone hated that house! Couldn't understand why the homeowners' association had signed off on it. Matilda's nails clicked on the sidewalk. Cicadas sang. The humid air clung to her skin like a wet blanket. She couldn't wait to retreat to the air-conditioning. Damn Matilda's tiny bladder and even smaller colon.

Matilda paused in the grassy strip between the sidewalk and street. She circled twice and hunched her back, bringing her back paws close to her front. "That's it girl. Do your doody and we'll go home for a cool drink. Mommy needs her bedtime spritzer."

Simone pulled a poop bag from the canister attached to Matilda's leash. As she bent to retrieve the little dog's nighttime deposit, she glanced at the Ames's

98

house. In that moment, she saw a flash in an upstairs window and heard a loud bang! She was so startled that she dropped the leash and had to lurch forward to catch it before Matilda darted away. In so doing, she stepped on the little dog's poop, which she scrapped from her shoe on the curb as she fumbled her smart phone from her back pocket.

"Sometimes, shit really does happen," she said, punching furiously at the keypad.

"911. What's your emergency?"

"I'd like to report a gunshot at 422 Rosemont Avenue in Country Club Hills where I'm walking my dog."

"We'll dispatch a cruiser. Can you stay on the scene to assist the officers?"

Simone tapped her foot impatiently. "I suppose so. How long will it be?"

"Wait one . . . five minutes."

Simone hung up. "Doesn't look like either one of us is going to get that drink anytime soon."

She sat on the curb in front of the Ames's house, crouching to minimize her shadow against the streetlights. She should have never agreed to wait for the police. Whoever fired that gun could show up at any minute and then what would she do?

Simone arose, tugged on Matilda's leash. "Come on girl. We're getting out of here!"

At that moment a police cruiser rounded the corner. Simone glanced at her smart phone. The response time was two minutes. The patrol car must have been close. Simone stayed put. She liked the attention her development received from police. It was something she would bring up at the next homeowners' association meeting—along with her I-told-you so regarding the abomination of the beer baron's palace.

The flashing strobe of the cruiser cast a cacophony of harsh light on the landscape. It was an epileptic's nightmare. Simone shielded her eyes and wondered why all that light was necessary. This was a dignified neighborhood. The police had no need to announce their presence so ostentatiously.

Two officers alit from the cruiser. Hiked up their pants and squared their gun holsters. The driver took the lead. Forty-ish, crew-cut, bulging biceps and the beginning of a beer paunch, the cop strode toward Simone, exuding the demeanor of a strip-club bouncer. "You the one who called in the gunshot?" He asked as his partner, a slender man in his early 30s, bent to greet Matilda.

Simone decided she like the younger cop better than the older one. The younger one had his priorities straight. Always greet the dog first. "That's right. Saw a flash from the upstairs window, far right."

"Good thing you were paying attention," The younger officer said, arising from his Matilda crouch.

"I was staring at the house, collecting Matilda's doody when I saw the flash and then heard the bang!" Simone explained.

The older cop nodded. "You know the people who live here?"

"The Ameses. Franklin and Jasmine and her son, Richard. Although I hear Franklin moved out recently. Marital troubles."

"Aren't you the nosey neighbor?" The older cop said.

"Are you a charm school drop out?" Simone responded.

The young cop sniggered.

The older one glared, then recovered. "I guess I deserved that."

Simone accepted the mea culpa. "Guess we're even."

"Hey Jed," the older cop said, addressing his partner. "Stay here and collect our witness's information. I'll check the doors."

Jed nodded. "I'm on it, Jake." He pulled a notebook from his back pocket as Jake crossed the drive, ascended the steps to the front door and rattled the door knob.

Jed pulled a pen from his shirt pocket and recorded Simone's name, address and telephone number. "Can I see some ID?" he asked when he was finished.

"Don't carry ID when I walk the dog. You'll just have to take my word for it."

"Sorry to be persistent, but some people lie when they don't want to deal with the police."

Jed pulled his phone from his pants pocket, consulted his notebook and dialed the number Simone had given him. Her phone rang. He nodded. "That checks out. You can go, Mrs. Maxwell. Thanks for being a good citizen."

Simone sniffed and tugged on the leash. "Come on Matilda."

"Cute dog," Jed said as they left.

"She likes you. So maybe you're all right," Simone replied over her shoulder as she headed home.

REPRISE-DEATH BY BEER

The two cops stood shoulder to shoulder on Franklin Ames's front porch. The cop named Jake leaned on the doorbell, which played a tune. His partner, Jed, couldn't quite place it. He hummed along for a few bars then exclaimed, "Anchors Aweigh!"

Jed leaned forward, cupped his hands and peered through the sidelight to the right of the door. "It's dark in there. Don't seen nothin'."

"Duh," Jake said, releasing the bell as the light in the foyer and the light above the door went on simultaneously.

Both cops were blinking as the front door swung inward to reveal a teen-age boy, bed-headed and wild-eyed. He was wearing sleep shorts. The right shoulder of his white T-shirt was blotched in crimson. "Oh fuck! Oh fuck! Oh fuck. She's dead. Musta shot herself."

The boy launched himself at Jake, grabbing him up in a ferocious bear hug. He pressed his face into the cop's shoulder and bawled. "Why would she do that? Why would she do that . . . to me? I thought she loved me."

To his credit, Jake made no effort to disengage. "Easy boy. We've got this. Where is she?"

"Master bedroom. Last door to the right up the stairs," the boy sobbed.

Addressing his partner, Jake said, "Why don't you go check it out. I'll stay here with . . . what's your name son?"

"Dickie."

Jed paused on the landing to call it in on his lapel mic. "Investigating possible 10-56 at 422 Rosemont Avenue in Country Club Hills." He made it to the top of the stairs, walked down the hall and through an open doorway on reluctant legs.

The overhead light was on. The woman lay on a chaise lounge positioned on the front wall between two windows. Harsh overhead incandescence cast the ghastly scene in silhouette on the front wall, which was spattered with blood and tissue.

Jed's cop brain recorded the scene dispassionately. The woman was nude and had been pretty. Short, well-endowed and obviously dead. Her right hand dangled inches from the floor. At her fingertips lay a handgun. Looked like a Ruger, probably a 9 mm. Her head was turned toward the wall. She apparently had shot herself in the right temple while stretched out nude on the chaise lounge.

Bile rose in his throat. He choked and swallowed his own vomit. Didn't want to foul the crime scene. He averted his eyes. Scanned the bedroom and noticed the door to the master bath was open. He poked his head inside and used his flashlight to find the light switch. The room was redolent. Jed recognized the odor. Beer. He switched on the light. A man's hairy leg was slung over the edge of a bathtub.

Jed forced himself forward to look into the tub. A fat man stared up at him from beneath several inches of amber liquid. Jed's nose told him the liquid was beer. The dead man's hair snaked out around him like Medusa's locks. The dead man's belly was a hairy island in a sea of beer. Jed had seen enough. He fled the scene, pausing on the landing to call it in. A 10-32 and a 10-56. Had to be a murder suicide. But, then, nobody could drown themselves in beer. Could they? The detectives would have to sort it all out.

When Jed got to the bottom of the stairs, there was no sign of his partner and the teenager. What was his name? Dickie. But he heard voices coming from a room to his left, which turned out to be the living room.

Dickie and Jake were sitting in armchairs situated with a love seat and sofa around a conversation carpet slung on hardwood. Jake had his notebook out and was writing in it. He looked up as Jed entered the room. "Watcha got, partner?"

Jed glanced at Dickie, assessing his mental state.

"It's OK. Dickie's got things under control. Don't you Dickie?" Jake said.

The boy wiped his nose with his right forearm and nodded.

"Two bodies," Jed said. "A man in the bathtub. Maybe a drowning. A woman on a chaise lounge. Gunshot wound to the right temple. Ruger at her fingertips. Probably a suicide."

"Dickie says the woman is his Mom, Jasmine Cox Ames. Who's the guy?"

"Didn't go into the bathroom. Didn't see him. Dunno," Dickie snuffed.

"Got any guesses."

"Maybe my stepdad. But he'd moved out."

"When?" Jake asked.

"They had a fight. Couple nights ago."

"You up to taking a look?" Jake asked.

Dickie took a deep breath. "Do I have to?"

Jake arose, knelt before the boy on one knee, and stared into his face. "I don't know how else we're going to ID him."

"OK."

Jake arose. Offered Dickie a hand up, which he accepted.

Addressing Jed, he said: "We need to turn this over to the detectives and the coroner. Call it in while I take Dickie upstairs."

It wasn't long before Country Club Hills was awash in the blue strobes of police cars and ambulances. Simone Maxwell, peering through her living room window was aghast. What would the neighbors think? Matilda, nestled in the crook of her left arm, whined, and licked her owner's hand.

SUDS NURSES A HANGOVER

Sunday, July 22, 2018

Suds Ferguson awoke to the sound of someone banging on a door. His head hurt. His feet stunk. He didn't love Jesus. But he still loved Jimmy Buffet.

"Open up! Police!"

He thought he recognized the voice, but he wasn't sure.

"I'm the police," Suds muttered.

He tried to sort things out. His eyes refused to open. It was as if they were stitched shut. He pried open his eyelids with thumb and forefinger. First the right and then the left. His vision was blurry. He recognized his situation. He was stretched out the sofa in the living room of his one bedroom condo.

The banging resumed at his front door. He struggled to his feet. The room swam. He lost his balance, pitched forward onto his glass-topped coffee table, the one he had acquired from Rent to Buy. Only three more payments and the table collapsed with a crash beneath him. The glass shattered. He felt a stinging on his left cheek. Not the one he sat upon.

The noise at his front door intensified. Bang. Bang. Bang. "Come on Suds. Open up. It's Evie. Open up for God's sake!"

Suds made it to all fours. His cheek was blossoming blood. He crawled forward and collapsed once again. Down for the count as his front door jamb splintered and uniform-trousered legs pounded into his abode.

"He's out cold," said a voice, not Evie's.

Mustering the last ounces of his resolve, Suds croaked: "Make sure you run tox tests."

And then he shook hands with his best buddy—unconsciousness.

The next thing he heard was a woman's voice, familiar, but not Evie's, at his bedside. "What makes you think he had anything to do with it?"

"He was seen with her last night at Murphy's Irish Bar on Second Street. At the very least he's a material witness," Evie replied.

The hospital sheets were pulled up tight around him. So tight there wasn't comfortable room for his feet. He kicked about trying to loosen them. He giggled *"Oh the agony of de feet."*

Stupid thought. Drugs must be involved.

His cheek hurt. His head pounded. Worst hangover ever. He groaned. "Someone slipped me a Mickey." The voice was his but it felt like it belonged to someone else. Hagar the Horrible, maybe, coming off a bender.

"That much he's right about," Evie said.

"Hey babe," Suds said, cranking opening his eyes. The light overwhelmed him. He raised a hand to his brow and squinted. Evie was one of two people staring down. The other was Linda Fontaine. His worst nightmare realized in broad daylight. "If the two of you are here to kill me, you're too late. I'm already dead."

"At least he's retained his sense of humor," Linda said.

Evie took his hand. "You were right about the tox screen. Came back positive for Rohypnol."

"The date rape drug? Babe you didn't have to resort to that. You could have had me for free."

Linda laughed. "I think both of us know that."

Suds studied Evie's face. She was amused too. "Look at you two, thicker than thieves. Something happen while I was out?"

"We've reached detente. Linda wants nothing to do with you and me? Well I've decided you're redeemable."

"For what? Valuable coupons?"

Both women laughed. "If it weren't for your sense of humor, I'd have kicked you to the curb long ago," Evie said, patting his hand to absorb some of the sting.

"So what this stuff about my being a material witness and Murphy's Irish Bar. I hate Jamison."

"You were seen there before you went missing in the company of the late Ernie Flowers and Jasmine Ames," Evie said.

"They're both dead?"

Evie nodded. "That's right. What can you tell me about last night? You may be the last person to have seen them alive."

"Nothing," Suds said. "I can't remember a damn thing."

ZACH DUNKEL BEATS FEET

Tall, willowy, razor cut, polished, cunning, and cowardly, the last among Zach Dunkel's attributes was not the least. He owed his continued sentience to cowardice. Pure and simple.

After their fateful confrontation with Zeke in his bedroom, something in Jasmine's demeanor had frightened him. He was terrified. She was, what was the right word? Livid.

Jasmine's lack of inhibition in the bedroom was exhilarating, but there was wantonness to her passion that bespoke a fundamental lack of restraint. She would be the death of them both. Dunkel's innate cunning told him this. The certainty of it resonated like a tuning fork in his gut. He feared her more than he feared Johnny Lewis's strong man. With Zeke you'd see the bullet coming. Jasmine was a pit viper. Her venom was time released.

Poisoned. Zach Dunkel was already poisoned by her, just as Boyd Porter had been. And look what happened to him. Dunkel had no idea who killed Porter. Jasmine feigned ignorance, but he was almost certain she was behind it. Jasmine may not have been driving the forklift, but she must have been driving the forklift driver. No doubt her venom also had infected Franklin Ames and her progeny, the feckless Dickie Cox.

Evidence that his cowardice had paid off, although he'd call it discretion, was written in 60-point type on the front page of The Harrisburg Telegraph. The newspaper had arrived on his doorstep not twenty minutes earlier, just in time to flavor the morning's first cup of coffee with two heaping tablespoons of bile.

Police investigate homicide in exclusive neighborhood. The headline screamed across six columns just below the banner. The story related how the nude bodies of Ernest Flowers Esq. and Jasmine Cox Ames had been discovered in Jasmine's boudoir after a neighbor reported hearing a gunshot at 10 the previous Saturday. Zach would have been square in the middle of the shit show that killed Jasmine and Ernie, had not his cowardice kicked in.

Details were sketchy. Other than the gratuitous revelation that their bodies were nude, no other details had escaped the net police and the DA had thrown about their investigation. The reporter, Alan Foster, pulled boilerplate from internet sources to assemble curriculum vitae for Flowers and Jasmine Cox. He called Flowers a prominent Harrisburg-based trust attorney and Jasmine, an ingénue who had landed the president of Hop Central Craft Brewery. Dunkel sneered at the use of Jasmine and ingénue in the same sentence. She was past 35 and about as innocent as the Ivory Soap girl.

Foster did score one coup. Dunkel imagined that he had cold-called the neighbors, until happening upon Simone Maxwell who was eager to share her "eye-witness" account of hearing the gunshot. Maxwell also let it slip that Franklin and Jasmine Ames were estranged. Maxwell avowed that she had seen him leave the house in a huff toting a big suitcase to his Subaru Forester. Doors were slammed and voices were raised.

Whether these details were true or hyperbole, Foster could not discern. He left such subtleties to the readers. Simone Maxwell said it and that was enough to go to press, with the appropriate attribution, of course. Matilda was not quoted in the story, but Simone's little dog was mentioned by name, affording her the requisite 15 minutes of fame.

Dunkel finished the story, snapped the paper, collapsing it on the fold and exhaled loudly. *"Whew! Talk about dodging a bullet."*

The story did not mention whether both Ernie and Jasmine had been shot. Dunkel wondered about the gun he had stumbled upon while in carnal embrace as he searched for a condom in Jasmine's nightstand. And now, just two days later, Jasmine's was dead.

He realized with a start that his fingerprints likely were all over Jasmine's gun. He had brandished it playfully and said: "My God Jasmine I had no idea you were armed and dangerous." To which she had replied "I don't need a gun to be dangerous. Now put that away. I'm more interested in YOUR weapon, which she had soon sheathed in latex.

Dunkel had left her soon thereafter, reluctant to stay for the meeting Jasmine had arranged with Franklin Ames later that evening. As he turned from Country Club Hills, a car was pulling onto the main drive. The driver's face was illuminated by a streetlight. Zeke Morrow! Zach eased on by, reasoning that any meeting where Zeke was a guest, was a meeting best avoided. It was long past time to abscond.

It took Zach about ten minutes to pack his kit, grab his passport and head for the bank to collect his emergency stash, $50Gs in cash he had secured by skimming clients accounts for the past ten or so years. He'd lay low in his hidey-hole on Grand Cayman.

But first he had a phone call to make.

His lover answered on the second ring. "What's up, Zach?"

"I see from the papers that the game is afoot," Zach said. "What's your next move?"

"Just follow the plan. Head to Grand Cayman. I want you to be out of the path of any more flying bullets."

"I'll stay in touch," Zach said.

Zach hung up and summoned an Uber.

STRONGMAN ZEKE TURNS UP WEAK

"God damn it Zeke. You weren't supposed to kill 'em you were just supposed to scare 'em. And, you killed the wrong fucking attorney, although killing any attorney is probably a service to mankind."

"I didn't kill 'em," Zeke said miserably. "But Jasmine damn near killed me."

"Huh?"

"When I showed up at her place, she pulled a gun on me right there on her doorstep. A 9mm Ruger, and she was close enough . . . there was no way she was going to miss if she pulled the trigger."

"What did you do?"

"I left her standing there in the doorway. My back was tingling when I walked away."

Johnny laughed. "Takes guts to turn your back on a crazy woman with a gun."

"Figured she wouldn't shoot me outside, with a witness. Some biddy was walking a yappy little dog out in front of her place at the time. Jasmine did have a message for you, though. She said tell Johnny Lewis that I've got things under control."

Zeke paused. "And here's a funny thing?"

"What's that?"

"Jasmine was wearing a surgical glove on her left hand. The one holding the gun."

"Hmm. That's odd. I wonder why? But I guess that doesn't matter. She's dead now, leaving us to pick up the pieces."

"Musta been a tough sum bitch who brought her down. There was steel in that one. When I confronted her before, at Dunkel's place. He shit the bed. But she kept a tight asshole. She wasn't scared. She was pissed."

"My source in the police department says Flowers was drowned in a vat of beer and Jasmine had a gunshot wound to the head. An eyewitness heard the gunshot that killed Jasmine at about 11:30. I wonder what happened?" Lewis asked.

"Somebody showed up after I left and killed 'em," Zeke said. "Or maybe she killed Flowers and then killed herself. But I don't see Jasmine killing herself. More I think about it No way she committed suicide. Too tough a cookied for that."

"So who killed 'em and why?"

"Dunno boss."

"Damn. This is an itch I can't scratch. I want to know, but I'm getting the idea that I'm better off not knowing. I wonder if Jasmine left a will and who gets her 200 shares?"

"My guess is that Jasmine's little puke of a son is her sole heir. But by the time her will clears probate our deal will be as dead as she is," Zeke said.

Lewis stroked his chin. "You know Zeke every time I conclude you're nothing but muscle, you say something reasonably intelligent."

"Gee thanks."

"And who knows, maybe Ames is her heir. I think it's time to give the bad new to our investors. Our payday is deferred. Time to cut losses. Time to move on."

THE BEER BATH COULDN'T CURE
WHAT ALED HIM

Monday July 23, 2018

Suds Ferguson and Evie Pinson were naked and lying abed in the master suite of his cheap condo. He had been released from the hospital. Evie drove him home. He invited her up for a drink. Water for him and a Manhattan for her. Then one thing led to another. Despite his chemical hangover Suds had been up to the task. Apparently he didn't need no stinking Viagra when the right woman was involved.

"So tell me again how you ended up at Murphy's," Evie said.

"Flowers called me at about seven o'clock. Asked me to met him at the bar, I was in the shower. Call went to voice mail."

"Seven o'clock and you were showering. What did ya have, big guy. A heavy date?"

"Yeah. With Franklin Ames. He asked me to attend a meeting with Zach Dunkel and Ernie Flowers at 9 that night at his house."

"About what?"

"Dunno. He was circumspect."

"Why did he want you there?"

"Same answer. But he did ask if I had a carry permit. I told him I did and he said it might not be a bad idea if I came prepared."

"He wanted you to bring your piece?"

"That's right."

"Odd."

"I thought so too."

"So did you? Carry?"

"Yep. The Walther. And it's missing. No idea where it is."

"That's not good."

"No it's not. I'll have to rely on my backup piece, the .38, but it worries me that my Walther's out there in the wind. Got my initials carved in the butt plate."

"So when you got out of the shower, you retrieved the voice mail from Flowers?"

"Yeah. I had enough time, so I agreed to stop by Murphy's."

"And?"

"And then I woke up on my couch with you pounding on my door."

"So, we know that there was supposed to be a meeting at Franklin Ames's house last night among Ames, Flowers, Jasmine, and Dunkel. Sure you can't remember anything else?"

Suds winced. "It hurts my head to think about it. Let it percolate. Maybe something will come to me. The thing that really bugs me is . . .

"Yes."

"There's no doubt about it. Ernie drowned in beer?" Suds Ferguson asked.

"That's right," Evie said.

"Who takes a bath in beer?"

"Apparently rich people do. It's all the rage. Technically it's called a beer spa. A European thing. Ames has the product to make it happen right here in the USA," Evie said.

"And why would Ernie Flowers wind up drowned in beer in his client's bathroom?"

"Franklin Ames might know. Where is he?" Evie asked. "He's off the grid. Musta turned off his cell phone cause we can't ping it."

Suds retrieved his phone from the nightstand and punched in the boss's number. He listened. Shrugged and hung up. "Straight to voice mail."

"Told ya. Anyway. Flowers tested positive for Rohypnol. A kitten could have held his head underwater. I mean under beer."

"The same Mickey they slipped me."

"Who's they?" Evie asked.

"I wish I knew."

"Wonder if Jasmine did it?" Evie said.

"Slipped me the mickey?

"No silly. Killed Flowers."

"You're thinking murder/suicide?"

"Maybe."

"Was her tox screen clear?"

"BAC was .6. There was an empty highball glass on the floor next to the chaise they found her on. Remnants of bourbon. Knob Creek if it came from the liquor cabinet downstairs."

"Dickie was home when it happened?"

"That's right."

"Don't much like that kid but I still feel sorry for him. He hear anything, before the gunshot, I mean?" Suds asked.

"Nope. Says he fell asleep playing video games. He was tired cause he'd worked after school on the bottling line. Then nothing until, bang!"

"So he was first to see the bodies?"

"Body. Didn't venture into the bathroom until after the police arrived. Cops found Flowers in the tub. Took Dickie upstairs to see if he could ID the corpse. He couldn't. ID came from his wallet. His pants were hung up in the walk-in."

Suds swung his feet over the edge of the bed, gathering up the sheet about him, exposing Evie's nakedness. His motive wasn't prurient. His cop brain had just kicked in. "You got pictures of the crime scene?"

"On my laptop . . . behind the driver's seat of my car."

Suds picked his pants off the floor, hopped on first one leg and then the other putting them on while Evie watched amused from the bed.

"Do you often go commando?" she asked.

"Only when I'm in a hurry," Suds said, his voice muffled by the T-shirt he was drawing on over his head. "I want to take a look at the crime scene photos. Where are your keys?"

"Clipped to the inside of my purse on your kitchen table."

"I'll be right back."

Suds descended the stairs, retrieved Evie's keys, and barefooted gingerly across the macadam to her car, which was parked on the far side of the street. When he returned to the bedroom, he was amused to see that Evie had donned one of his T-shirts, fluorescent yellow and emblazoned with the Hops Central Craft Brewery logo. She was sitting cross-legged on his bed and had taken the time to brush her hair.

"I like the shirt," Suds said. "Looks like it would be easy to take it off of you."

"You might not be so amorous after you see the crime scene photos," Evie said.

Suds sat down next to her causing the cheap mattress to rise and fall. He handed her the laptop.

Evie powered up and selected a folder that indexed 30 or more jpegs. She clicked on the first image and handed the laptop to Suds. The slide show feature allowed him to click through the images quickly. He took note of the sequence of the image numbers so he could return to ones that seemed to be particularly telling.

When the run was finished, Suds paused to consider. "So a beer tap opened straight into the tub?"

Evie nodded. "That's right. But it's a spa, not a tub. The keg is in a closet behind the spa."

"Room temperature beer?"

"Nah. Spa comes with heating coils."

"What kind of beer?" Suds asked.

"Dunno. That's your wheelhouse. A porter, I think."

Suds wrinkled his nose in distaste. "Waste of good beer. Might be the fountain of youth, but I prefer applying beer to the inside of me."

Evie shrugged. "Rich people."

"Any sign of injuries to Flowers?"

"Nothing other than the Rohypnol and the beer in his lungs."

"So he wouldn't have fought if someone held his head under water . . . beer, I mean," Suds said, thoughtfully.

"That's right."

"Hmm. Tell me how does a small woman like Jasmine get an unconscious man of Flowers's size into a . . . spa?"

"Maybe he got in himself . . . before the drug took effect."

Suds shifted on the bed. Scooted so his back was resting on the headboard, which groaned in protest. "I'll circle back to that. Something bothered me when I cycled through the pictures of Jasmine's death scene."

He rubbed his forefinger over the touch pad until the 2600 sequence of jpegs was highlighted. He opened the photos and clicked through them one at a time. "You told me Dickie had blood stains on the shoulder of his T-shirt and on his arms. So that means he probably embraced his dead mother, disturbing the crime scene. Any chance he cleaned things up?"

"In what fashion?"

"I dunno. There was no suicide note, right?"

Evie nodded.

"Maybe Jasmine left a note that contained something Dickie didn't want to be public. Or maybe there was evidence of sex play he removed to avoid dishonoring his mother."

"Is that what's bothering you?"

"Nah. Just filling empty air while my brain idles. There's something off here. It has something to do with the gun. Did you confirm that the Ruger was the one she bought at the gun store the day we saw her on the indoor range?"

"Yep."

Suds closed his eyes. Concentrated. He straightened suddenly. "That's it." He enlarged one of the pictures centering the frame on the gun lying on the carpeted bedroom floor just beyond Jasmine's fingertips. "The Ruger is just beyond the reach of her right hand as if she dropped it after shooting herself in the right temple."

"That's right," Evie said.

"Well. The other day when we saw Jasmine practicing with her new gun at the range . . ."

"Yes."

"I am absolutely, 100 percent, positive that she was shooting left-handed. Hitting the target more often than she missed. Almost certainly a southpaw."

"And a left-handed shooter would have to tie herself in knots to shoot herself in the right temple," Evie said.

"That's right! Coupled with my reservations about how Flowers ended up in the spa, I'm almost certain that what we have here is not a murder/suicide but a double homicide."

"That occurred while Dickie Cox was fast asleep in his bed?" Evie said.

"Yeah. Hard to figure. Either he's a sound sleeper. A liar. Or . . ."

Evie finished the sentence for him. "A murderer. That doesn't feel right. Dickie might be strong enough to lug an unconscious fat man into a spa. But from talking to the cops first on the scene I get the sense that he was guileless and that his grief was genuine."

"Maybe they mistook remorse for grief," Suds said. "But you're right. Despite his surname I don't think Dickie has the balls to kill his mother and her lover. Unless there's a powerful motive here that we are missing."

"Besides. Dickie had to know his mother was left-handed. Would he have been stupid enough to stage a right-handed suicide?" Evie asked.

"He's not the sharpest tool in the shed. But I agree. We need to look elsewhere for suspects and motive."

"But where?"

Suds thought about that for a while. He rolled to one hip and retrieved his smart phone from the nightstand. Returning to his former position on the bed he scrolled through menus on his phone for a while before remarking: "Here it is."

"Here what is?"

"Flowers voice mail. He left it at 7:05 and I returned his call at 7:22, according to my phone log." Suds stabbed an index finger at his phone taking the voice mail to speaker so Evie could hear it too.

"Hey Suds. Give me a call back when you get this message," Flowers said. "I'm at Murphy's with Jasmine Cox. She's been telling me some things about our mutual client that I think you need to hear for yourself. Any chance you can stop by?"

Suds closed his eyes, concentrating. Evie knew him well enough to let him brood.

"I remember the trip to the bar," Suds ruminated. "The car was cold and the air was warm. Fogged up my windows. Had to use the defogger on the Harvey Taylor Bridge. I found a parking space right in front of Murphy's. Place wasn't busy. Only five or six people at the bar. Jasmine and Flowers were sitting knee to knee talking to the bartender when I arrived. I got the sense that Flowers knew the bartender. They were bending close, talking in low voices."

Suds paused, scratched his chin and stared into space. Evie said nothing.

"I pulled up a barstool next to Flowers," Suds continued. "Jasmine reached over Flowers to shake my hand. I thought that was weird. Women don't do that."

"Do what?"

"Shake hands. It's is a masculine thinge," Suds explained. "The bartender set a highball glass in front of me. Said: 'Your friends have bought you a drink.'"

"Remember what the bartender looked like?"

Suds though about it. Then shook his head. Pretty sure it was a dude. But that's all I've got."

"You don't recall sipping the drink?"

"I'm more of a gulper than a sipper when it comes to hard alcohol. Why prolong the agony? But no. My memory ends there."

"You think Jasmine, Flowers and the bartender were complicit in drugging you?"

Suds nodded. "Maybe they didn't want me to attend that meeting."

"But why?" Evie asked.

"And why did they end up dead?" Suds wondered.

GOOD NEWS AND BAD

Franklin Ames awoke to a hangover and a sudden resolve to call Suds Ferguson. He was ensconced in the airport Hilton. He fumbled about on the nightstand until his hand encountered his cell phone. He powered it up, waited for the home screen to appear, and punched in Suds's number. The phone rang and rang and rang.

Just as he was about to hang up, Suds answered.

"Hello Franklin. Man am I glad to hear from you."

"And I you. Where the hell have you been?"

"Drugged to unconsciousness and pumped full of fluids at the hospital. Then home in bed."

"Sounds like I have a lot of catching up to do," Franklin said.

"You got that right boss. Listen. I've got some news. Some of it good. Some of it bad."

"OK. Lay it on me."

"Not over the phone. This demands a face-to-face."

Franklin considered. "Where?"

"How about your office at the brewery?"

"OK. Sure you can't give me at least a hint?"

Franklin heard a rustling sound as if Suds had covered the microphone. After a moment he was back. "Let's just say it's a matter of life and death."

"Is there someone there with you?" Ames asked.

"Yeah. Evie's here. For a sleepover. I popped into the crapper to answer your call. Don't want you to think I'm sleeping with the enemy."

"Gotcha. How soon can you meet me?"

"Give me two hours. Want to catch some breakfast first."

Franklin laughed. "Post coital munchies?"

"Something like that."

"See you then," Franklin said, and disconnected the call.

EVIE PITCHES A HISSY

Suds's kitchen smelled of bacon. It would continue to smell that way for at least two days. The exhaust fan in his condo kitchen wasn't up to the task. It didn't vent to the outside. The fan just moved the odor around inside.

But Suds was OK with that. He loved the smell of bacon. It reminded him of the domesticity he had once enjoyed with Evie who at this moment sat at his cheap walnut laminate kitchen table with a cup of Dunkin Donut's French vanilla coffee in front of her, steam rising gently from it.

Scenes such as these were what he missed most about their marriage. Morning is an intimate time when you are at your most vulnerable with bad breath and bed head. Suds missed sharing those moments with Evie almost as much as he had missed the sex, although he would never tell her that for fear that she would think his priorities were too wussy.

Suds turned off the stove and siphoned the bacon grease into a tin can, Dinty Moore beef stew from two nights ago. "Eggs over easy?"

"You know me," Evie said, her words muffled by the coffee cup she had just brought to her lips.

Suds nodded, and busied himself with the rest of her breakfast. He put two slices of whole wheat into the toaster, wiped bacon grease residue from the fry pan, turned on the heat, and poured himself a cup of coffee while the pan reheated. He cracked two eggs and was gratified by the sizzle when they arrived in the pan.

"What do you think about our moving back in together?" he asked.

"Too early," Evie replied.

"For me to move back in?"

"No. For us to have a heavy conversation. Need more coffee."

"Coming right up, Ma'am."

Suds replenished her cup, retrieved a pint of half-and-half from the fridge, and plopped it down in front of her. A plateful of eggs and bacon soon followed.

Suds was sitting down with his own plate full when Evie's phone went off. She glanced at the display. "Gotta take this. It's the office."

She listened for a while. Her face grew red. "God damn it Linda. It's a wonder we catch any bad guys at all."

Evie listened for a while longer. "OK. OK. I get. Shit happens, but the shit seems particularly deep right now. Doesn't smell good, either."

Evie moved the phone a couple of inches from her ear and Suds could hear the plaintive tone of Linda Fontaine's voice, even if he couldn't make out her words.

"Gotcha," Evie said. "We'll talk more about this when I get into the office."

She stabbed at the phone with her index finger. "I miss landlines," she said.

"Why's that?"

"It's so much more satisfying to slam a handset down than to punch an effing button!"

"So what's up at the office?"

"We fucked up. Missed some pretty important evidence the first go round on Jasmine/Ernie murders."

"Whadda miss?"

"The fact that there were five rounds missing from a seven-round clip in the Ruger."

"Maybe Jasmine didn't have a full load to begin with."

"Yeah but that wouldn't explain the four empty casings someone finally got around to finding in the garage. Not to mention three bullet holes in the drywall, shattered safety glass and the side view mirror from what turns out to be a Subaru Forester on the ground just outside the garage."

"Ouch!"

"I can't believe we were that incompetent," Evie railed. "It's no wonder only stupid people end up in jail. We're not sharp enough to catch anyone else."

"That's accurate. Sad. And probably racist, given the fact that 70 percent of the prison population is non-white," Suds observed.

Evie's face softened. "Point taken. I won't say that sort of thing in public."

"Here's something else to consider . . ." Suds paused considering his options. "Oh the hell with it . . . Franklin Ames drives a Subaru Forester."

"Another reason why we really need to talk to Franklin Ames," Evie said.

'SPLAININ' THINGS TO DA BOSS

Suds used his ID badge to open the electronic lock to the executive suite at Hop Central Craft Brewery. Evie was right on his heels as they walked past the cubicles, the ping-pong table, and corn hole set to Franklin's office.

The boss was behind his big desk. Alarm registered on his face when he realized that Suds was not alone. "Relax. Evie is here as a friend of the court. I've persuaded her that you are the victim not the perpetrator."

"The victim of what?"

"Good thing you're sitting down boss cause I got bad news."

"Shoot."

"Poor choice of words. Jasmine is dead."

Franklin couldn't help himself. "Is that the good news or the bad?" he asked.

Suds grimaced. "Depends on your perspective, I suppose. There's no way to sugar coat this. She died of a gunshot wound to the right temple. Staged to look like a suicide, but we're suspicious."

"Why."

"No note. And she's left-handed. Be hard for a left-handed person to kill themselves in that fashion."

Franklin said nothing.

Suds didn't fill the dead air. Evie did. "Your wife was lying, naked, on the chaise lounge in the master bedroom. And Ernest Flowers was in your bathroom, drowned in your beer spa."

Franklin buried his face in his hands. "Oh my God. That explains why I haven't been able to get in touch with Ernie."

"There's more," Evie said. "Jasmine's corpse showed signs of recent sexual activity."

"You didn't share that with me!" Suds said. "Was DNA run on the semen?"

Evie nodded. "No results yet. This is hard to ask, but did you and Jasmine have sex recently?"

Franklin dropped his hands fixed Evie with a hard stare. "We haven't had sex in three or four months. Another reason why we're getting a divorce."

Suds and Evie looked at each other. "You realized that husbands make prime suspects," Evie said.

"We had grown so far apart that I didn't care who she slept with," Franklin said. "In fact I was glad she was unfaithful so I could invoke the morals clause in our pre-nup."

"What advantage is there in that?" Suds asked.

"She would have had to return 200 shares of common stock in the brewery that I gave her as a wedding gift. She and her dirty lawyer, Zach Dunkel, were organizing the minority stockholders into a block that could have sold the company out from under me. Jasmine's 200 shares would have tipped the balance."

"Boss, I don't know how to say this other than to say it, you realize that gives you even more motive to kill Jasmine?"

"But Ernie, too? He was representing my interests, not hers. How does he play into this?"

"We'll know more when the DNA results on the semen come back from the lab," Evie said.

"Why would Ernie Flowers have brokered a meeting with me and Jasmine?" Suds asked.

"Whoa! Where did that come from?" Franklin asked.

"Ernie called me, asked if I could meet him and Jasmine at Murphy's Irish Bar at 7 P.M. two nights ago. I did and to make a long story short, I'm thinking the bartender slipped me a mickey. I ended up in the hospital with no memory of what had happened. Tox screen showed that I'd been doped with Rohypnol."

"What's that?" Franklin asked.

"A date rape drug. Makes you zombie like, compliant. Unable to resist," Evie explained.

"It also induces amnesia," Suds added.

"Ernie Flowers was poisoned by the same thing," Evie said. "That's what made it so easy to drown him in the beer spa."

Franklin shook his head. "Death by beer, what a way to go."

"There's been a lot of that going around lately," Suds observed. "First Boyd Porter, then Chuck Dubbel, and now Ernie Flowers and Jasmine. All of their deaths are suspicious."

"You think they are related?" Franklin asked. He paused, then added, "You know in a strange way this weakens the hands of the minority stock holders. The bad PR of late has reduced the value of the company. Reduces their incentive to sell."

"Four suspicious deaths related to the brewery? Strains the boundaries of coincidence," Evie chipped in. "But so far, we haven't been able to connect the dots. And here's another thing that's bothering us."

"What's that?" Franklin asked.

"The three bullet holes in your garage, the side view mirror in your driveway and your shot-up Subaru Forester in the employee parking lot," Suds said.

Franklin's laugh was brittle. "I was wondering when you would get around that. Simple explanation is that Jasmine tried to kill me. She asked me to meet with her at our house on Friday night. She was waiting for me in the garage and fired four shots at me. One shattered the windshield of the Subaru. I didn't stick around to see where the other three had landed. Lost the mirror backing out of the garage under fire."

"Why didn't you call the police?" Evie asked.

"Thought about it, but I decided the threat of arrest might tip the balance in my divorce negotiations with Jasmine. I saw it as a way to protect my interests in the brewery. Sword of Damocles. That sort of thing."

"Why didn't the neighbors hear the shots and call the police?" Suds asked.

"She used a silencer. Gun was no louder than a handclap. Extra weight may have fucked up her aim. Lucky for me."

Evie frowned. "Four bullets were missing from the clip of the Ruger we found at Jasmine's fingertips. If she fired four at you . . . the math is all wrong."

"Maybe I lost count. Numbers don't make much sense under fire," Franklin said.

A thought occurred to Suds. "You test for gunpowder residue on Jasmine's hands?" he asked Evie.

She nodded. Nada."

Franklin raised his right index finger. An ahha moment. "Just remembered Jasmine was wearing a laytex glove on her shooting hand."

"Leaves us with a real who-done-it, don't it?" Suds observed.

Evie's smile was ironic: "That's my man. Sharp as a paper cut."

SUDS FOLLOWS HIS NOSE

The brewery was in full swing as Suds and Evie made their way down the stairs from the executive suite to the factory floor. Suds led Evie past the bottling line and fermenting tanks. He paused at the scratch beer lab as his olfactory senses were overwhelmed by a familiar scent. He'd encountered that aroma somewhere before, but where?

Joe Farrell, one of the biologists happened by and noticed Suds's nose-in-the-air attitude.

Farrell grinned. "It's overpowering isn't it? It's something Chuck Dubbel was working on when he died. Care to guess the ingredient?"

"Give me a minute. In the meantime, I'd like you to meet . . ."

Evie finished the sentence for him. "I'm Evie Ferguson," she said, thrilling Suds because she had reverted to her married name.

Evie offered her hand. Farrell shook it, then looked expectantly at Suds. "You telling me the man with the golden nose is stumped?"

Suds inhaled deeply and nodded. "Got it!"

"And?"

Instead of answering, Suds addressed Evie. "Joe is in charge of the scratch brewery. That's where we test out various combinations of yeast, barley, hops, and aromatic additives to come up with new beers. I'm among the official testers here and I can tell you I've encountered this before—it's hibiscus, isn't it Joe?"

Farrell laughed. "Yep. The nose knows. It was Chuck's pet project, an IPA blended with hibiscus tea. I think it has a lot of promise. I'm trying to bring it home for him, in homage, you might say."

Suds took in one more deep lung full, then grabbed Evie's hand. "Nice talking to you Joe. Let's go Evie."

He practically dragged her toward a door. When they were out of earshot, she hissed: "What the fuck, Suds. That was abrupt."

"Shh. I'm processing something here."

He led her outside into the parking lot and stood for a full minute looking skyward. "Hibiscus is the key."

"To what?"

"To who killed Boyd Porter."

"I'm listening."

"When I bent over him on the loading dock right after I discovered his body, I caught a whiff of something that didn't belong. Cans of Hoppy IPA had exploded all around him. Should have smelled like grapefruit and it did, but there was something else there."

"Hibiscus?"

Suds nodded. "That's right. I think Chuck Dubbel did it. I think he killed Boyd Porter. If he'd been working on his pet project that day, he'd have been infused with hibiscus. I think Lisa saw her father kill Boyd Porter. I think Lisa lied and implicated Franklin to protect her dad."

"If that's true. Who killed Dubbel? And more than that, what was Dubbel's motive for killing Porter?" Evie asked.

"I don't know. I'm just spit-balling here," Suds said. "But just suppose Porter and Dubbel conspired to mix up the DNA samples that ostensibly showed Dickie Cox to be the father of Lisa's unborn child."

Evie picked up the thread. "And suppose that Porter had second thoughts and was about to come clean with the boss. That would have screwed up Dubbel's gravy train."

"Yeah but is that motive enough? Dubbel was a skillful brewer and by all accounts a well paid one. Wouldn't his job at the brewery be worth more to him than he could extort from Ames for child support?"

"Good point," Evie acknowledged. "There has to be something deeper here. Something we've missed. Where do we go from here?"

"My house. I'd like to take a second look at those files I purloined from Porter's computer."

"You mean the files you can't admit you stole."

"And the ones you can't admit I possess? The very same."

"It wouldn't hurt to re-interview Lisa and Julie Dubbel," Evie said.

"That's the cart. Let's not put it before the horse," Suds said.

"Huh?"

"I've got a suspicion those computer files just may confirm. I want to take a look at them before we confront Lisa and Julie. If I'm right we'll have enough leverage to solve Porter's murder."

"What about Dubbel, Jasmine and Flowers?"

"One murder at a time," Suds said.

WHOSE DNA IS IT ANYWAY?

Settled in behind the walnut-veneered table in Suds's kitchen in matching ladder-back chairs, Suds and Evie poured over the files he had copied from Porter's computer.

The files were as he remembered, one for each of the samples Porter had submitted for analysis. They included: Franklin Ames, Cloyd Jackson, Richard (Dickie) Cox, Lisa Dubbel, Chuck Dubbel, and Julie Dubbel. They had all been compared against a sample taken during amniocentesis on Lisa's unborn child.

Suds opened a file titled Sample Key and tapped on the screen with his index finger. "See here? Porter assigned a letter to each sample so he could send them off blind for the analysis," Suds said.

"I'm just remembered something that bugged me about you during our marriage," Evie said.

"What's that?"

"The way you put your fingertips all over a computer screen. Move the cursor to highlight the info you want to point out. Don't smudge the screen with your fingerprints."

"My computer. My fingerprints. If that's the only thing I did that bugged you then maybe we should get back together."

"You forgetting fucking Linda Fontaine on camera?" Evie said.

"Apparently you aren't," Suds rejoined. "Haven't I been pilloried enough?"

"Not quite."

"Let me know when."

"Forgiveness is a process. I'm processing."

Suds opened another file without touching the computer screen. "OK. Here's the report Porter received from the lab. Let's review what's in it."

They skimmed through the document. Suds was a faster reader. Evie placed her hand on his wrist before he could scroll deeper into the document. "Let me catch up first."

Suds waited impatiently until Evie said "OK." He scrolled to the last paragraph of the analysis, bulleted CONCLUSION: *There is a familial relationship among samples D, E, F, and G. Specifically, there is a mother/daughter relationship between F & D and D & G and a father/daughter relationship between E and G. The samples submitted as A, B, and C have no relationship to each other or to the samples D, E, F and G. Furthermore . . .*"

"Why does it end with 'furthermore' and what does that mean?" Evie asked when she'd caught up with Suds.

"Dunno. We'll have to check the key," Suds said.

"That's only part of what I mean. Why does the conclusion end with furthermore when there is no furthermore?" Evie asked.

He opened the file marked "key" and they read the following:

A - Ernest Ames

B - Cloyd Jackson

C - Chuck Dubbel

D - Lisa Dubbel

E - Richard Cox

F - Julie Dubbel

G - Fetus.

They studied the key in silence for a while. Suds began toggling back and forth between the two files. This annoyed Evie. "Will you please stop that? You're giving me a headache."

Suds toggled back and forth one more time. "Wait a minute. I'm on to something here."

He pushed back in his chair and threw up his hand in exultation. "That's it! How could Porter have been so stupid? Franklin, too, for that matter. He would have arrived at the same conclusion if he had read Porter's report as carefully as I just did."

"I'm confused," Evie said miserably. "I feel like I used to when you beat me by 50 points in Scrabble. The report seems to say pretty conclusively that E, Richard Cox, and D, Lisa Dubbel are the parents of G, Lisa's fetus."

"Yep. But like in Scrabble the key is in considering the entire board, how the words interconnect. There is a tile out of place."

He dragged the cursor over the Conclusion portion of the lab report Porter had forwarded to Ames highlighting the sentence: *The samples submitted as A, B, and C have no relationship to each other or to the samples D, E, F and G.*

"Yeah. So?"

"Substitute the names from the key into the sentence I just highlighted it would read:

Evie concentrated hard and said aloud "The samples submitted for Franklin Ames, Cloyd Jackson, and Chuck Dubbel have no relationship to each other . . ."

Suds nodded in encouragement. "That's right. Keep going . . ."

Evie continued: "Or to the samples submitted by Lisa Dubbel, Richard Cox and Julie Dubbel."

She thought about what she just read and slapped herself on the head. "Report says that Chuck Dubbel is not related to Lisa Dubbel. That doesn't make any sense."

"You got it kid. Even more than that. It says there is a familial relation-ship among Lisa Dubbel, Julie Dubbel and Richard Cox. Don't you see what a stupid thing Boyd Porter did?"

"Got it!" Lisa said. He switched the letter codes for Chuck Dubbel and Richard Cox in his report to Ames . . ."

"Which means?"

"Mother fucker! Chuck Dubbel must be the father of his daughter's unborn child. That low-life son of a bitch!"

"I'm betting that the sentence that begins and ends with 'Furthermore' in its entirety noted a father/daughter relationship between E, which we now know is Chuck Dubbel, and G, Lisa's unborn child. Porter was both careless and stupid," Suds said.

"Wonder why Franklin Ames missed that? He's a pretty sharp guy."

"Probably distracted by the hostile takeover bid, his paternity of Alex, and the infidelity of his bitch of a wife."

"Whoa! Who's Alex? What's up with that?"

Suds winced. "Oops! That was supposed to be covered by my non-disclosure pact executed by Flowers. But I guess that cat's out of the bag now."

"Explain please," Evie said.

"Franklin's DNA results ended up on an anonymous website and got a hit from a woman in Charleston who was searching for a bone marrow donor for her sick kid who has a really rare blood type Rh-null. That happens to also be Franklin's blood type. Its so rare, in fact, that it is next to impossible that Franklin isn't the boy's father."

"He's acknowledging paternity?" Evie asked.

"More than that, he's already been to Charleston and submitted to the bone marrow procedure. Alex should have already received it. He's praying for the best."

"Who's the mother?" Evie asked.

Suds sighed. "Here's where it get's dicey. She's a former prostitute now married to the prominent pastor of a mega church in Charleston. The relationship between Franklin and the woman, Gerry Smith, has to be kept secret for both of their sakes. And for the sake of their son, too."

Suds paused, giving Evie a chance to process the new information.

After a minute or so, she circled back, saying "there's our motive."

Suds didn't make the trip with her. "Motive for what?"

"If Chuck Dubbel had an incestuous relationship with his daughter and Boyd Porter found out about it, he's just the sleazy sort to resort to blackmail."

"Atta girl, Evie. Follow it to the end."

"And if Dubbel was unwilling to pay, or got tired of paying, he just might have decided to settle things by dumping a skid of beer onto Porter's head."

"I think you just solved murder number one," Suds said.

"But who killed Dubbel, Jasmine and Ernie Flowers?" Evie asked.

Suds retreated to default: "One murder at a time," he said, adding, "I think it's time to confront Lisa and Julie Dubbel with what we now know."

LISA AND JULIE DUBBEL
COME CLEAN

Tuesday, July 24,2018

Lisa and Julie Dubbel sat uncomfortably on rickety folding chairs that had been dragged into Police Chief Evie Ferguson's office. The folding chairs both had a half-inch trimmed from one of their legs. Evie had replaced the usual upholstered visitors' chairs with a specific purpose. She wanted the Dubbels to feel off balance, unsure. She could tell by their demeanor that she had succeeded.

She and Suds had discussed whether they should double-team the interview. They had concluded that it was more seemly for Evie to go it alone. Suds was tarnished goods in police headquarters. He'd cool his heels at the diner down the street until Evie arrived to debrief him.

That he was willing to make such an accommodation spoke volumes about the degree to which their relationship had been repaired. The death of their son was the elephant in the room, but the two of them realized they had sought solace on different paths leading to the same place. They needed each other because dealing with the grief separately was a one-way street leading to chronic depression and, probably, alcoholism. Evie's newfound affection for Manhattans was evidence enough. She needed a high alcohol jolt unavailable in wine coolers to get through some of her days.

Suds had turned to sex with a coworker as a balm for his grief. Evie understood the imperative of human touch. That he had to turn elsewhere for that release was on her as much as it was on him. She wasn't quite prepared to admit that to him, but she was inching closer. That revelation, she supposed would complete his absolution and repair their relationship, she hoped, forever.

But the issue at hand in this moment was not her relationship with Suds, it was dragging some sort of confession out of Lisa and Julie Dubbel. Clearing her throat, Evie said:

"Thank you both for coming in today. Some new information has come to light and I need your help understanding it."

Julie Dubbel was not reassured by Evie's reassuring tone. "Should I have brought my lawyer?"

"And why would you need a lawyer?"

Lisa studied her shoes. Julie fiddled with her purse which she clutched on her lap. The lawyer moment passed.

"What do you want to know?" Julie asked.

"State police computer specialists have been pouring over Boyd Porter's computer, which we recovered during a search of his home and we've uncovered some startling information."

Julie clutched at her purse even harder. "What did they find?"

"I'll get to that in a moment. The search of Porter's home turned up evidence that, although he was reputed to be a bachelor living alone, he had regular congress with a female, size six by the intimate apparel she left behind."

"What's that got to do with us?" Julie asked as Lisa continued to study her shoes.

"You look to be a size six," Evie observed.

Julie sputtered: "You're not suggesting that I . . . Boyd Porter was vermin, a disgusting human being. I'd never . . . How could you imagine such a thing?"

Evie, in truth could not, but the observation had tipped Julie off balance just as she hoped it would. "Obviously, you knew Boyd Porter."

"I didn't, but my husband did."

"Really? How did the two meet?"

Julie's worrying with her purse became even more frantic. Lisa looked up from her shoes. "He came to our house coupla of weeks ago, carrying a briefcase.

I answered the door when he rang the bell. He said he was a private investigator hired by Mr. Ames and that he needed to talk with Dad," Lisa said.

Lisa ran out of steam. Julie shot her a dirty look and picked up the story. "I came into the room as Lisa was talking to Porter at the front door. I didn't like the look of him, but I invited him in. Sent Lisa upstairs to get her father and told her to stay in her room until we told her to come out."

"Why did you do that?" Evie asked.

"Like I said. I didn't like the look of Boyd Porter. Didn't know what he had to say but I was pretty sure Lisa shouldn't hear it."

"Why's that?"

"The whole paternity issue. I figured that Porter was there to reveal the paternity of Lisa's baby. And I was pretty sure it was bad news."

"Why?"

Julie cut her eyes at her daughter. "I love Lisa, but she's a slut. It's not her fault, but she's a slut."

Julie dropped her purse to the floor and buried her face in her hands, sobbing while her daughter shot eye daggers at first her mother and then at Evie. "You couldn't leave it alone, could you, you bitch," Lisa hissed, venom dripping from her words.

Evie's maternal instinct kicked in. It was all she could do to keep from arising and throwing an arm around Lisa in comfort. But her cop brain shouted down her empathy. Evie let her stew. Julie, too.

Julie composed herself. Picked up her purse, opened it and rooted around until she found a tissue. She blew her nose lustily.

Evie moved in for the kill. "As I was saying, I've had a chance to review Boyd Porter's report to Franklin Ames, which concludes that Dickie Cox, Mr. Ames's stepson, is the father of Lisa's child. We've compared that against a key he left behind, which ascribed letter codes to each sample he sent off to the lab."

Evie paused. She had both women's attention now. They were staring at her like spectators in the front row of a horror movie.

"What we found is Porter reversed the codes for Dickie Cox and your husband before he sent his report off to Mr. Ames. When we restore the proper order, the lab results indicate that your husband is the father of your daughter's child."

There it was. The bald-faced accusation. The late Chuck Dubbel was an incestuous lecher. Implicit in that accusation was an obvious conclusion. Boyd Porter was a blackmailer.

Julie and Lisa glared at each other. Two boxers touching gloves before the opening bell.

Julie drew in a deep breath and relaxed her shoulders.

"How long had the relationship been going on between your husband and your daughter?" Evie asked.

Julie laughed bitterly. "That's sort of like asking do you still beat your wife?" She blew her nose on the tattered tissue, which wasn't up to the task. Snot smeared Julie's left cheek and she wiped her face with her wrist. "I found out about it about five months ago. Got up to go to the bathroom in the middle of the night. Chuck wasn't in bed. I heard a commotion from Lisa's room, peeked inside and . . ."

Julie could go no further. Evie didn't want to intrude on that bedroom scene. She let it go. "So Boyd Porter showed up on your doorstep to . . ."

"Blackmail my husband and to conspire with him to strong arm Mr. Ames. Porter wasn't stupid. He knew he couldn't extort much from Chuck, the son of a bitch. And he knew Ames is loaded."

Turning to her daughter she said: "Lisa I am so sorry. Your father was a sick man, a pervert, and I enabled him because it was easier to live with him than in a cheap hotel room or worse, a battered women's center."

Julie reached out to take Lisa's hand. Lisa squeezed Julie's hand, dropping it quickly as if it carried an electric charge. "Dad was a good provider," she said, almost choking on the words. "I loved him."

"So who do you think killed him?" Evie asked.

"I did," Julie said.

"No, I did!"

Evie didn't know what to say. But her mouth was on autopilot: "One thing is certain, I didn't," she said.

The comment startled Lisa and Julie. It was incongruous, but they both laughed. Evie joined in.

After a moment, Evie said. "You two worked this out in advance, didn't you? Think I saw an episode of *Law in Order* on that theme. But this isn't TV. The more I think about it, the more likely it is that neither of you did it."

Both women looked at the floor.

Evie filled the silence. "A pretty good cause could be made that Chuck Dubbel's death was a suicide. Everyone says he was too smart to enter a closed space where CO_2 was likely to be present. Remorse made him do it. Set you guys up for a solid wrongful death suit in the process, isn't that right?"

Julie raised her gaze, met Evie's eyes head on. "This is the part where I probably could use a lawyer, but what the hell." She opened her purse, withdrew an envelope and pushed it across the desk to Evie.

"What's this?" Evie asked, picking up the envelope.

"It arrived in the mail, two days after Chuck died. It's a suicide note. Also includes information on where his will is, bank account numbers, that sort of thing. Chuck advises me not to tell the authorities to avoid compromising his life insurance policy, which apparently contains a suicide clause."

Evie thought about it for a moment then dropped the envelope onto her desktop and slid it back toward Julie. "I'll make a deal with both of you."

"What's that?" Julie asked.

"Lisa signs a statement recanting her testimony that put Franklin Ames on the loading dock at the time of Porter's death. Both of you avow that Chuck confessed to you that he had killed Porter because Porter was threatening to reveal that Dickie Cox was not the father of Lisa's child. Then you can destroy his suicide note, which I never have seen. No one will be the wiser."

"What about the murder investigation? I hear the coroner is involved." Julie asked.

"I'll tell Gregg Taylor I've stumbled upon the perfect crime," Evie said. "We'll never know who killed Cock Robin."

She opened the top drawer of her desk, withdrew a yellow legal tablet and a pen, which she slid across the desk to Julie.

Evie arose and started toward the door. "My office is yours. Get busy on those statements," she said, closing the door behind her.

GIRTY'S SNATCH GETS RELIGION

Sunday, July 29, 2018

The Rev. Graham Smith railed about the wages of sin from his pulpit high above the huddled masses in the sanctuary below. Gerry Smith crossed her legs in the front pew affording Graham a quick peek up her skirt. He loved it when she did that, because it affirmed his possession of her. She smiled at him and licked her lips. Only he could see.

Smith's topic was the generosity of strangers. He told the congregation about the kindness of Franklin Ames, the beer baron of Hershey, Pennsylvania. He told them how nice sometimes arises from vice. Graham was particularly proud of that turn of phrase. Gerry found it puerile but he would not be dissuaded. Graham told his flock that God had forgiven Franklin Ames for purveying demon rum. He told them both Alex and Franklin had been saved by the grace of God and the redemptive power of Jesus's love.

Gerry let her husband's words wash over her without paying them heed. She had endured a mock run the night before. This gave her time to reflect. Gerry had no illusions about what she had been. She had sold herself wantonly (often enthusiastically) mostly to high-ranking officers of Uncle Sam's Navy. Her body had been her ticket out of a life of abject poverty, reared in a trailer park in North Charleston that catered to people on their way down from rock bottom.

Her father was a career Navy man, an absent-at-sea gunners mate. Dear old dad maxed out at Petty Officer First Class forever resentful. No matter how hard he tried, he couldn't pass the chief's exam.

Her mother was a career alcoholic who drank up her husband's meager allotment by the middle of the month and turned tricks when he was at sea so she could continue to float along on a river of booze and regret about what she could have been had she married better.

The devil himself had cast Gerry's fate with fire and brimstone. She had become a whore like her mother before her. But she was a lucky whore who rose to the top rung of an escort service by virtue of her unparalleled beauty. No STDs because she was meticulous with condoms. No opiates because she had witnessed first hand the agony of addiction. Two arrests. But no convictions. Her clients had the clout to spring them quietly from the hoosegow, staving off public humiliation—theirs, not hers.

One of those arrests swept up her client de jour, a young minister named Graham Smith. His father, a prominent minister in his own right, had intervened when Gerry and Graham were collared in a police sting orchestrated by a politician who had been elected on a platform of cleaning up Charleston.

The elder Rev. Smith had insisted that his son make amends. He forced Graham to seek Gerry out after they had been released from jail (under cover of darkness). His instructions were simple. Invite the whore to church.

Hat in hand, figuratively speaking, Graham had done just that, after tracking her down through her escort service. Gerry was hung-over and remorseful when Graham arrived on her doorstep. It was against all rules, but she invited him in, gave him a cup of coffee and listened to his spiel. She accepted his invitation and soon found her self as nervous as a whore in church. To this day, Graham snickered at that old cliché when the two of them got to reminiscing about the way they were.

It took several years, but Graham finally admitted what had drawn him to her. Their arrest came after the fact while he was lingering in the afterglow and she was looking at her watch timing her next assignation. Sex with Gerry was the best he had ever had. His appearance on her doorstep might have happened without his father's intervention. He was a young bear who'd gotten a taste from the honey pot and wanted more. Much more than sanctimonious female congregants with their knees welded together could ever afford.

What he got was Alex, who arrived seven months later and at full term; the offspring of God knows whom. Graham accepted Alex as his own because what other choice did he have for propriety's sake? Early on, as Alex grew and prospered and Graham inherited the mantle of shepherd of his father's flock, Gerry often wondered how a prayer she had never uttered had been answered. She was rich and, for the most part, happy—an outcome denied her father, who was stabbed to death in a barroom brawl, and her mother who finally succeeded in drinking herself to death.

Gerry's illusions were not about what she had been. Her self-deception began with what she had become, the suave, polished partner of a Southern religious icon. She could not admit even to herself that her reverence for the trappings of her husband's faith was a facade that protected the very essence of her being. She was a fake. She did not believe that God had ordained her salvation. She had been saved by her carnal impulses not her spiritual ones.

The words of the Apostle's Creed and Lord's Prayer flowed effortlessly by rote from her mouth but they left the bitter aftertaste of hypocrisy upon her tongue. When Alex got sick, Gerry was not surprised. She considered it a whore's just desserts.

And when Franklin Ames appeared on her doorstep with proof that he was Alex's father and that within his bones lay Alex's salvation, Gerry began to believe that maybe, just maybe, Jesus did love her after all.

No. That wasn't right. The stain of prostitution made her unlovable by deities great and small. Jesus loved Alex. That had to be it. Proof of that would abide in his recovery with his immune system bolstered by the infusion of bone marrow from his father who art on earth, Franklin Ames.

Gerry contemplated these things as she sat in the front row of the grandiose sanctuary believers in Jesus and in Graham Smith had erected as evidence of their own salvation. The congregants were rich and willing to pay penance for their own success by footing the bill for lavish accouterment like thick pile carpeting, stained glass, pipe organs, lush robes, and a sound system that blared out the truth: God resides here!

Gerry wasn't so sure of that but Graham sure was. At the moment he occupied his pulpit, exhorting the congregation to trust in God's love. His voice was rich and baritone and caromed off the vaulted ceiling in the heavenly tones of Charlton Heston descending the mountain with his tablets of stone. His words had little meaning for Gerry who was absorbed in her own thoughts, which centered on Alex. When would he return home? When could she sweep the little boy up in her arms and hug him without the fear of his breaking?

Gerry was overwhelmed by gratitude, but Graham would say her gratitude was misplaced because it was directed not at God but at Franklin Ames, a beer baron, a man who made his fortune by peddling a product with the potential to do more harm than good. And at the end of the day a man who lay down with whores, and without penitence, all irony aside.

Gerry had trouble giving credit to something she could not see, hear, feel, touch, or taste. God was a concept. Franklin Ames was real and it looked like he had saved their son. Gerry sensed that her gratitude was not misplaced but that Graham's was. He gave credit to God, not because God deserved it. People opened their wallets because Graham had convinced them that salvation lay in honoring God by depositing gold in the alms box.

Graham withdrew that gold considerably for his own purpose. And therein lay his gratitude to God. Gerry knew this because she was party to his conversations with his accountants. She listened at the formal teas Graham orchestrated to twist the arms of wealthy parishioners. And she listened as he discussed their finances with their broker.

Why Graham afforded her this access to his private business escaped her. Perhaps he realized at the end of the day that they were both prostitutes. That they had both sold themselves for their own profit and not for God's.

GRAHAM SMITH MAKES A DEAL WITH THE DEVIL

The scam was elegantly simple. Wealthy parishioners made large contributions, in cash. In turn, the church proffered a receipt worth twice as much as the donation. A devout parishioner in the 30 percent income bracket could give $5,000 to the church, receive credit for a $10,000 contribution and receive a tax credit worth $3,000. The discrepancy was offset by whatever anonymous cash was piled into the collection plate on Sunday.

Smith's father had devised the scheme. Graham perfected it by raising the ceiling far beyond what the church could offset through the collection plate. The same connections that had led Graham to Gerry's door gave him access to the men and women who profited by drugs, whores, extortion, and other crimes against humanity. He offered to launder their cash.

He assembled a cast of the ultra wealthy who numbered between 20 and 30 as they dropped into and out of the program. Each agreed to contribute $50,000 a year and receive credit for $100,000. The subterfuge afforded the opportunity to launder an equal amount from sources unsavory. Graham took a finders fee of 20 percent.

The plan worked at peak efficiency for five years. And then a bookkeeper with more savvy than she exhibited on her resume sniffed things out. She demanded hush money and Graham had no choice but to comply.

The bookkeeper became greedy and asked for ever more. It had to stop. He approached his clients in the cleaning business and they agreed to stop the bleeding. The bookkeeper got an offer she couldn't refuse, but Graham had to pay the piper. His 20 percent commission dwindled to 15 and then to 10. But his appetite for creature comforts continued unabated. Something had to be done. He needed to nail down another source of income. The church council already was tapped out, offering him a $75,000 per annum salary. There was no more to be had there. His income of $350,000 per annum now diminished $200,000, while his expenses accrued at their usual pace.

Alex had become a millstone. Medical expenses were eating him alive. Contributions to Alex's go fund me page helped but couldn't staunch the hemorrhaging of his personal accounts.

Best he could hope for was that the fruit of another man's loins would die before Graham was bankrupt. Meanwhile, he prayed publicly and loudly for Alex's salvation.

And then, first Boyd Porter and later Franklin Ames, had showed up on his doorstep. Porter was scum. But Ames was rich and he was Alex's father. There had to be an opportunity there. How could he tap into that wealth for his own benefit?

The people for whom he laundered money would know the answer to that question. Alone in his office, Graham picked up his cell phone and called Mike Weisse, whilst fearing for the worst and hoping for the best.

DOUBLING DOWN ON A DEAL
WITH THE DEVIL

Monday, July 30, 2018

You called this meeting," Graham Smith said. "What's on the agenda?"

"Preserving your lifestyle," Mike Weisse said. "Check that. Preserving your life. You're into us for 100Gs."

"The hell I am!"

"Save that for the suckers in the front pew. That's how light you've been on the last three payments."

"The money's there. In escrow. I can't release it until we take custody of the new organ. It's a $300,000 deal. Gives me the opportunity to wash an equal amount of your money once we get through burying your cash in the contract."

"I hear the money's not there. That you've diverted it to your personal account."

"Who told you that?"

"Your bookkeeper. Buying her silence bought us quite a bit more."

"I thought you threatened to break her legs."

"Sometimes you catch more flies with honey."

"The bitch!"

"Tch. Tch. Such talk from a man of the cloth."

"So what do you want from me?" Smith said, backing down on the vitriol.

"Franklin Ames. We bounced his name off some people we know in Pennsylvania."

"And?"

"It seems that someone else is trying to milk that cow."

"What do you mean by that?"

"Ames's business is a cash cow. Someone else is trying to milk it."

"Who?"

"His soon to be ex-wife and an attorney who's into the loan sharks for nearly a half mill. They're trying to engineer a hostile takeover."

"So what do we do about that?"

"Take some aggressive action to quiet title."

"Huh?"

"We hear that Franklin Ames is rewriting his will to name your son as his sole heir. We're thinking the lawyer and Ames's wife may take preemptive action . . . before the new will is executed."

"I take it you plan to forestall that?"

"Correct. We see an opportunity to use his brewery to clean up even more money. But we need to keep Ames safe until that new will takes effect."

"How do you propose to do that?"

"Better you not know."

"What's in it for me?"

"We forgive the 100 G arrears. You accept a 7 percent skim on the church scam . . ."

"I'm already struggling at 10 percent," Graham sputtered.

"You can collect another 7 percent on the brewery scam if it pays out. Accountants think they may be able to pump even more money through the brewery's books. You could come out of this smelling like roses . . . if you accept our offer."

"And if I don't?"

Weisse's grin oozed menace. "You really don't want to find out, do ya?"

GERRY SMITH SUFFERS
A VISITOR

Tuesday, July 31, 2018

Alex Smith was almost a pale as the hospital sheets he lay upon. But his eyes sparkled and he greeted his mother enthusiastically. His bed was in sitting mode and an episode of Sponge Bob Square Pants was playing on the TV as Gerry swept into his hospital room carrying a bouquet of flowers.

"Mommy! Doctor Dave says I can leave after four more sleeps. Where's Daddy?"

Gerry was fresh from a similar conversation with Dr. David Englehart out in the hall. "That's great news, sweetheart. Daddy's too busy to visit. But he loves you very much."

"Which Daddy? The real one or the pretend one?"

The frank innocence of the question made Gerry gasp. She deferred on an answer as she busied herself arranging the flowers in a vase next to the sink.

"Which Daddy?" Alex repeated as Gerry pulled a visitor's chair to his bedside and sat down.

Gerry spoke softly to clear her words of dismay. "Why the man who raised you of course."

"Where's the one who made me all better?"

"I'd say another father was responsible for that," Gerry said.

"Another father?" The little boy repeated.

"That's right. Our Father who art in heaven," Gerry replied. The hypocritical sanctimony burned her ears.

Alex had sat in on enough church services to catch the allusion. He wrinkled his nose. "You're just like Daddy. Always talking about God."

"Which Daddy?" Gerry said, trying to divert with humor.

Alex stuck out his tongue. "You know what I mean. Where's . . ." he searched for what to call him . . . "Mr. Ames?"

"I don't know where he is right now sweetheart. Back home in Pennsylvania. At work I imagine. But he has been in touch, through email. I've been giving him updates on your condition. He's glad you are feeling better."

"I wanna see him again to . . ." Alex touched his fingertips to his chin, signing the word "thank you." It was a throw back to his toddler days. Gerry had taught him a few words of sign language so he could communicate without getting frustrated. The gesture brought tears to her eyes. He was so young and had suffered so much.

"Now that he knows about you, I'm sure we'll be hearing from him regularly."

They were interrupted by a commotion out in the hall. A man's voice said: "I'm looking for Alex Smith. Is this his room?"

A woman's voice, probably that of the duty RN said. "Yes it is. How nice of you to bring balloons."

Helium-filled balloons in bright colors of red, blue, orange, and yellow bumped on the doorframe and wafted into Alex's room followed by a large man sweating in a too-small, department-store suit. He released his grip on the balloons, which rose, elbowing each other noisily, to the ceiling.

He was crew cut. Tattoos showed on his neck and forearms, which the suit jacket strained to conceal . . . and failed. His voice oozed southern charm, but his demeanor was menacing: "Hello, Mrs. Smith. This must be Alex. I understand that he is feeling much better now. It's amazing that you were able to find a marrow donor and just in the nick of time."

"How do you know that?" Gerry asked as Alex stared wide-eyed at their visitor.

"Graham's sermon this week. Said the donor owned a beer factory in Pennsylvania. Ain't the internet great?"

"What do you mean by that?"

"Without it you would never have tracked this guy down."

Gerry nodded. "You're right about that."

"Franklin Ames must be a special kind of guy."

"You know his name?"

"No secret there. Graham thanked the beer baron and the congregation . . . for their prayers for Alex."

"Franklin is a saint."

"I hear he's more than that. I hear he's Alex's father."

"Graham didn't mention that in the sermon."

"A private conversation . . . a sidebar you might call it."

"Graham really does have a big mouth."

"Occupational hazard," Weisse said. "I hear that Ames isn't quite the cuddly philanthropist you think he is."

"What do you mean by that?"

"I hear he financed the most recent expansion of his brewery with dirty money."

"I won't know anything about that. All I know is that he saved Alex's life. More than that, when I visited him right after he awoke from the anesthesia, he told me that he was making Alex his sole heir. Said his lawyer already was working on the papers."

"Interesting."

"What's your interest in all of this?"

"Let's just say that I'm one of Graham's investors. You know. One of those guys who cleans up nicely for his Sunday services."

"Investor? That's an odd way to refer to yourself. I've never seen you at church."

"I'm a back pew sort of guy. Like to arrive late, sit in the back. Keep tabs on my investment."

"You keep using that word. What's your investment?"

"I'm invested in your husband. His success is my success, if you know what I mean."

"I can assure you I do not," Gerry said, affecting the lofty tones she had perfected to survive in her new environment.

The big man laughed, extended a meaty hand, which Gerry ignored. He scowled dropped his hand. "Don't be all high faultin' with me, Girty, he said.

We crawled out of the same sewer, you and me. Tell Graham that Mike Weisse paid you a call. Tell him cold feet can be fatal."

Gerry's heart pounded. She wrapped herself in the only security available to her. In true southern-belle attitude she replied. "I have no idea what you are talking about, Mr. Weisse and I can't imagine my husband would consort with the likes of you. But I will pass along your message."

"See that you do," Weisse said. He approached Alex's hospital bed. Gerry arose to block his way, but he pushed her, none to gently, aside. He bent over Alex, breathing in the same air, and kissed him lightly on the forehead. "Y'all get better soon. I'll be praying for you, just like your Daddy does."

And with that, Mike Weisse lumbered from the room.

FRANKLIN AMES IMPOSES HIS WILL

Ernest Flowers's young associate Les Benson, welcomed Franklin Ames and Suds Ferguson to his late boss's big office. He motioned toward the two chairs he had arranged on the visitor's side of Flowers's big desk.

He sat down, gingerly in the boss's executive chair. Benson was short. Flowers had not been. The chair was still adjusted for Flowers. It bothered Benson that his feet didn't touch the floor. He could have adjusted the chair, of course, but that was something he should have done before his visitors arrived. To do it now would be unseemly. So he put up with feeling like the little boy suddenly called to dine with the adults at the big table.

Franklin Ames was not inclined to ease Benson's suffering. He could have expressed his sorrow at Ernie Flowers's demise. Suds wondered about that. He could understand Franklin's callous reaction to the death of Jasmine. But Ernie? Franklin and Ernie were asshole buddies. Or so it had seemed. Franklin's lack of remorse just didn't make any sense. He was all business. "You've reviewed the appropriate files, I trust."

"Too bad about Ernie," Suds interjected.

Benson smiled his gratitude. "What an awful way to die," he murmured.

"You mean there's a good way to die?" Ames observed.

Nonplussed, Benson shuffled the papers arrayed on the desktop. "I've reviewed Ernie's notes on how you wanted to revise your will," Benson said. "He actually had completed most of the work. I've finished things off. The new will and attendant trust documents are ready for your signature. To recap. The will names Alex Smith of Charleston, South Carolina, as your sole heir and upon your demise moves all of your assets into a trust for his exclusive benefit. You'll need to change the beneficiary on any life insurance policies you may hold if that is your desire.

"Sidney Ferguson is executor?" Ames asked.

Benson nodded. "That's right."

"I'm honored, but are you sure you want to do this, Franklin?" Suds asked.

"Yes. There are too damn few people in this world I can trust. Can't think of anyone, other than you, who would be likely to hold Alex's interests above their own. You have a unique perspective on Alex's . . . needs."

The allusion to Rufus had Suds blinking back tears. "What about, Alex's mom?"

"An unknown quantity. She's a good mother. But the whole religion thing is off-putting. Don't want the fruits of my labor to wind up in a collection plate. Are the trust documents ready as well, Les?"

"Yes. Your assets will move to the trust upon your demise. Mr. Ferguson holds your proxy at the brewery with the sole rights to vote your shares until such time as a majority of stockholders agree to its final disposition. Income from the trust is earmarked for the support of Alex until he reaches his majority. The trust allows withdrawals of principal to pay for Alex's college education. He shall take sole possession of all trust income upon his 21st birthday and shall have control of 50 percent of the corpus when he reaches the age of 30. He shall have unfettered access when he turns 35."

Benson paused. "All right so far?" he asked.

"One addition."

"What's that?"

"I'd like to name Miles Karfan as an alternate executor for both the will and the trust. He also would take over guardianship of Alex should Suds be unable to discharge his duties."

He cut his eyes at Suds. "Always have a backup plan."

"Very well." Benson pressed the intercom button on the landline. "Eleanor please add Miles Karfan as alternate executor and trustee to Mr. Ames's will."

He covered the mouthpiece. "How is that spelled?"

Franklin spelled it for him one letter at a time.

"Interesting name," Suds said.

"A second cousin," Franklin said. "A lawyer of some sort."

Benson waited for the sidebar to end. He spelled the name of the alternate executor for Eleanor's benefit and said: "Reprint the executor page. We'll need you as witness. Collect Amy. Tell her to bring her notary seal."

SHARON TILLIS WEIGHS IN

So what went wrong?"

Sharon Tellis, Ph.D., looked at Suds and Evie over the top of tortoise shell reading glasses.

"I got out of bed this morning," Suds said, cutting his eyes toward Evie, who was sitting next to him on Tillis's shrink couch.

Suds's arms were crossed over his chest. He had cast one leg nonchalantly over the other. His body language screamed, "I don't want to be here!"

Evie, on the other hand, was engaged. She leaned forward on the sofa, elbows on knees, and stared intently at first Dr. Tillis and then Suds. Evie lay a warning hand on Suds's wrist. "You promised to keep an open mind," she reminded him.

Suds took a deep breath. "OK. I'll try again. We are here because Rufus died; Evie retreated into herself and I got tired of trying to knock down the walls WE had built between us. Then I charged into an ill-advised relationship with a co-worker. Evie got pissed and threw me out."

He cast his eyes back on Evie. "Does that about sum it up?"

"Rufus was your son?" Tillis asked, just to keep the conversation going. She already knew the answer to the question.

"That right," Evie chimed in. "He died of leukemia."

"I'm so sorry. How old was he?"

Suds's voice was thick with phlegm, but he chocked out the words. "If he had lived another week, he would have been 5."

"Was it a long decline?"

"That's an insensitive question," Suds snarled.

"On the contrary. It addresses a fundamental problem that may have driven the two of you apart. Getting to the bottom of that is the first step to putting you back together. That's why we are here, isn't it?"

"What problem?" Suds asked, sullenly.

"The longer he lingered, the more pain you have to deal with. Oftentimes ripping the bandage off is much preferable to removing it slowly."

Evie nodded. "I get it. He died seven months after diagnosis."

"Well I don't . . . Get it." Suds said.

"Grief is like a tsunami," Tillis said. "In a lingering death, the wave builds slowly. You see it coming and the grieving begins a long time before the fact. But that never seems to make the aftermath any easier. In a sudden death, the wave arrives without warning. Sometimes, it's easier to deal with a disaster you don't see coming."

"The disaster I didn't see coming was the worst one of all," Suds said.

"What was that?" Tillis asked.

"Rufus died, right after his physicians had identified a bone marrow donor. We were elated and then . . . if he only could have held on just a little longer." Suds buried his face in his hands.

Evie threw an arm around his shoulders.

Dr. Tillis smiled. "That's a good start."

Suds composed himself. "What do you mean?" he asked.

"Evie is offering you emotional support. That's fundamental to restoring your relationship. Grief can either isolate or build bridges. The either-or is entirely up to you."

"So the solution is a simple as choosing *or* rather than *either*? That sounds awfully glib," Evie said.

"There are multiple *ors* to choose among," Tillis replied.

"Such as?" Evie asked.

"Well right off the top of my head, there are these: either you don't forgive Suds for unfaithfulness, or your do; either Suds doesn't apologize, or he does; either you don't accept his apology, or you do. In sum, your choices are predetermined by the strength of your relationship before Rufus got sick and before Suds fooled around."

"So you're asking us to go back in time? Do a reboot on our relationship?" Suds asked.

"Something like that," Tillis said, "but even more."

"How much more?" Evie asked.

"I'm asking you to think back to your lives before Rufus arrived. To remember what brought the two of you together and then to ask yourselves if that spark is still there. If it is, you can rekindle your relationship. If it isn't, the best outcome is that the two of you can become friends."

"I want to be more than friends," Suds said.

"Me to," Evie said.

"Well, then, let's get started," Dr. Tillis said.

SUDS RETURNS TO THE SCENE OF THE CRIME

Murphy's Irish Bar was somnolent as Suds Ferguson slid onto a barstool at 2:30 in the afternoon. The lunch crowd had left. He had the place to himself. The jukebox was quiet. There was neither clatter of utensils from the kitchen nor murmur of voices from the dining room at the end of the bar. The advice Sharon Tillis had offered circled in his head like buzzards over a fresh kill.

The bartender was restocking the coolers in anticipation of happy hour. Slender and dressed in tight shorts and a scoop-necked shirt to enhance tips from male patrons, she looked up from her task. "Be with you in a minute, hon."

"Take your time. I'm not that thirsty."

Suds scanned the tap tops, studying the available draft beers. Hop Central was well represented by a summertime shandy and light-bodied pilsner, but an IPA called Voodoo Ranger caught his eye. He knew the brewery, New Belgium. He liked their beer.

The bartender finished her task and wiped her hands off on a bar towel. She walked toward Suds, teetering a bit on platform shoes, which he supposed she wore to make her legs look long and slender. "What'll ya have?"

"Give me a Ranger. Kitchen open yet?"

She looked at her watch. "Fred just came on. Give him a few minutes to get set up. What-a-yah thinking?"

"It's way to early for corned beef. Chicken fingers and fries?"

She nodded and busied herself with pouring his beer and tapping his order into the computer. "You want to start a tab?"

Suds dug his wallet out of his back pocket, opened it and slid a credit card to her side of the bar. "Sure."

She plopped the Voodoo Ranger in a chilled 16-ounce glass in front of Suds, who bent over to inhale the essence of beer. He sniffed appreciatively picked up the glass and swirled the contents about a bit, sniffing again. He took a tentative sip and smacked his lips in appreciation.

"Beer-o-phile, huh?"

"That's right. Hey. Tell me something. You guys have a lost and found here?"

"Yeah. Box under the bar. Whadda ya missing?"

"I was in here coupla days ago. Can't find my business card case. My wife gave it to me. Has my name embossed on the cover. I'm thinking maybe I left it here on the bar."

She bent over, giving Suds an opportunity to enjoy the view. Looking up at him from her task she said: "Not much in here, hon. No card holder that I can see."

"Thanks anyway. Tell me. Who was the big guy behind the bar that night? Man bun, sleeve tattoo on both arms. Black glasses."

"Sounds like Todd. Todd Rudy." She spat the words.

"I take it you don't like Todd."

"Used to date him. Took me a while to figure out he was a real asshole. A beer-o-phile just like you."

"Gee. Thanks."

"Not that I mean that you're an asshole or anything. It's just that Todd cared more about his man bun than my buns, if you know what I mean."

"Self-absorbed?"

"Narcissistic know-it-all. Especially when it comes to beer. Also works as an assistant brewer over at Hop Central."

Suds cocked his head as the bartender's words sunk in.

"Interesting."

"Huh."

"Never mind. When's Todd's next shift . . . just in case he might have picked up my business card holder?"

The bartender checked a laminated sheet taped to the top of a beer cooler where employees' names and shifts were recorded in grease pencil. "He's supposed to come in at seven."

"How long has Todd worked here?"

"Dunno. He was here when they hired me. I started dating him cause we both work out. But it turned out he was more into his body than mine."

"Like you said. Narcissistic."

"Yeah. Right. Why all the questions about Todd?"

Suds took a long draught of beer, set the glass carefully down on a Budweiser coaster, and riffed a big fat lie. "Watched him for awhile the other night. He was just a little to chatty with some of the customers. Sort of like he had some action going on the side."

"Whadda mean? Drugs? Could be if the drugs were steroids."

"True confessions. I used to be a cop. My cop sense said maybe he had some action going with broads or the ponies."

"I never heard nothing like that, but I do know that he got into a tight scrape with finances. An ex-girlfriend hits him up for a grand in child support every month. That's why the job at the brewery ain't enough. Todd used to cry in his beer a lot about that, back when I was dating him, I mean."

"Listen. I wouldn't say anything to management. My impression of Todd may be out of whack and I'd hate to jam up an innocent man."

The bartender guffawed. "Todd's a lot of things but innocent ain't one of them. But I'll keep my mouth shut."

"Good girl."

A buzzer sounded at the end of the bar. "That means your food is up. Be right back."

Suds tuned into the big screen TV on the wall behind the bar. The Phillies were down 3-2 to the Nationals in the bottom of the ninth in the first game of a double header.

Suds ate his chicken fingers in silence as the bartender continued her happy hour prep and the Phillies loaded the bases with one out, only to ground into a game-ending double play.

He glanced at his watch. He caught the bartender's eye, made a circling motion with his right index finger. "Ring me out please. I have an appointment to keep."

SUDS SWEATS A NARCISSIST

Suds's position as director of security gave him access to the personnel files of Hops Central employees. He pulled up Todd Rudy's curriculum vitae on the computer and skimmed through it.

Rudy was 34 years old. He had served as a Marine Corps MP for eight years before coming to work as a bottling-line employee six years ago. His quarterly reviews were excellent and he had made his way through a progression of jobs, learning the beer business from the ground up. He had been promoted to assistant brewer two years ago.

His supervisor was the head brewer, Mike Riley. Suds consulted the in-house directory and picked up his phone. Riley answered on the third ring.

"Zup?"

"Hey Mike. Suds here. Is Todd Rudy working today?"

"Yeah. He's about to go off shift."

"Good. Could you have him swing by my office before he heads out."

"Sure. Mind telling me why?"

Instead of answering, Suds said: "What's your assessment of Rudy? Is he a good worker?"

"He shows up on time, and does his job without complaint. He's not the most talented man on staff, but he shows potential. Guess that's why Mr. Ames encouraged me to take him off the line."

"Mr. Ames told you to promote him?"

"That's right. I guess you could say Todd is the boss's protege. Again. Why the interest? Is there something about Todd I should know about?"

"Nah. His personnel file says he served as an MP in the Marines. So he has a skill set I might be able to use."

"You're not thinking about hiring him away from me?"

"What I have in mind for Todd is ancillary to what he's doing for you. No conflict whatsoever."

"OK. I'll catch Todd before he goes off shift."

"Thanks," Suds said. But he was talking to dead air. Riley had already hung up.

—◆—

Suds arose from his chair when Todd Rudy tapped at his office door about 15 minutes later. Todd was a big guy, 6 feet, three inches, 220 pounds, according to the paperwork. Suds opened his office door, and stepped back beckoning Rudy to enter.

A tall man is often disquieted in the presence of an even taller one. Suds had Rudy by a good four inches. He accentuated the height difference by stepping close to Rudy, invading his personal space. "Come on in Tony. Have a seat."

"It's Todd."

"Right. Just seeing if you had the balls to correct me."

Suds extended his right hand. Rudy gripped it. Hard.

Suds held the handshake for a long time without speaking, allowing an uncomfortable silence to build in the hope that the assistant brewer would reveal his guilt at having slipped Suds a mickey. The man was stonefaced. No tell. Time to move on.

Suds let go. "Have a seat Todd."

Suds retreated to neutral ground behind his desk. Sat down in his office chair, which was extended to its highest setting. He had set Rudy's seat at the lowest setting, making it seem like he was a first-grader called to the principal's office. Another gambit in the chess match Suds was about to commence.

Suds had Rudy's personnel file open on his laptop in front of him. He waved a hand at it. "I see from your file that you were a Marine MP."

"That's right."

"I'm a retired captain in the Army MPs," Suds said. "That's how I got my start in civilian law enforcement."

This was dangerous territory. Suds would lose some of the intimidation factor if Rudy had read the bad press that had accompanied Suds's abrupt dismissal as Derry Twp. Police Chief. Rudy's blank face demonstrated he was not a newspaper reader.

"Semper Fi," Rudy responded, mustering some Corps bravado.

"Yeah. Yeah. Marines eat Army grunts for lunch. You're a tough bunch, I'll give you that, which is one of the reasons I wanted to talk with you."

"How's that?"

"Part of my job as director of security is to protect Mr. Ames and I need your help doing that."

Rudy scrunched around a bit in his chair. "What do you need?"

"Your advice. I'm assisting Derry Twp. Police in their investigation into the murder of Boyd Porter. Police may be willing to drop the charges against Mr. Ames if we offer them another plausible suspect."

"I take it you've settled on a suspect."

"That's right. What's your impression of Chuck Dubbel?"

"He's dead."

"Ha. Ha. I mean, do you see him as the sort of fellow who could commit a murder and then kill himself in remorse?"

"That's your theory?"

"Yep. What can you tell me about Chuck?"

"Well. You know his wife, Julie. She used to work here, too. And sometimes when she showed up to work . . . she had bruises. On her throat, arms. Once she showed up with a black eye. She tried to cover it up with makeup but you could still tell. Someone hit her. And I'm betting it was Chuck. He had a temper."

"Interesting. You have a read on his relationship with his daughter?"

"Lisa the pump?"

"Ouch."

"I'm not talking out of school here. She's fucked every other guy on the bottling line."

"Including you."

"Hey. I'm no pedophile. She's what 16? I like more mature women."

"Like the bartender at Murphy's. What's her name?"

163

"You know Bernice?"

"Introduced myself just this afternoon. Pretty girl."

"Yeah. Bernice's all right. Sorry things didn't work out with her."

Suds studied Todd carefully. Questions about Bernice had unnerved him. Todd's upper lip was beaded with sweat even though the a/c was cranked up. His fingers were clinched on the armrests and he'd pushed back as far as possible in his chair, trying to maximize the distance between them.

"Bernice tells me you got screwed on child support by an ex?"

Rudy pushed back even harder on his chair, which creaked in protest. "Damn. The two of you asshole buddies, or something?"

"Nah. Just some friendly conversation over lunch. I go into Murphy's once in a while. You ever see me in there?"

"Uh. Dunno. Maybe. Lotta people pass through."

"I was at Murphy's the night Mr. Ames's wife shot herself in the head," Suds said, making it sound like an aside. He paused, made a tent of his fingertips. This didn't make the papers, but the night before Jasmine died, she tried to kill her husband. Fired off four rounds with a 9mm. Missed."

Todd shifted his weight in his too-short chair which squeaked in protest. Glanced over his shoulder at the door. Then returned his gaze to Suds. Finally, he said. "No shit."

"You don't seem surprised," Suds observed.

"I'm not surprised because Jasmine was a real bitch."

"How would you know?"

"Mr. Ames complains bout her all the time."

"You know the boss, socially?"

"We go way back. I was a Marine MP stationed at Charleston same time he was. I looked the other way on a DUI and the boss figured he owed me one. Got me this job at the brewery when I got out."

"Interesting. You know police have decided Jasmine didn't kill herself."

"They're investigating it as a murder?"

"Yes. Funny thing. I was at Murphy's the night Jasmine shot herself."

Rudy looked at his watch. "That right? Hey listen. I'm working the late shift at Murphy's tonight. Can we wrap this up? I need to get home and clean up."

"Almost done here. Just have one final question for you."

"What's that."

"I met Ames's lawyer and Jasmine at the bar that night. I can't remember much about the evening because someone slipped me a mickey.

But what I do remember is that the bartender who served me my drink had tattoo sleeves up both arms just like you."

Rudy stood up; shoving his chair back, so hard it toppled to the floor. He stooped, righted the chair and said: "I don't know nothing about anyone slipping you a mickey. So whatever you think you know. You don't know shit!"

And with that. Rudy stormed from Suds's office.

"There goes a guilty man." Suds said.

A CONFEDERACY OF MISCREANTS

Johnny Lewis was a major shareholder in Hop Central Craft Brewery, but he did not have the voting shares to effect its sale. Jasmine's demise had taken her shares out of circulation until her will, if she had one, cleared probate. The one million he had invested in the brewery in 2012 to facilitate its expansion, which included Franklin Ames's palatial office in the sky, was now worth twice as much. But the profit was untouchable because Ames refused to sell and didn't have the cash to buy Lewis out. Lewis would have to pay the usurers, diminish his lifestyle for a while, and ride the whole Goddamn mess out to the bitter end.

It was as simple as that.

And then, his office intercom buzzed.

His secretary, Jeremy, lisped: "A Mr. Mike Weisse of Charleston, South Carolina is on line two. Says he'd like to talk to you about acquiring your shares of Hop Central Craft Brewery. You want to talk to him?"

The name was unfamiliar, but the prospects of unloading his Hop Central shares at a fair price were intriguing. Lewis decided to take the call.

"Start talking," he said.

Weisse chuckled. "I like a man who gets to the point, which in this case is to offer you 750K for your shares in Hop Central Craft Brewery."

"They are worth three times that," Lewis snarled, and slammed down the phone.

In 30 seconds his intercom buzzed again. "Mr. Weisse is on the line again. He says he's prepared to sweeten the deal."

Lewis picked up the phone. "I'm listening," he said.

"OK. We've measured dicks and yours is longer," Weisse said. "I've done some digging around and I know that you invested one mill in the brewery six years ago and that your shares are worth $2.25 million, given Hop Central's most recent financial statement. Thing is you can't cash in until Franklin Ames agrees to sell. Kinda devalues your investment, don't it?"

"All I have to do is remain patient. Ames will come around."

"But will it be soon enough? I hear the wolves are at your door. I'm prepared to double my initial offer."

"I'll have to do some refinancing, but I can handle the debt on my other projects. You're going to have to do a lot better than a million and a half."

"What will it cost you a year to service your debt on the Hillcrest housing project?"

"Damn. Don't know this guy, but he seems to know me. Far too well," Lewis thought to himself.

"400Gs a year," Lewis said.

"Ha! Hear it's twice that. And you're cash strapped, right? That's why you were trying to force the sale of the brewery."

"Yeah. So?"

"I represent financial interests with an opposite problem. We have lots of cash and nowhere to hide it from the dad gum gubment."

"I can't be associated with money laundering," Lewis said. "I'd rather declare bankruptcy than end up in prison."

"Oh come on, Mr. Lewis. I've looked into your situation. You've been skimming from kickbacks on public works projects in Pennsylvania for years. Your political connections make you bulletproof."

"I'm listening," Lewis said.

"Good. Here's my counterproposal. You keep your shares in the brewery until it is sold, and we handle your debt services on the housing project. All you have to do is vote with us at Hop Central board meetings."

"Mr. Ames is going to sell to you?" Lewis said. "Find that hard to believe."

"Let's just say we have some leverage and let it go at that," Weisse said. "Do we have a deal or not?"

"We have a deal, provisionally."

"Providing what?"

"I'll need some due diligence on you. I think my political connections can fill me in. If I see something I don't like. I walk. Deal's dead. No questions. No recriminations. Got it."

Weisse chucked. But his words exuded menace. "Have a nice day, Mr. Lewis."

He hung up, leaving Lewis to ponder a deal with the devil.

MORE PILLOW TALK

"I'm scared. Graham. Really scared."

Gerry Smith addressed those words to the ceiling above the king-sized bed she was at the moment sharing with her husband, who was as rigid as a board between the sheets beside her.

Graham had just initiated sex with his wife and found himself not up to the task. It was the first time that had happened. Failure gnawed at him like a bubonic rat.

"It's a scary world," Graham replied. "That why we need to abide in the Lord."

"Abide in the Lord!" Gerry shrieked. "Don't you spout that religious pabulum at me. Not now. God didn't get us into this mess. You did. And you're going to have to get us out!"

"Whatever are you talking about, dear?"

She rolled on her side to face him. "I'm talking about Mike Weisse. And don't you pretend you don't know who he is."

"Oh I know who he is. Sweetness. I'm just surprised that you do, too."

"I didn't until he visited Alex and me at the hospital."

Graham gathered up the sheets in his fist and flung them from him. He swung his feet to the floor, presenting his back to his wife. He hung his head and began to sob.

This was aberrant behavior for the patrician preacher. Gerry's surprise drew her to his side. She threw an arm around his naked shoulders and drew him close. "Tell me about it," she said.

"I'm not sure where to start."

"Try the beginning."

"I guess it all started with my pride. I wanted to be even more influential than Dad. I wanted to take his solid foundation and build something bigger and even more beautiful upon it."

"Your church is certainly that," Gerry murmured.

"Oh, but the cost. To pay for it, I had to let the devil worship with us."

"What do you mean by that?"

"I've been laundering dirty money through the church's books. Weisse is the principal in a group of congregants who approached me about reinvesting some of their money in the church."

"Explain."

"I don't know where their money comes from and I'm certain I don't want to know, but it worked like this. We launch a big fund-raising campaign to erect a school wing, to expand the sanctuary, to build the performing arts center," Graham said ticking off a recent string a building projects at the church.

"Fund-raising among the congregants was not nearly up to the task, so this group of investors made the funds available. At a price. I had to ensure that their select contractors got the work at exorbitant rates. I paid the contractors with money from Weisse and . . ."

"And the contractors made kick-backs to Weisse, laundering the money," Gerry said, finishing the sentence for him.

"That's right. In return I got to keep a skim that amounted to a quarter of a million a year on top of my salary at the church."

"Which is how we can afford the mortgage on this palace," Gerry said, raising her arms and drawing the air toward her.

"That's right. Anyway. We're running out of plausible projects and Weisse isn't running out of cash to launder. The new organ is my last gasp. And . . ."

"Well?"

"Lately, I've been skimming a little more than I should have from Weisse. I've been using it to pay Alex's hospital bills, mainly."

"What about that big boat?"

Graham hung his head. "Well, that, too. Anyway. Weisse is wise to me. I think he expected it all along, encouraged it, actually, as a way to sink his hooks into me even deeper. Now he wants me to do something that's totally reprehensible."

"What's that?"

"He wants me . . . us to exploit our relationship with Franklin Ames. He's done some sniffing around and found out that Ames's brewery is a cash cow poised for expansion and a prime spot to clean up even more money."

"I may be responsible for Weisse's interest in the brewery," Gerry said.

"How so?"

"When he visited us in the hospital, I let it slip that Ames had made Alex his sole heir."

Graham exhaled explosively. "That explains a lot."

"How so?"

"Come on Gerry. Think. With Alex as Ames's heir that opens up all sorts of leverage, we can apply as Weisse's proxy."

"Such as?"

"Suppose he kills Ames and installs us as his puppets in another money laundering scheme?"

Gerry shivered. "I get the sense that Weisse won't shy from murder if it serves his purpose. What's the risk for us if Weisse is doing the dirty work?"

Graham considered. "I don't think he'd want to implicate us in a murder. He needs us to front the money laundering. Although, he could bury proof of our complicity somewhere and hang it over us like a sword of Damocles. More I think about it . . . that probably will be his play."

Gerry mulled over their options for a while, stroking Graham's thigh absently with her left hand. He responded in typical male fashion, but Gerry paid it no heed, although her smile played hide and seek with the bad news at hand.

"Alex is recovering," she said thoughtfully. "We owe Franklin Ames a great debt. What I am weighing is whether my debt to Franklin Ames outweighs my debt to you. I used to sell my body. You saved me from that. To save you, it appears I'll have to sell my soul."

"You have me by the balls in more ways than one," Graham said.

"How's that?"

"You could save yourself, Alex, too, by selling me out to the feds."

That was at that moment that Gerry's resolve stiffened.

Her distracted stroking of Graham's thigh had stiffened something else. This time he was equal to the task at hand.

CHARLESTON CALLING

The mound of paperwork in front of Suds Ferguson was formidable. A three-hole binder bearing the company's most recent financial report was open on its center spine before him. He was 200 pages into a 500-page report, and his head was stuffed with gobbledygook.

Franklin Ames, apparently, was serious about bringing Suds onto the management team. It was hard to ascertain his motive. Suds shoved the binder aside. He had other more pressing things to consider, such as Todd Rudy's relationship with Ames and what his ex-wife was up to at this moment.

Suds knew that Evie still was preoccupied with the murders of Ernest Flowers and Jasmine Cox-Ames. She had not entirely eliminated Franklin Ames as a suspect. Franklin was, however, off the hook in the Boyd Porter investigation. The District Judge had dismissed the charges on Evie's initiative.

A report generated by Linda Fontaine, who had re-interviewed Simone Maxwell, added grist to the mill of Evie's discontent with the Jasmine/Ernie investigation.

Simone avowed that earlier on the evening of Jasmine's noisy death, she had witnessed an angry confrontation between Jasmine and a tattooed and crew cut man on Jasmine's front porch as Simone happened by with Matilda.

The man stalked away and settled behind the wheel of a Jeep Cherokee. Simone noticed a magnetic placard on the front door panel of the Jeep visible under the street lights. It read Hi-Lo Construction Inc., the corporate entity headed by Johnny Lewis, a local developer with an unsavory reputation and a not-so-silent investor in Hop Central Craft Brewery.

That revelation, along with Suds's report on the truculent Todd Rudy and Rudy's apparent friendship with Franklin Ames, had embroiled Evie in a frenzy of what-ifs. For his own part, Suds was almost certain that Rudy had drugged him, taking him off the table at a critical time. Suds might, otherwise, have prevented the murders of Ernie Flowers and Jasmine Ames. If Rudy had poisoned Suds' drink, was it at his initiative or upon the orders of someone else and for what purpose?

Suds was worried about that. And so was Evie.

These thoughts swirled about in his head as he tried to concentrate on balancing the cost of hops, barley malt, yeast, personnel, debt services, and utilities against beer-sale revenues.

The ringing phone was a welcome relief.

"Hello," a woman's voice said.

Suds picked up the nuances of that hello quickly. "Gerry, how are you? And more importantly, how is Alex?"

"We are both fine. Alex is feeling so much better since the bone marrow transplant. He's asking for you."

"For me? I can't imagine I made that much of an impression on him."

Gerry laughed. "OK. You ratted me out. Actually, Alex has been asking about Franklin. It's me that wanted to talk to you."

"Why's that?"

"Something's bugging me and I wanted to bounce it off you before I took it to Franklin."

"OK. Shoot."

"Well, it's like this. When he was coming out of the anesthesia, Franklin told me that he was making Alex his heir. I'm not sure I'm comfortable with that."

"Franklin is full of surprises, lately. The murder of his wife has him considering his own mortality, I suppose."

"Murder?" Gerry's voice was shrill. "I hadn't heard anything about a murder."

"A double murder actually. A sordid affair. The naked bodies of Jasmine and Ernest Flowers, Franklin's personal attorney, were discovered in her boudoir. Police initially suspected a murder/suicide, but the evidence now seems to suggest that they both were murdered."

"Wow. I had no idea. With all that going on, how could Franklin even think about changing his will?"

"Franklin obviously can multi-task. It's a done deal. It's official Alex is Franklin's sole heir, and this is the part that makes me uncomfortable . . . I'm the executor of his estate."

"You two that close?"

"Didn't think so, but he says that doesn't matter. He plans to live forever."

"You don't keep Franklin's calendar, do you?"

"No. Why?"

"Well. It's just that Alex is feeling so much better now. I'm wondering if maybe, Franklin would like to come down for a visit. You'd be welcome, too. Graham and I would be glad to put you two up."

"I'll bounce that off of Franklin. When are you thinking?"

"Maybe the weekend? Sooner the better."

"I'll check with Franklin and get back with you."

"OK. Thanks. I guess that's it. I just want to say thank you again."

"For what?"

"For facilitating Franklin's visit to us. It really was a lifesaver. Literally."

Suds felt the lump rising in his throat. "For me, too. Helped me come to grips with . . ."

"Your loss? I'm so sorry a Franklin Ames didn't show up for your son. What was his name?"

"Rufus. And a donor did show up. Just too late. I am so happy that your outcome was better than mine."

"I don't know how to respond to that."

"Just be grateful that Alex is still alive. There is no better response than that."

"I know. Thank God."

"I'd thank Franklin Ames first."

"And you second. You're a fine man Suds Ferguson."

"I have my moments," Suds said.

WHITE KNUCKLES AT A
BOARD MEETING

Friday, August 3, 2018

"Gentlemen," Franklin Ames said. "I've called this meeting to introduce you all to Suds . . . Sidney Ferguson, whom I'm bringing on as CEO. Mr. Ferguson is a former police chief who joined us some time ago as director of security. He possesses a discriminating palate and a love for craft beer in addition to considerable management experience as erstwhile chief of the Derry Township Police."

The gathering in the main conference room at Hops Central Craft Brewery included eight people, among them Les Benson, Suds, Johnny Lewis, and Jan Murphy. Ames's secretary owned 25 shares of stock in appreciation of her dedication to Franklin Ames.

There was a commotion in the hall outside the conference room. The voice of an angry woman, probably Franklin's receptionist, rose above the hubbub. "I'm sorry sir, you can't go in there without an invitation."

"I've got my invitation right here," a low, southern, masculine voice rumbled as the conference room burst open to reveal a large, crew-cut, and tattooed man stuffed into a cheap suit two sizes too small. "My name is Mike Weisse," he announced to the surprised assembly.

Franklin rose from his executive chair. "What is your interest here?" Mr. Weisse?"

Weisse waved a Number 10 envelope, which he deposited on the conference room table in front of Franklin. "This is my proxy to vote 200 shares of common stock belonging to the estate of one Jasmine Cox Ames," he announced.

"Ownership of those shares have reverted to me under the morals clause of my prenuptial agreement with my late wife," Franklin rejoined. "Now's your chance to leave before I have my director of security escort you from the room."

Taking his cue, Suds arose to his full height and squared his shoulders.

As Suds approached Weisse smiled and raised his hands in mock surrender. "My attorney's opinion is appended to the proxy. You can have your lawyer review it, but my guy is certain the last will and testament of Jasmine Cox Ames supersedes the prenuptial agreement. You can't enforce a moral's clause on a woman who died while still lawfully married to you. The shares belong to her estate and her attorney, one Zachary Dunkel esquire, has ceded executorship to me. It's all there in the envelope."

Franklin motioned Suds to stand down, collapsed into his chair, and shoved the envelope across the table to Les Benson. "What do you think, Les?"

If Les could have swallowed his Adams apple, he would have. He gulped several times before replying. "I'll have to review the paperwork, but if it is in order . . .'

"I assure you that it is. I've paid handsomely to ensure that," Weisse interjected.

Benson opened the envelope and withdrew a thick wad of papers. Shuffling through them, he came to the proxy, which he skimmed and then dropped on the tabletop. "The proxy is in order, duly notarized and executed," he said. "My advice is to allow Mr. Weisse to participate in the meeting. At your direction, I can ask the court to decide which document should prevail, the pre-nup or Mrs. Ames's will."

Franklin sighed. "Eleanor. Please roll another chair in here so Mr. Weisse can have a seat at the table."

Weisse sat down in and empty chair, rubbed his hands together in anticipation, and said: "OK folks. What's on the agenda?"

Franklin cleared his throat, glaring at Weisse. "I was just introducing the board to our new chief executive officer, Sidney Ferguson."

"I don't know much about Roberts rules of order. But doesn't the hiring of a CEO require an affirmative vote on the part of the board of trustees?" Weisse asked.

"I hold a majority interest in the brewery, so I don't need the consent of the board," Franklin sputtered.

"Not if Mr. Lewis and I decide otherwise. He holds the proxies for 48 percent of the shares. My proxy for the 3 percent owned by the late Mrs. Ames gives us a 51 percent majority. To move things along, I move that we name Sidney Ferguson CEO."

Ames looked a Benson for advice. Benson had the look of someone who had just sampled rancid sushi. "There is a motion on the floor, is there a second?" he asked.

"I'll second the motion," Lewis said.

"There is a motion and a second," Benson said. "Roll call vote?"

"Point of procedure?" Lewis asked.

"Yes, Mr. Lewis."

"I'd like some assurances of Mr. Ferguson's qualifications for the job. I propose we defer voting on this motion until I've had a chance to review Ferguson's qualifications and consider his references. He does have references, doesn't he?"

"I didn't think he'd need them," Franklin said, miserably.

Lewis leaned forward in his chair. "I would say they are a necessity, given the circumstances, and the recent press reports regarding Mr. Ferguson's departure from the Derry Township Police Department."

"I move we table my motion to hire Mr. Ferguson as CEO," Weisse chimed in.

"Second," Lewis said.

"Roll call vote," Benson said. "Mr. Weisse?"

"Aye."

"Mr. Ames?"

"Nay!"

"Mrs. Murphy?"

"Nay!"

"Mr. Lewis?"

"Aye."

Benson looked to Franklin for guidance.

"Get on with it Les," Franklin said, wearily.

"The motion to defer action on Mr. Ferguson's promotion to CEO is carried," Benson said.

"Is there any other business to come before the board?"

"I'll have some suggestions to bring before management," Weisse said, "but nothing that requires board action at this time."

"Oh get on with it, damn it," Franklin snapped. "I know Johnny Lewis has been wanting to sell the company and cash in his investment for some time. I'm sure you've got a buyer in your back pocket."

"On the contrary, Mr. Ames. "We don't want to sell Hops Central Craft Brewery. I represent financial interests that want to double down on your success. I think an expansion is in order and I've lined up $10 million in venture capital. I've got some ideas on how we can spend it that we can discuss in private," Weisse said.

Franklin was dumbfounded. "You on board with this Johnny?"

Lewis nodded. "Mr. Weisse has my cooperation, 100 percent."

Ames shook his head as if trying to dislodge a swarm of bees. "In that case, I move that we adjourn."

"Second," said Jan Murphy.

Adjournment was unanimous.

THE PLOT THICKENS

The ballistics report on the bullet that killed Jasmine Cox-Ames landed on Evie's desk first thing Friday morning, turning the murder investigation on its ear.

The ballistics expert concluded that Jasmine had died from a single shot from a .380 caliber handgun. There was no way the 9 mm found at her fingertips could have been the murder weapon.

The revelation only deepened the mystery of who killed Jasmine Cox-Ames. Evie ran over the list of suspects in her head: Dickie Cox? The mysterious visitor Simone Maxwell reported seeing on Jasmine's doorstep the evening of the murder? Franklin Ames? The late Ernest Flowers, who then drugged and drowned himself in a vat of beer?

Nothing seemed to fit.

She read through the ballistics report a second time, carefully. Looking for some nuance she'd missed on first reading. There was none. The result was simple, not subject to interpretation. Jasmine had been killed by a .380 not a 9mm. The Ruger at her fingertips had to be some sort of misdirection on the part of whomever killed her.

"Who does the .380 belong to?" Evie asked herself, drumming her fingers on her desktop. Only person she knew who owned a .380 was Suds, but for obvious reasons, Evie was loathe to add Suds to the suspects' list.

Her office line buzzed. "Your ex is here to see you," the desk sergeant reported.

"Speak of the devil."

"Huh?"

"Never mind. Send him on back," Evie said.

Suds arrived in a bluster, slamming her office door closed behind him.

"I take it you have something on your mind," she said, mildly.

"Yeah. My promotion got shit-canned."

"Shit-canned," Evie repeated.

"Yeah. Mike Weisse, a yokel in a too-small suit, showed up at the board meeting with Jasmine's proxy. Threw his shares onto the table alongside those of Johnny Lewis's and the two of them were able to defer my promotion until such time as I passed a security check."

"Security check. They said that?"

"Not in so many words. But Lewis reads the newspapers and brought up my recent dismissal from the police department as a concern that warrants investigation before I ascend to the front office."

"God damn. I'm sorry, Suds."

"It's not your fault."

"Isn't it? I spread your indiscretion abroad."

"You mean my indiscretion with a broad? That's all on me."

"Just trying to soften the blow."

"Gee thanks."

"I've got some other troubling news," Evie said.

"What's that?"

"Ballistics is just in. The bullet that killed Jasmine is a .380."

"Shit. You sure?"

Evie stared him down.

"Sorry. You wouldn't make a mistake on that."

"I know. Floored me too."

"So what's with the 9mm?"

"I don't know. Misdirection on the part of the murderer?"

"Or maybe Jasmine confronted the killer with her own gun and he . . .

"Or she?"

"Shot first."

"Coroner says the bullet was an impact wound."

"So no gun play?"

"That's right. No gun play."

"What then?" Suds asked.

"Maybe the killer was hoping we wouldn't check."

"Incompetent killer?"

"Or competent killer hoping the police would be incompetent."

"Which you aren't."

"Gee thanks."

"I own a .380," Suds said.

"I know. I was kicking that around in my head when you arrived. I was just about to compare it to the personal weapon inventory you started when you were chief."

"I'm a little nervous about that because I was packing the Walther the night I was drugged and Jasmine was killed."

"I know," Evie said.

"I don't know where my Walther is."

"I know," Evie repeated.

"That make me a suspect?"

"Not you. Toxicology has you in the clear. But it might make your Walther a suspect."

"Rohypnol incapacitates your will and obliterates your memory. Could I have pulled the trigger and not remember it?"

"Don't want to even consider that," Evie said.

"So other than me. Who's on your list of suspects for Jasmine's murder?"

"Dunno. Want to spitball?"

"Well. There's Dickie of course. He was in the house at the time of the murder."

"That's right. But I still have trouble seeing him as the doer," Evie said.

"Too wimpy," Suds agreed.

"And I guess that it's conceivable, although highly unlikely, that Flowers killed Jasmine and then offed himself in remorse."

"Yeah. But pretty far-fetched that he'd drug himself with Rohypnol and then drown himself in beer. And if he did, where's the murder weapon?" Suds asked. "Then there's Franklin Ames, but I don't see much of a motive there. As it turns out, he has more to lose than to gain by Jasmine's death."

"How so?"

"Weisse had a copy of Jasmine's will, which made her lawyer, Zach Dunkel, her executor and guardian of Dickie until he reaches his majority. Dunkel ceded Jasmine's voting proxy to Weisse who joined forces with Johnny Lewis to out-vote Franklin."

"What then?" Evie asked.

"Weird. Franklin was certain Lewis and Weisse would move to sell Hop Central out from under him, but instead Weisse announced that he was bringing $10 million in venture capital to the table. Wanted to invest it in expanding the brewery. Has no interest in selling it."

"So what now?"

"Franklin adjourned the stockholders meeting and agreed to sit down with Weisse to discuss what he had in mind for the brewery." Suds looked at his wristwatch. "They should be talking right about now," he said.

"But you still have a job, right?" Evie asked, anxiously.

"As director of security, yes. Franklin assured me that I would not be fired. Franklin was well-aware of why I was dismissed from the police force. That's not a skeleton in my closet as far as he's concerned."

"Whew."

"Something else just occurred to me, regarding Jasmine's murder. Franklin did not have a financial interest in her demise, but maybe her infidelity was enough to put him over the edge."

"Hard for me to see Franklin as a cuckold inflamed to avenge."

"But still not something to take off the board entirely. Agreed?"

"Agreed."

"I would like to get the skinny on Mike Weisse. He hails from Charleston . . ."

"Now there's a coincidence," Evie said.

"No kidding. Think I'll give my buddy Harrison Ford a call and see if Weisse has a rap sheet."

"Good idea," Evie said. "Why don't you try him right now?"

Suds nodded. Dug his cell phone from his back pocket, scrolled through his phone book and selected Ford's number from the queue.

He listened for a minute. "Voice mail."

Evie nodded.

Suds left a message: "Hey Harry. Suds here. Mike Weisse, a big guy in a cheap suit, is muscling in on Hops Central Brewery. Holds proxies on a majority of the shares. Says he's from Charleston. Wondering if you've heard of him. Give me a call when you get the chance."

Suds hung up. "And now we wait and see."

Evie unclipped a key ring from her belt, selected a key, and unlocked the bottom file-size drawer in her desk. She dug out a file folder and opened it on her desk.

"Let's check the staff ballistics' list," she said.

Dread built in Suds' gut as Evie extracted a sheet of paper from the file folder and compared the ballistics profile on Suds' Walther to that of the bullet the coroner had extracted from the late Jasmine Cox.

She looked up from the task. "Shit," she said.

"No shit?"

Evie nodded. "Sorry Suds."

HARRISON FORD IS A MOVIE STAR

Saturday, August 4, 2018

"I can't afford this," Police Lieutenant Jarrod Fisher said as he addressed the ball on the first tee at The Plantation Course at Edisto.

"I know. Neither can I, really. I picked up a corporate membership to entertain wealthy clients. Get to write it off as a business expense," Harrison Ford said.

Fisher stepped back from the ball. They had a mid-afternoon tee time. It was as hot as balls, so they had the course pretty much to themselves. No pressure behind, and a foursome three holes ahead.

"I've never played this course. What's the distance again?"

Harry bent over the golf cart to examine the scorecard. "Par four. Three-seventy to the center. Trouble left and right. Sand trap, center, live oak, left, and water right protect the green."

"Not sure my 20 handicap is up to this," Fisher muttered.

He readjusted his stance and his grip and ripped his tee shot hard right into the trees. "Fuck!"

Harry laughed. "One mulligan on the front, one on the back. You must like to get those out of the way first thing. Go ahead. Hit another one. Try a stronger grip to correct that slice."

Fisher dug a ball out of his pocket, pulled a tee from behind his ear and set up for another try. He stepped his right foot in the bucket and squared his shoulders.

"Let it rip!" Harry said.

Fisher did, with better result. He got a little too much air under it. Drive carried about 170 yards and ended up two club lengths from the trees on the right side of the fairway.

Harry, a lefty, pulled a three wood from his bag and teed it low on the right side of the tee box. His shot flirted with a tree on the left of the fairway then came back to the right, landing in the middle about 130 yards out.

"Nice shot asshole," Fisher said. "Is this the part where you suggest a gentlemanly bet on the outcome of the game? How many strokes are you willing to spot me?"

"Actually, I don't want your money. What I would like is some information."

"I knew you had an agenda other than golf with an old buddy."

"You'd rather I ask about Cindy and the kids?"

"Cindy's bitchy and the kids are assholes. Enough said?"

"I'll tell her you said that."

"No you won't. You're just as afraid of her as I am. Besides I invoke the guy rule. What happens on the golf course stays on the golf course."

The two men climbed into the golf cart and made their way to Fisher's ball. He walked to the back of the cart to make his club selection.

"You're 220 yards out with water right at about 150 yards. Unless you've got a 220-yard club in your bag, I'd suggest laying up and coming in from the left."

Fisher grunted. Pulled a club from his bag and addressed the ball. He topped it a bit, but the ball traveled right to left putting him in good position about 90 yards out for an approach to the green unimpeded by water or sand.

"Nice shot," Harry said, as Fisher settled into the cart.

"So what is it you want to know?"

"In a minute."

Harry drove to his ball. Stopped. Set the brake, alit and pulled an eight iron from his bag.

Before taking his second shot, he paused. "Got two names to bounce off you. I'll let you think about 'em as I take my shot."

"OK. Shoot."

"Mike Weisse and Graham Smith."

"There's an unlikely paring."

"Shh. Shoot first. Ask questions later."

Fisher laughed. "The cop's mantra."

"Yep."

Harry's eight iron just cleared the sand trap. It hit a sprinkler head, bounced high in the air and settled about six feet from the flag. He smiled at Fisher. "If you can't be good. Be lucky."

"The duffer's mantra," Fisher said.

"Yep."

Harry settled back behind the wheel. "Now about that dynamic duo?"

"I really shouldn't be talking about this, because the feds have told us to stand down," Fisher said.

"Which is why you're going to tell me anyway. To fuck with the feds?"

"Fuck the feds," Fisher agreed. "We got suspicious when the gangster got religion."

"The gangster, I take it is Mike Weisse."

"That's right. He's got a piece of the pie on just about every racket in the city. Broads, loan sharks, extortion, drugs. He looks like a thug but he's got brains. He's insulated himself so far up the food chain that we haven't been able to get a nibble . . . until he began going to a local mega church, the Rev. Graham Smith presiding. Weisse began by making large cash contributions to the church. I'm guessing that he was washing money and the good reverend was complicit in kicking a lot of the cash back to him. We were about to close in when the feds told us to cease and desist."

"Why, do you figure?"

"My guess is the feds have themselves a confidential informer. They're chumming the water hoping a big shark will rise to the bait. It was frustrating because we'd just gotten a line on Weisse's new scam."

"What was that?"

"Washing money through church projects that were drastically over bid. We're thinking kick back from the contractors to clean dirty cash."

"How bad a guy is this Weisse?"

"We had him on a murder rap 10 years ago. Walked when a witness got cold feet, bought a brand-new boat, and enrolled his kid in an expensive private school. Weisse is seven years or so removed from doing the strong arm work himself. He has other people do it, but I think he bares his teeth occasionally just to prove that he still can."

"So if you're a civilian like me, you'd tread carefully around Mike Weisse?"

"You got far more teeth than your average civilian. But yeah. I'd steer clear. Why the interest?"

"Favor for a buddy who lives in Pennsylvania. Weisse is strong arming my buddy's boss."

"Tell him to hire some muscle."

"My buddy has his own muscle. He's six seven, two forty, and he used to be a cop."

"Formidable. But I still tell him to step carefully."

Harry stopped on the cart path next to Fisher's ball. "You're up."

Fisher took a full swing at his ball with a wedge. Got plenty of air under it and the ball landed on the fringe 15 yards from the flag. Fisher sighed. "So best I can do with an out-of-bounds is a double bogey and you'll be standing over a kick bird. Your wife's prettier than mine and you make more money than me. Life is so unfair."

"At least you've got a pension."

"Not if I keep blabbing to ex-cops like you," Fisher said.

A HOMECOMING FOR SUDS

Suds set his big suitcase down on Evie's doorstep. He still had a key, but he rang his doorbell for propriety's sake. Evie answered, wearing sweatpants and a Ben Roethlisberger jersey. She stepped back so he could enter.

"You sure about this?" Suds asked, dragging his heavy suitcase inside.

"Yes, but on a trial basis. If I get tired of your sorry ass, you're out. Just like that. Those are the ground rules."

Suds smiled. "I'm OK with that. I'm just glad to have a foot in the door."

"Well don't sell your furniture. You're on probation."

"No worries. I'm paid up with Rent America through the next month," Suds said.

"Before you unpack, I've got a couple of things to discuss with you," Evie said.

"Got a couple of thing on my talk-about list, too," Suds rejoined.

"Let's sit in the living room."

"Where my bowling trophies used to be."

"They're in the basement. Couldn't make that phone call to the Aurora Club," Evie said.

They sat. She on the love seat. He on his former recliner, which still was ensconced in prime TV-watching position.

"So talk," Suds said.

"Linda Fontaine is on board. She knows that your Walther was the Jasmine Cox murder weapon and she's got our backs, for the moment, anyway."

"Why is she sticking her neck out?" Suds wanted to know.

"Reparation. For screwing you . . . and thereby screwing me."

"Damn woman. You've got a way with words. But relax. I may have another suspect."

"Who?"

"Mike Weisse. He's a gangster."

"I'm taking it Harry got back in touch with you."

"That's right. Says I owe him two hundred bucks in green fees and bar tabs. Expenses for entertaining a lieutenant on the Charleston police force."

"Cheap at twice the price if it gives us a suspect, other than you."

"You're right about that," Suds agreed. "And thanks for inviting me back . . . for a sleepover or whatever you want to call it."

"I'd call it the first step of a reconciliation, but there something else we have to do first."

"What's that?"

"We've got to go into Rufus's room."

Suds blanched. "I haven't opened that door since the day he died."

"Neither have I. It's sort of emblematic of the thing that drove us apart."

"Linda Fontaine?"

"No silly. Our grief. We tried to handle it separately. We needed to embrace it together."

"We blamed Rufus for dying and ruining our lives," Suds said. "I've thought that for a long time but it's just now that I figured out how to articulate it."

Evie's eyes filled with tears. "That's remarkably insightful for a beer-loving dude named Suds."

"I have my moments," Suds said. He stood offered Evie his hand. She took it and they made their way up the stairs to Rufus's room. They embraced outside his closed door. And then they opened it and stepped inside, confronting their grief head-on and hand-in-hand for the first time.

FRANKLIN AMES PLAYS
HIS CARDS RIGHT

At first, Franklin Ames celebrated the day he welcomed the nefarious financier Johnny Lewis into his business. He soon came to rue it. Lewis's one million dollars had leveraged the brewery's expansion of 2012. It was the helium that lifted Hop Central to new heights in production and in market share.

Now, the company was at a different crossroads. It was large enough to attract the interest of investors who could sweep Ames off the board while transforming him from a millionaire to a multi-millionaire. That was Johnny's vision for the company. It contrasted wildly with Franklin's.

Franklin was captain of his own ship and he intended to maintain iron-fisted control. He had come up in a military culture. He was Navy through and through. Even though he had left the active service more than a decade earlier, his leadership model was military. Hop Central grew upon his initiative and at his directive alone. He could not abide rule by committee.

His management style was to find diamonds in the rough like Suds Ferguson and Todd Rudy and smooth their climb up the ranks in true military fashion. Mike Weisse was an enigma. Franklin needed to know what resources Weisse had tapped to line up a majority of stockholders against him. His next move, obviously, was to turn Suds loose on that problem. Let the former cop do his cop thing and report back to his captain.

He was beholden to Ernie Flowers who had helped negotiate the Lewis deal. But he had come to learn that Ernie's handling of his marital contract with Jasmine had not been nearly as deft. Jasmine's 200 shares were in the wind and there was nothing either Franklin or Ernie's feckless underling Les Benson could do about it. That's why Weisse's offer to infuse the brewery with even more investment capital was so bewildering.

God damn his decision to offer such a generous wedding gift to that buxom gold-digger with the sexual appetites of a sailor on liberty and the morals of a politician on the take. The thing that nagged at him the most was her infidelity's tacit rebuke of his manhood. Her wandering insinuated he was less than a man.

His inadequacies in that regard were never far from his mind but were ineffable. It was an insecurity he held close to his heart where it festered, poisoning his relationships with all women. Jasmine had become a surrogate for all of womanhood.

Emma had been a nurturer. One of a kind. In Franklin's experience, all other women were either whores or baubles. Jasmine was both. That certainty fueled a misogyny that he tucked away carefully lest it tarnish the paternalistic relationship he had fostered among his employees. But a careful review by a modern-day HR specialist would have revealed heavy gender lopsidedness among the management ranks at the brewery. That was a dirty secret that could escape abroad were corporate management to be wrested from him.

Even dirtier, at least in the mores of the times, in which he had grown up, was his attraction to men. That was a secret he held even closer.

Peculiar proclivities aside, like every man Franklin wanted to bequeath his essence upon future generations. It was a biological imperative hardwired by genetics that knew no sexual orientation. That's why the news that he was not, after all, sterile had come as such a thunderbolt and elicited in him an unprecedented generosity.

The whore now called Gerry Smith thought that his largesse was directed at her. But he had another purpose altogether. He wanted her son . . . no, his son. He wanted something of himself to endure through the ages. He might not ever get a second chance. Now was the time to strike.

Suds, despite his size and background, could not be the tip of the spear in his plot to claim Alex as his own. For the assault on the Charleston redoubt Gerry and Graham Smith had gathered about themselves, Franklin would need a blunter instrument. He could think of no more likely candidate than his former shipmate Todd Rudy.

Years ago, in a steroid-induced rage, Rudy had torn apart a whorehouse bar in Charleston. He had broken a prostitute's jaw and shoved the whorehouse enforcer, an off-duty SEAL down a flight of steps. The damage to the SEAL's body and to his machismo was so profound that the SEAL had to be cashiered from the Navy. To be bested by a Marine was the ultimate humiliation.

Cowering in an alley nearby as the police descended on the whorehouse, Rudy did the first thing that came to his mind. He called his CO, Commander Franklin Ames, who had driven his personal vehicle to the alley and opened the back door so Rudy could slip inside, thereby escaping the wrath of a certain police lieutenant who rushed to the scene when he learned his favorite girl had been brutalized.

Rudy was grateful then and even more grateful years later when Franklin offered him a chance to learn the beer business from the bottoms up. Rudy was the boss's go-to guy when the bottling line staff had tried to organize a union. No legs were broken, but the children of union organizers were followed home from school by a black van with dark windows. Rudy was aided an abetted in this enterprise by Sampson Reeves, a tall, bald and black bad ass who handled the graveyard security shift at the brewery.

The union effort stalled and Franklin rewarded Rudy with promotions at a quicker pace than other long-time employees. Middle management got the hint. Todd Rudy was the golden-haired boy. Complaints against him died on the boss's desk.

Franklin was about to pick up the phone to summon Rudy to his office when Jan Murphy buzzed him on the office intercom. "A Mr. Weisse to see you, sir. Says he has an appointment."

Franklin sighed. The other shoe was about to drop. "Send him in."

Weisse sauntered across his portal with the aplomb of a circus bear wearing a clown suit. He was big, burly, crew cut, and tattooed. He carried the demeanor of a master chief petty officer gone to seed, a giant among lesser enlisted men.

Weisse sat down without being asked. He cast his eyes about Franklin's office, taking in the panorama of the tasting room, bottling line and brewing tanks arrayed below, beyond the one-way glass walls. "Nice office. Play your cards right and you'll get to keep it."

"By that I take it you think you hold the superior hand," Franklin said. "Huh?"

"Never mind. Poker allusion. What's your deal?"

"My deal is this. I'm sure you got expansion plans tucked away somewhere around here. I want you to execute them and let me take care of the bidding, contracts, and billing."

"What's in it for me?"

"I keep Johnny Lewis off your ass."

"What's in it for him?"

"I'll be handling the debt services on a certain municipal project delayed by an environmental impact assessment. Something about the loss of habitat for hellgrammites or some such shit."

"And what's in it for you?"

"You let me worry about that."

"Your intent is pretty obvious. You've got dirty money you're trying to clean. I'm thinking over-billing and some sort of kick-back scheme with the contractors."

"Smart guy. But don't get too smart. Too smart can get you killed," Weisse warned.

"And if I don't play ball?"

"I throw the late Jasmine Cox Ames's proxy on the table alongside Lewis's proxies and we sell the brewery out from under you."

"Figured it was something like that. How much money are you planning to invest?"

"I'm thinking ten million over five years."

"For what? Five million worth of brick and mortar?"

"I like the way you do math," Weisse said.

"So let me get this straight. You want me to develop plans for a five million expansion that can be billed at $10 million?"

"That's the gist of it," Weisse said. "At the end of the five years, I'll return your late wife's shares and buy out Lewis. Five years is pretty much the maximum term of a laundering scheme like this. Longer than that and the feds get interested."

"I'll do it. With one caveat."

"What's a caveat?"

"One condition. You've got to get good builders. I don't want to end up with a falling down factory five years from now."

"That's where Mr. Lewis comes in," Weisse said. "He's got some good builders who are willing to play ball. We got a deal?"

Weisse extended a pudgy paw across the desk. And Franklin shook it.

"I'd call that a royal flush. Poker allusion," Weisse said. And then he winked. "One more thing."

"What's that?"

"There's a brewery in Charleston I'd like you to take a look at. They make a good brew. I think the owner would benefit from our investment and your expertise. I'd like you to take a look."

Franklin nodded. "What's the brewery called?

"Palmetto State Craft Brewhaus."

"I'll have a look," Franklin said.

TODD RUDY COMES CLEAN BUT IS STILL DIRTY

Monday, August 6, 2018

One of two visitors' chairs in Franklin Ames's office was already occupied when Suds arrived for a meeting called by the beer baron himself. Two men were chatting amicably as Suds knocked on Franklin's office door. The visitor turned and Suds was surprised when Todd Rudy's sullen eyes settled upon him.

"Come on in and have a seat, Suds," Franklin said, beckoning Suds forward. "I wanted to get you two together for some strategizing since you both have experience in military law enforcement. But before we get started, Todd has something to get off his chest."

Suds settled into the chair and eyed Rudy warily. The obvious familiarity between Franklin and Todd was unsettling. There was a bond here that ran contrary to Suds' long-held belief that Franklin was a good guy and his certainty that Todd Rudy was not.

"Tell him, Todd," Franklin said.

"I doped your drink . . . at Murphy's," Rudy said.

"I had already arrived at that conclusion," Suds said, icily, "but why?"

"Cause Mrs. Ames paid me to."

196

"Why?"

"I got the idea that she wanted you out of the way for a while. That's all."

"Why?"

"Dunno. But I figured Franklin was on board with it because his personal lawyer was with her. The two of them were tighter than ticks on a dog's ass that night, I'll tell you."

"I'm pretty sure they did it to keep you from acting as my bodyguard," Franklin said.

"Which cleared the way for Jasmine to take those pot shots at you," Suds said.

"That's right. I was uneasy about Jasmine. Couldn't understand her play. That's why I asked you to bring your piece that night."

Suds almost blurted out the news that a bullet from his gun had killed Jasmine. He bit his lip. Instead, he said: "So how did I end up back in my own place with the world's worst hangover?"

"Jasmine and the lawyer musta taken you home," Rudy said. They steered you out of the place. One of 'em on each elbow. Anyway. Sorry. My ex-old lady is bustin' my rocks on child support. I really needed the cash."

"How much did Jasmine pay you?" Suds asked.

"Two hundred."

"Cheaper than 30 pieces of silver, I suppose."

"Huh?" Rudy said.

"Biblical allusion."

"You two guys OK now?" Franklin wanted to know. "I want you to work together on a project and I can't have any in-fighting."

"I'll not work with that son-bitch. No way!"

"Tut. Tut. Suds," Franklin said. "Need I remind you of second chances? I certainly gave you one."

Franklin's riposte hit the mark. "What project?" Suds gulped.

"I need the two of you to find out whatever you can about Mike Weisse."

"The fat guy in the cheap suit who strong-armed his way into the board meeting?"

Franklin nodded. "That's right. I need to know how he lined up all those proxies against me. I need to know who he is and where his money comes from."

"His money?" Rudy asked.

"That's right. He's offering to invest $5 million in an expansion project at the brewery. But he wants to let the contracts himself. Lewis is on board. He has all sorts of connections in the local building industry."

"Money laundering?" Rudy asked.

"That would be my guess," Franklin agreed.

"I think I can help you out with that. I've got a guy in Charleston. He's already turned over some rocks and Weisse crawled out," Suds said.

"Explain," Franklin said.

"My guy is an ex-cop with the Charleston PD. He's a private security consultant now but he knows people. Golfed with one of them, on my dime."

"And," Ames said, his impatience palpable.

"Weisse's is a sort of ombudsman for organized crime in Charleston. He's got connections with all the rackets. Numbers, drugs, broads, extortion. He looks like a biker gone to seed but he's got financial smarts and owns enough muscle to get dirty jobs done on the QT."

"I think I could handle him," Rudy said, cracking his knuckles. "Just say the word, boss."

"Thanks for the enthusiasm," Franklin said. "What else you got, Suds?"

"It's a good guess Weisse has cash to clean. He's been working a sweetheart deal with someone already known to us."

"Who. Come on Suds. Don't spoon feed me!"

"The evangelist Graham Smith."

"Mother fucker!"

"Who's Graham Smith?" Rudy asked.

"I'll tell you later. What was the scam, Suds?"

"My guy says Weisse was scrubbing cash through Smith's church, which has been growing by leaps and bounds far beyond the reach of the parishioners."

"Let me guess. The church expands. Weisse pays the contractors twice the cost of the project and gratefully accepts the kickback of clean cash."

"That's the gist of it," Suds agreed.

"So I jump up on Smith's radar when I ride into town to rescue his son. But how does Weisse get wind of me?"

"A sermon. Smith named you as his benefactor. "Told his congregants that the Lord works in mysterious ways moving a purveyor of sin, a manufacturer of demon rum, to do good in the world."

"Demon rum? We brew beer," Todd interjected.

"Poetic license," Franklin snapped.

"Biblical allusion," Todd said, thinking himself witty. Alas, he was but half right.

"So Weisse gets wind of that and seizes on another way to clean up some cash. Doesn't that make him a suspect in the murder of my wife and my attorney?" Ames asked.

"Yep. Evie is running down some leads right now."

"Such as?"

"What has become of Zach Dunkel, Jasmine's attorney? He held her will and her proxy on those shares of Hop Central. I'm thinking someone made him an offer he couldn't refuse," Suds said.

"Godfather allusion," Todd exulted.

Franklin ignored him. He arose. Slapped Suds on the back. "I knew I did the right thing when I pulled you off the scrap heap. Love the initiative. But I gotta ask: Why did you decide to check up on Weisse without my telling you to?"

"Dude pissed me off. Fucked with my promotion. Wanted some payback," Suds said.

Franklin nodded. "Glad I called this meeting. Now I know how to proceed. Suds I want you to hang close to your wife see if you can tie Weisse or one of his associates to Jasmine's murder. I'll give you a name to start with, Zeke Morrow."

"Who he?"

"Muscle in the employ of Johnny Lewis. If any foreign talent has come to town lately, Morrow would know it."

"What about me?" Todd asked.

"You're coming with me to Charleston. I want to collect intelligence of Mike Weisse and visit my son."

"Huh?"

"I'll explain later. I'm going into the lion's den on Weisse's home court. And I want some muscle backing me."

"Sounds like you're putting me on the bench," Suds complained.

"Don't look at it like that, Suds. You're my designated hitter. I need a singles hitter in Charleston. We haven't reached your spot in the batting order. OK?"

Suds nodded, grudgingly.

"Meeting adjourned," Franklin said. "Todd I'd like you to stay a few minutes longer so we can discuss our trip and what I'd like to accomplish."

Suds left them alone to plot, feeling like a bench warmer despite the boss's disclaimer.

SUDS ENJOYS A STEAK OUT

"I'm going to Charleston," Suds announced over dinner at Nicks 114 Cafe, a culinary and social institution in downtown New Cumberland, Pennsylvania. "First thing tomorrow morning."

"How come?"

"Because I think Franklin Ames is sending me off on a wild goose chase while he and Todd Rudy take care of some serious business down in Charleston."

"What sort of business."

"They're are going to confront Mike Weisse on his home turf because they think he is trespassing on ours."

"What's that mean?" Evie asked, picking at her crab cake, a Nick's specialty.

They were sitting in a booth at the back of the restaurant, next to a long, high-top table. Around the high table was gathered a group of a dozen or so men. The noise volume rose as friendly voices discussed a burning issue, which was, apparently, who is the best male actor of modern times? Dustin Hoffman seemed to be carrying the day.

Their waitress, Stevie, approached. "Need refills on your drinks?" she asked.

"What's with the noisy crew next door?" Suds asked.

Stevie laughed. "That's the Premier Philosophy Club of Lower New Cumberland. A bunch of old farts who meet here once a week."

"Well they are wrong. The greatest actor of modern times is Robert Duvall," Suds said.

"I heard that, said a tall fellow at the apex of the Philosophy Club. Duvall lost in the quarter finals, even though I voted for him."

Suds smiled. You've got good taste in actors. Sorry for interrupting."

The tall fellow laughed. He returned his attention to the meeting. "Next on the agenda is a our guest for the evening. Gentlemen, I'd like to introduce Lawrence Knorr, publisher of Sunbury Press and our series of books Keystone Tombstones."

Suds redirected his attention to Stevie. "I'll have another Nimble Giant. Evie?"

"Nothing for me."

Stevie smiled and left with Suds's order.

Suds leaned forward, re-engaging Evie. "Franklin thinks Mike Weisse, or someone who works for him, is behind Jasmine and Ernie's murders."

That perked up Evie's ears. "What's their motive?"

"To claim Jasmine's shares and set Hop Central Craft Brewery up for a money laundering expansion scheme."

"Jasmine strikes me as the sort who'd be eager to play ball with a scheme like that. Why kill her and Ernie, too?"

"Maybe a falling out among thieves. Maybe Jasmine and Ernie were in cahoots. Maybe they wanted too big a cut. I just can't figure out why Franklin is cutting me out of the action."

"What does Franklin want you to do?"

"Check to see if any known associates of Mike Weisse showed up in Harrisburg ahead of Jasmine's murder."

"Seems like a reasonable request. But how would you know who works for Weisse?"

"Franklin gave me a name. Zeke Morrow. Says he's muscle for Johnny Lewis. Says Morrow would know it if any foreign talent had shown up in town."

"So are you going to reach out?"

"Already have. Morrow wouldn't say shit if his mouth was full of it."

"A dry hole?"

"One that would require a lot of dredging to reach pay dirt."

"Want me to take a crack at it? That's the sort of thing Linda Fontaine loves to do. Bust the balls of ball busters."

"She certainly busted mine . . . wait a minute. That was you."

Evie stuck out her tongue. "You deserved that and I suppose I did, too. So, when do you leave?"

"First thing tomorrow . . . direct flight out of Baltimore. I'll have to get on the road by 5 A.M. if I want to beat Ames to Charleston. He's leaving out of Harrisburg an hour later and has to change in Greensboro."

"How would you know that?"

"I asked Jan Murphy. She knows everything."

"And she told you because . . . ?"

"She thinks I'm one of the good guys. I'm also one of the suspicious guys. Franklin's behavior of late has been erratic. There's something on his mind that has nothing to do with the brewery."

"What?"

"Dunno. Hope I'll find out in Charleston."

"I take it Harry is on standby to help you out."

"Yeah. Harry says Weisse rents space at a big construction company. Our plan is to stake out his office and see who turns up."

Stevie showed up with Suds's third beer, a Gentle Giant brewed by Troegs Independent Brewing, also of Hershey. Suds bent over it waved the aroma into his nose. And took a sip. "Ahh. Perfect."

"Aren't you sleeping with the enemy? Drinking a Troegs' beer?"

"I'm willing to do that if the enemy is good in bed. And Troegs certainly is," Suds said.

"Slut."

"That's beer slut to you."

Evie laughed. Reached over and covered his hand with hers. "Be careful down there."

"Harry will have my back."

"I'll let you know what we turn up from Zeke Morrow. Probably shake Johnny Lewis's tree too."

"Enough shop talk," Suds said, attacking his sirloin with gusto.

SUDS ENJOYS A STAKE OUT

Tuesday, August 7, 2018

Suds grumpily rang up the rental fee on a perv van on his Visa card, two hundred and thirty-eight dollars and forty-one cents with tax and insurance. The clerk said: "Return it full or pay a $50 filling fee."

Harrison Ford knew that Suds was tight with a dollar. The pain was written across his face in ALL CAPS.

"Waste of good beer money," Suds said, as the clerk returned his card. "You sure you don't have a stakeout van in your fleet?"

"Nope. I haven't chased cheating husbands for years. I'm a security consultant."

"Lah de dah."

Suds checked his watch. Franklin's flight was due to arrive in forty-five minutes. "How long to the airport?"

"Bout a half hour," Ford said.

"Better get going then. I'll drive cause you'll need to pick up surveillance at the arrival gate. For obvious reasons I can't do that."

They settled in the van, a five-year-old Econline, blue with a dent on the right door panel. "You get what you pay for from Rent a Wreck," Harry observed.

Suds balanced his briefcase on his knees. "Sure weren't wreck prices," he grumbled as he popped the latches. Rooting around in his briefcase, he withdrew a file folder opened it up, found two pictures, and handed them to Harry. "Ames on top. Rudy below. From their personnel files at the brewery."

Harry studied the photos and returned them to Suds. "Got it."

Suds returned the photos to the file and the file to the briefcase, which he stowed next to his overnight bag behind the driver's seat. "Let's go." He fired up the engine and backed out of the parking space at Rent a Wreck. Dropping the van into drive, he said. "Where to?"

"Right out of the parking lot and follow your nose. Next turn is an on ramp in a couple of miles. I'll tell you when."

With Suds settled into the right-hand lane, with his mirrors properly adjusted, Harry commenced his interrogation.

"So why the cloak and dagger?"

"I get the sense that Franklin is lying to me. And I don't like to be lied to."

"About what, specifically?"

"His reasons for coming here."

"What's Weisse's play?"

"He holds Jasmine's proxy on 200 shares of Hop Central and has lined up enough other stockholders to sell the brewery out from under Franklin unless Franklin plays ball."

"And the ball playing?"

"Money laundering. Weisse wants to take point on an expansion of the brewery. To let the contracts, pay the bills . . ."

"And accept kickbacks from the contractors to clean his money."

"Just like he did with Graham Smith's mega church."

"Aren't we a pair of de-tectives?" Harry said.

"On that note."

"Yes."

"Just how desperate do you figure the Smiths are?"

"Jarrod Fisher, my detective friend, tells me the feds are sniffing around the mega church's books. Don't know if a deal has been offered but my guess is they're ramping up the pressure on the Smiths to cooperate in some sort of plea deal."

"So Weisse is the prize? And the Smiths are the bait?"

"Something like that. I get the sense that the Smiths, or Graham anyway, had his hand in the till. They are cash hungry, what with Alex being sick and all."

Suds eased the van to a stop behind a line of cars waiting for the light to change. He drummed his fingers on the steering wheel. "If the Smiths need cash. I know someone who has some."

"Who dat?"

"Franklin Ames. I don't know for sure, but I think some money already may have changed hands."

"From Weisse to Ames?"

"That's right."

"How much?"

"Don't know. Just spit balling. But the obvious question is: What do the Smiths have that Ames wants?" Suds said.

"I have a feeling that's a rhetorical question."

"Alex."

"A sick kid?"

"Doesn't matter that Alex is sick. Besides, he's getting better, by all accounts. I think Franklin is trying to leverage the money he got from Weisse to claim some sort of joint custody arrangement for his son."

"Why would he want that?"

"A legacy. He doesn't have an heir. Thought he was shooting blanks. Turns out there was at least one bullet in the chamber. And here's anothering thing. He has made me the executor of his estate. He named Alex as his sole heir."

"Jesus. That's spooky."

Suds was startled. "Why?"

"I get Alex. But why you? As executor, I mean. Unless he was trying to set you up for something farther down the line."

"Set me up? For what?"

"Dunno. Just suspicious. Occupational hazard. On ramp is just ahead on the right."

The two men fell silent as Suds merged with a steady stream of traffic. Signage told him that the airport exit lay ten miles ahead. He looked at his watch and increased his speed. Valves knocked as the Econoline labored under the increased demand.

"I can't think of any scenarios dangerous to me should I end up the executor of his estate," Suds said.

Harry laughed. "Sorry to have made you paranoid."

"My missing gun makes me paranoid."

"Missing gun!"

"Yeah."

Suds told him the story about his being drugged and waking up on his own couch with his Walther nowhere to be found.

"You sure you were carrying that night?"

"Positive. Know what's worse?"

"What?"

"The specs on my personal weapon are on file with Derry PD. Ballistics show that my Walther was the murder weapon for Jasmine."

"Man are you fucked!"

"Evie's got my back. Toxicology shows I was incapacitated that night. And Todd Rudy, the bartender has confessed to doping my drink. Says Jasmine paid him to do it."

"The same Todd Rudy who's traveling with Franklin Ames."

"The very same."

"Why would Jasmine want to drug you?"

"Maybe to take me off the board so she could take a shot at her husband without my interference."

"Damn. A tight juxtaposition that."

"Huh?"

"You think Franklin is your buddy, but he's also the buddy of your enemy."

"Yeah. One of many reasons I'm suspicious of this field trip. One of the many reason I asked for your help."

"Who took you home from the bar?"

"Rudy says I left with Jasmine and Ernie Flowers."

"The dead lawyer?"

"Don't forget the dead ex-wife."

"So where is your Walther?"

"Wish I knew."

Suds followed the signs, exited the expressway. It wasn't long before the rattily Econoline gasped to the curb in front of a sign that said passenger drop-off. Suds looked at his watch. "Arrival in five minutes. We cut that close. Let me know when you spot them."

Harry nodded. Checked his smart phone. "Strong signal. And I've got you on speed dial."

"I'll hang here until the gendarmes get nervous. Then circle til I hear from you."

Harry grunted his assent and climbed from the van. "Stay close Sherlock." He slammed the door and eased his way through the automatic doors into the terminal.

LOST AND THEN FOUND

On his fourth circuit around the airport, Suds's cell rang.

"They're at the Avis counter," Harry said.

"I'll meet you at the curb."

Harry was jingling his pocket change when Suds arrived. The van was still moving when Harry wrenched open the Econoline's door. "Do the loop one more time and come up behind the rental lane. Should put us right behind them. They've rented a Lincoln Navigator."

"Big SUV."

"They'll need it. There are three of them. Third is a black guy, almost as big as you, with twice as many muscles and half the fat."

"Sampson."

"You know him, or are you describing him?"

"Know him. Sampson Reeves. Shaved head. Hoop earring in the right ear. Diamond stud in front tooth."

"Don't know about the tooth, but right on the other accounts. Who he?"

"Night watchman at the brewery. Tough guy. Another of Franklin's reclamation projects. Personnel file shows he's got a record. Assault and battery. Makes me nervous to be in the same room with him."

"Why would Franklin need that much muscle on this trip?" Harry asked.

"Not too much if he's gonna tweak Weisse's beard."

"Suppose not."

Suds navigated two right turns and snugged the van along the curb in the car rental lane. They didn't have long to wait. A dark blue Navigator with deep tinted windows pulled onto the road from the rental lot. "That them?" Suds asked.

"Hard to tell through the tinted windows. But how many Navigators with Avis decals could there be leaving the rental lot?"

"Good point," Suds said, and gave chase.

He followed the Navigator for three or four miles, before it pulled into the lot of a Hampton Embassy Suite. A young woman, not more than 27 or so, blonde and long-legged climbed out of driver's seat.

"Shit! Wrong Navigator!" Suds fumed.

"No shit!"

"What now?" Suds asked.

"I'm betting they're heading to Weisse's office," Harry said.

"Which is where?"

"Not to far from here, but lots of twists and turns, so why don't I drive?"

The two men traded places. Soon, they arrived at an industrial park close to an airport runway. The name on the building read Novinger Construction. No Navigator to be seen.

"Guess we should wait here," Suds said.

"I don't have a better idea," Harry admitted.

And so they waited. Before long, Suds's bladder told him he should have used the bathroom at Rent-a-Wreck.

"Damn it! I need to pee."

Harry scrunched around behind the wheel. "You know, it wouldn't hurt me to squeeze one off myself."

"Never pass up a chance to pee," Suds said. "We'll just have to take our chances."

Both men alit from the van, made their way to the front door, opened it and went inside where they were confronted by a long counter behind which stood Mike Weisse. He was leaning over a young woman who was assaulting a computer keyboard.

"The accounting software portal won't let me in," she complained. The bell fixed to the front door jangled.

Weisse looked up. "Son of a bitch. What brings the would-be CEO of Hop Central Craft Brewery to my front door?"

Suds said the first thing that came to his mind. "Me and my associate need to pee. And then I need to talk to you about Franklin Ames."

"There's no up side to getting between a urinal and two big men with full bladders. This way gentlemen," Weisse said, beckoning them forward.

While they were peeing in side-by-side urinals, Harry asked. "How we going to play this one?"

"I'm the brains. I'll introduce you as the muscle. Glower and agree with everything I say."

"Yassa. Massa."

"Cool the black face. It's politically incorrect even in the deep South. Just follow my lead."

They washed their hands and left the bathroom. The young woman behind the counter directed them to Weisse's office where the man in a cheap suit waved them to visitors' chairs. "Now what about Franklin Ames bears discussing?"

"Why he would be visiting Charleston with enough muscle to tag team Andre the Giant," Suds said.

"Interesting."

"More than interesting. Ominous would be the word I'd choose," Suds said.

"How so?"

"Don't know if you'd had the chance to measure the man, but Franklin is not someone to trifle with. He's knocked heads with the union. His cohorts left some bruises that some tough guys in hard hats are still ruing."

"I've got my own tough guys," Weisse said. "Hell. I'm one of them."

"So I've heard. But forewarned is forearmed."

"And you're warning me of?"

"The likelihood that Franklin is not going to be your bitch. His balls are too big for that."

"He tell you to deliver that message?"

"Nah. The warning comes from an entirely different spot."

"What spot is that?"

"The spot where the would-be CEO of Hop Central starts looking out for his own interests when they diverge from those of Mr. Big Beer."

"And you're warning me because?"

"I thought it was a good idea to form an alliance with the man who could be controlling the purse strings at the brewery for some time to come. What I'm saying is I'm willing to help do some cleaning if cleaning is in order. And don't pretend you don't know my meaning."

Weisse arose from his office chair. "This has been an interesting encounter, but we're done here. I'll consider what you've said. Go home Suds. See to our brewery. I'll be in touch."

"Don't wait too long. And do be careful. One of Mr. Ames's associates, one Sampson Reeves, is a black man of about my size, considerably more muscle and enough attitude to out-bitch a roller derby team."

Suds paused with his hand on the door handle. "One more thing. I'd appreciate if you didn't tell Franklin that I had stopped by. I don't want him to think that I'm disloyal."

"I'll play the cards you've dealt me in my own best interest. But off hand, I can't think of any reason Franklin Ames needs to know that you stopped by," Weisse said.

Suds nodded and made his way to the exit with Harry close on his heels.

DEAD RECKONING

Suds snugged the Econoline to the curb in front of Graham Smith's palatial McMansion. They had circled the block several times looking for a Lincoln Navigator to no avail. "I wonder where the fuck they went," Suds said.

"Seems like a couple ex-cops could find an SUV as conspicuous as a Lincoln Navigator."

"Franklin Ames has two Charleston connections, Weisse and the Smiths. He's got to be at one or the other," Suds mused. Then he snapped his fingers. "The U.S. Navy!"

"Gonna have to help me with that."

"Goose Creek."

"Duck. Duck. Goose, Still no help."

"I remember Franklin saying he'd pulled reserve duty at the Goose Creek Naval Weapons Station. I wonder if he has some connections there he's been exploiting."

"Such as?"

"Dunno. But I'm pretty sure Todd Rudy pulled MP duty as a Marine at Goose Creek. Think that's where the two of them met."

"Rudy and Ames?"

"That's right."

"Think it's worth driving to Goose Creek? It's not that far."

"Nah. I'm grasping at straws," Suds said. "We're here. Let's knock on the door and see what the Smiths are up to. Maybe Franklin has stopped by."

They alit from the van, walked through an open gate up the drive, and ascended the steps to the front door, which was ajar.

Suds studied the door and frowned. "This is an exclusive neighborhood. So I imagine the police are always nearby, but I don't think the Smiths would leave their front door open."

"I'd say that's a clue," Harry said.

"But of what?"

"Betting the answer lies inside."

"You got gloves?"

"Nope."

Suds dug a handkerchief from his back pocket and covered his hand with it before he pushed the door open. "Hello! Anyone home?"

There was no answer. Save for a meow.

"They got a cat," Harry said.

Suds made hissing sounds. "Pss. Pss. Pss." And was rewarded with another plaintive "Meow!"

Suds said: "Apparently so."

Padded footfalls on the hardwood from the floor above. An orange tabby appeared at the top of the stairs.

"Here kitty, kitty," Harry said.

"Didn't know you were a cat person," Suds said

"I've always enjoyed a little . . ."

"Don't go there. What are you, thirteen?"

Harry's laughter soon hollowed. The cat descended, leaving bloody footprints on the hardwood of the stairs.

"Fuck!" Suds said.

"Should I call the police? Or do you want to have a look-see, first?"

Suds considered. "Right now the only evidence we have is a cat with bloody feet. I say we reconnoiter before we call your buddies."

The tabby circled Harry's ankles, purring lustily.

They ascended the stairs, careful not to step on the cat's bloody footprints. They followed the trail down a hallway into what obviously was the master bedroom suite. There, face down on the king-sized bed, lay a woman. Her head dangled over the edge of the bed. Her hair formed a crimson halo about the back of her head. Blood had pooled on the floor beneath her.

Suds retrieved his handkerchief and covered his right hand. He stepped forward, avoiding the bloodstain, crouched and cupped the woman's chin in his handkerchiefed palm. Raising her head gently, Suds confirmed that the dead woman was Gerry Smith.

He lowered her head and stepped back. Behind him he heard Harry talking on his cell phone.

Harry said: "That's right. That's the address. Dead woman is Gerry Smith. Looks like a single gunshot wound to the forehead. No I won't disturb the crime scene. I'm not some bootlick rookie. OK. OK."

Harry hung up and stepped forward as Suds studied a handgun lying on the bed beside the body.

"A Walther PPK," Suds said. "Chambered for .380 ammo. Max load is seven in the clip one in the chamber."

"Aren't you the quick study."

"I'd recognize that gun anywhere."

"Why?"

"Cause it's mine."

"You shitting me!? How can you be sure?"

"My initials are engraved on the butt plate. I can see them from here."

"If I were you, I'd pick up the gun and stow it in the van while we wait for the police."

"Really?"

"Yes. Really. I know you didn't kill Gerry. You've been with me for the past five hours and this is a fresh kill. We've got to figure out who did this and we can't do that if you're locked up in an interrogation room."

Suds nodded. Used his handkerchief to pick up the gun. He checked to make sure it was safetied and shoved the gun, handkerchief and all, into the waistband of his trousers.

"Let's go downstairs and wait for the police," Ford said.

The cat met them at the bottom of the stairs. He, or she, meowed and trotted off toward the back of the house, trailing bloody footprints. They paused in the foyer. Suds shrugged. "We've got a few minutes before the police arrive. I'm going to follow that cat, which they did to a backroom study, where they found Graham Smith collapsed face up on the carpeted floor.

"Exit wounds mean three pops to the chest," Harry said.

"Probably with my Walther," Suds said, miserably.

"Let's go," Harry said.

The cat followed them outside where sirens rent the air, startling the cat, tail twitching, into the shrubbery. "There goes our material witness," Suds said. He pulled the Walther carefully from his trousers, sniffed the barrel. "Freshly fired." He ejected the clip, made sure the chamber was empty, and thumbed three rounds into the palm of his left hand. "Four rounds missing, unless there was one in the chamber," Suds said. He stowed the gun and loose ammo in his briefcase, which he returned to its spot behind the driver's seat.

"I'm fucked Harry. No matter how you slice it."

"How so?"

"Ballistics on my personal piece are on file with Derry Twp. Police. It's a policy I instituted myself when I was chief. Evie's got my back. But her sergeant is also in the loop and her loyalty is less certain."

"Who her?"

"Linda Fontain is her name. And it gets worse."

"How so?"

"I had an affair with Linda. It's what wrecked my marriage to Evie."

Harry whistled. "You are indeed fucked. We'd better figure out who did this. Sooner than later."

"I could sure use a beer," Suds said.

"I know just the place. We'll go there right after the prostate exam."

Suds laughed. "Yeah. You can bet our comrades in blue will be crawling up our asses for a least a couple of hours."

TOEING THE THIN BLUE LINE

The proctology was gentler than it would have been for lesser men. As ex-cops, Suds and Harry got kids-glove treatment. The interrogation room was Lieutenant Jarrod Fisher's office. There was no denial of bathroom breaks or of coffee. But the inquisition was thorough and conducted in one-and-one sessions with first Harry and then Suds.

Harry and Suds were allowed to drive the Econoline to the police station rather than suffer the ignominy of riding in the back of a patrol car with the windows and doors perpetually locked tight and the lingering odor of piss and vomit that no amount of cleaning could ever obscure.

That gave them time to get their stories straight. They agreed they would tell nothing but the truth on everything, except Suds's Walther, and hope to hell Charleston PD didn't ask to search their rental van.

They parked on the street outside headquarters in a tow-away zone, hoping a do-not-disturb decal would keep the van un-impounded. "Put this on the dash," Fisher said, handing them a cardboard cutout in the shape of a detective's badge. "Your ride will be safe in the tow-away."

As they disembarked from the Econoline, Suds was torn. Should he bring the briefcase into the police station, taking a chance he could brazen his way past security on the thin blue line? Or should he leave it (and the Walther) inside the van where an unattended briefcase might be a tempting target for a smash and run?

Suds decided that losing his briefcase to a vandal would be better than facing the Visigoths inside.

When it came time for Suds's interview, he was ushered into Fisher's office. He rubbed shoulders with Harry who was on his way out. Harry smiled, winked and gave Suds a thumbs-up, which he took to mean that Harry had sailed through the interview with flying colors.

Fisher tried and failed not to be intimidated by Suds's size. He shook hands briefly, and sat down quickly trying to minimize the psychological effect of confronting a much larger man in such a small space. Fisher had the demeanor of a man greeting a circus bear in a telephone booth. What would happen if he pissed off the bear?

"Harry tells me that he is helping you with an investigation of one of our local luminaries, Mike Weisse, on behalf of your employer," Fisher said, without preamble.

Suds nodded. "That's right."

"How did that investigation lead you to Graham Smith's doorstep?"

"How much time you got?" Suds asked.

Fisher checked his watch. It had been a long day and he was, in fact, hoping to wrap the interview up and get home in time for dinner with his wife and their two brats.

He exhaled lustily through his nose. "Tell me what time it is. Leave the how the clock works for a follow up interview, if need be."

Suds nodded. "OK. I'll summarize." He told Fisher about Boyd Porter's death on the loading dock at Hop Central; how his boss Franklin Ames was a suspect in Porter's murder; how Porter fiddled with DNA samples to fudge Dickie Cox's paternity of Lisa Dubbel's issue; how Chuck Dubbel's suicide note cleared his boss; how the DNA testing had revealed Franklin's paternity of Alex Smith; how Franklin's bone marrow had saved Alex's life; how Mike Weisse had strong-armed his way into a Hops Central board meeting; and how he had followed Franklin Ames to Charleston out of fear that his boss was getting himself into more than he could handle with Mike Weisse.

Suds buried Fisher in extraneous details in the hope that it would divert the lieutenant's attention from the thing Suds feared most, the murder weapon that resided in his briefcase behind the front seat of the Ford Econoline parked at the curb outside police headquarters.

It wasn't long before, Fisher had enough. He raised a hand. "My turn," he said. "That gibes pretty closely with what Harry told me. I've run out of questions for you. But stay close to your phone. I may need you to clear up a point or two. Gimmie your cell."

Suds rattled off his cell phone number, which Fisher recorded on a notepad.

"OK, Now I have a question for you," Suds said.

Fisher eyed him suspiciously. "Shoot."

"What has become of Alex Smith?"

"Social services have already kicked in. He's still in isolation at the hospital. They don't want to expose him to germs until his immune system has recovered from the bone marrow transplant."

"What will become of him?"

"Dunno. That's up to social services. I suppose they'll try to track down next of kin. See if a relative is willing to take on responsibility for the boy. Why?"

"Just wondering. I lost a son to leukemia and I must say I feel a real connection with that little boy. I've been praying that his outcome will be better than Rufus's."

"Rufus was your boy?"

Suds blinked back tears. There was no artifice in his bringing up Rufus. He wasn't angling for sympathy. It just happened. "That's right. He died six days before his fifth birthday."

Fisher had two kids of his own. He could imagine the pain. He stood, signaling the interview was over. As Suds arose, Fisher stepped forward, invading the sanctity of personal space and ignoring the intimidation factor of the dancing bear. He patted Suds' awkwardly on the shoulder. Bit his tongue on the words "There. There." And ushered the big man out of the office into the detectives' room where Harry was seated at a desk, chatting with a former colleague.

Harry arose. "All done?"

Fisher interjected. "Get out of here the both of you. I'm late for dinner."

Harry grinned. "Fuck you Jerry. Never did like ya."

"The feeling is mutual," Fisher said.

The two men shook hands, disconnected, and Harry led Suds outside to the street, where the Econoline waited with Suds' Walther still snugged comfortably in the briefcase behind the driver's seat.

Suds settled behind the wheel. "I think it's time for that beer," he said.

THIRSTING FOR KNOWLEDGE, SUDS FINDS SOME

"So where is this notorious cop bar?" Suds asked.

"Justin's Place. Bout 10 minutes from here. Just drive. I'll tell you where to turn."

Suds shivered. "I hope Justin is an ex-cop with good sense about beer. I hate Budweiser, or worse yet, Miller Lite."

"My haven't you become the beer snob."

"Not a snob. Just cursed by a gourmet's palate. Wish I did like Bud. It certainly would be cheaper."

"So you and Evie?"

"Back together. On a trial basis. So far I'm passing muster."

"How are you guys coping? With Rufus. I mean."

"Gingerly. Losing a kid. Harry, man, it's worse than a hard one to the nuts. Makes you wanna puke. The ache and the nausea never go away. Not entirely, anyway."

"Not sure Evie would describe it in those terms."

"Yeah. I'm a closet chauvinist. Most cops are, at least the ones who stand up to pee."

"Which explains the other woman."

"Nah. Hormones are to blame for that. After Rufus died, Evie became remote. Unapproachable, both emotionally and sexually. My grief didn't suppress my desire. In a perverse sort of way it enhanced it. I wanted to crawl inside Evie and forget the world. She wanted nothing to do with me . . . with anything other than her anger and her grief."

"And the other woman?"

"Linda was empathetic. Going through some serious shit in her life, too. And to make a long story short, we connected. We were discreet, but . . ."

"Don't tell me. Cops talk. Among themselves. If not to others. And word got passed along the thin blue line and made it back to Evie's ears."

Suds nodded. "That's right. We . . . Linda and I used the evidence room to you know . . ,

"Got it."

"Evie sniffed it out. Set up surveillance cameras, shared a video with borough council. Edited the clip to obscure private parts and Linda's face, but not mine. Sisterhood of the pants sort of thing. The clip was PG 13, but it was pretty clear what was going on. Evie was pissed. Leaked the PG version to the media."

"Evie got you fired and took your job."

Suds smiled ruefully. "That's pretty much what happened. I was mad for a while but then I concluded that I got pretty much what I deserved."

"Which explains why you're willing to move back in with Evie."

Suds nodded. "I was ready to forgive her, long before she was prepared to forgive me."

"Turn left at the next light."

As Suds made the turn, he noticed two things, a sign that read "Palemetto State Craft Brewhaus," on the marquee above a storefront in a strip mall. Parked in front of the storefront was a midnight blue Lincoln Navigator.

He made a hard and quick left into the parking lot, ignoring an angry horn sounding behind him and screeching tires ahead as oncoming traffic braked to avoid a collision.

"Jesus Christ, Suds. What gives!"

"The Navigator and the brewery. Just playing a hunch."

"Come on. What are the odds?"

"It's a long shot, but worth exploring, don't you think?"

'Doesn't seem to matter what I think."

"Come on. Worst case scenario . . . we get to sample some good beer."

"Or some bad beer. I'm a Bud man," Ford lamented.

"I won't hold that against you."

The brewery occupied a 75-by 120-foot slot in a strip mall with a Dollar General on one side and a coffee shop on the other. Parking was out front and jam-packed around the Navigator, which somehow had secured a spot not too far from the front door. Suds found a parking spot behind the mall next to a Dumpster.

They climbed from the van, walked around the end of the strip mall and went inside the brewery. The space was windowless and illuminated by a garish incandescence. Noise from the crowd bounced off the concrete floor and cinderblock walls unsoftened by wall or floor treatment. Drinkers were packed around a 30-foot bar and jammed elbow to elbow around a desultory collection of high-tops.

The smell of perspiration and the cacophony of revelers did nothing to obscure the aroma of hops, yeast and barley malt. Suds inhaled deeply and sighed in satisfaction. Silenus was in the house and Suds felt at home among the god of beer's minions.

Harry did not. "Come on Suds. This place is a zoo. Let's get out of here. Justin's is just down the street and much quieter."

"And full of cops. I've had enough of them for one day, haven't you?"

"We are cops," Harry observed.

"Ex-cops," Suds corrected. "Look two places just opened up."

Suds used his six feet seven inches to carve out enough elbow room for the both of them at the bar. They sat on rickety barstools and examined the beer list, which was scrawled on a blackboard with chalk marks through the beers that had kicked. Pads and pencils positioned on the bar top gave patrons the opportunity to select a flight of beers for tasting.

The beer list, even with the expungements, was impressive. Three IPAs, four bocks, an amber, a golden amber, couple of goses, a porter and a pilsner or two. The beer styles were as familiar as the Lord's Prayer for Suds, but Harry felt as if he had stumbled into Greek orthodoxy in the original language. "I want a Bud," he said, after perusing the blackboard.

"Then try one of the pilsners, or better yet get a flight. Given your pedestrian tastes, I'd suggest the IPA with the lowest IBU and ABV, number seven on the list, the Pilsner, number four; the amber, number 11; and the bock, number 15. A flight of four, four-ounce pours is seven bucks. It's a good deal."

Harry continued to study the beer list like it was a menu in a Chinese restaurant. "I don't know Suds . . ."

Suds grabbed a pencil and a beer-tasting pad. "Here, I'll take care of ordering for you." He checked off four beers for himself on one list, tore it from the pad and checked off four more for Harry.

It was an efficient way to take orders. A harried bartender was grateful when Suds handed him their beer selections. "Welcome," the bartender said. He was a big dude two or three inches shorter than Suds. He sported a handlebar mustache and a prodigious beer belly. His pants defied gravity with an assist from red suspenders.

"Is it always this crowded?" Suds asked.

"Happy hour."

"You must make good beer."

"I'll let you be the judge of that," the bartender said, leaving to pour their flights.

He returned and plopped down the beers, which were arranged on wooden boards with indentations to accommodate the bottom of the four-ounce glasses. "Beers are arrayed in ascending number order from left to right," the bartender yelled over the happy hour cacophony.

"Thanks. You own the place?"

"Nah. My brother. He's the brewer. I'm a cop. Jud Simpson's my name. I help out when I'm off duty." Jud patted his stomach and winked. "Ralph pays me off in beer."

"You appear to be well-paid," Harry said. "You look familiar. How long you been on the job?"

Jud caught the allusion. "Joined the force here, four years ago, came in from out of town to help my brother when he started up."

Harry nodded. "After my time."

"You a cop, too?"

"We're ex-cops, the both of us," Suds said. "I'm head of security for a brewery."

"Oh yeah? Where?"

"Hop Central Craft Brewery in Hershey, PA."

Jud rubbed his hands together. "Now that's odd."

"How so?"

"Ralph is in a meeting with three guys from Hop Central in the back room right now."

They were interrupted by a clamor four patrons down at the crowded bar. "What does a guy have to do around here for a refill?"

"Keep your pants on," Jud yelled. To Suds, he said. "Gotta go."

And off he went to slake the thirst of happy hour revelers who cared more about consuming beer than coincidence, which was what was consuming Suds Ferguson at this particular juncture.

Suds downed his beers in record time, hating himself for doing it. The beer was delicious. Chugging it was sacrilege.

"This beer tastes like shit," Harry grumbled.

"Come on. Drink up."

"What's your hurry?"

"I'm not ready for Franklin to know I followed him to Charleston. I want to watch outside to see who climbs into the Navigator."

Harry nodded. "Gotcha."

With a wave of his hand, Suds summoned Jud Simpson. "Hey listen. I'm not supposed to be here. In Charleston. My boss thinks I'm minding the store back in Hershey. But something came up I had to deal with. It's personal. I'd I appreciate it if you didn't say anything to my boss. About my being here. I mean."

Jud nodded. "Mum's the word." And then he was off to fill another order.

The two men drank up and returned to the van.

The parking lot had thinned out considerably and they were able to secure a parking spot with a good view of the front door of the brewery and of the Lincoln Navigator. They waited with Harry behind the wheel and Suds in the passenger's seat.

In about a half hour, five men emerged from the bar and stood before the Navigator: Sampson, Rudy, Ames, Weisse, and a man who looked like a smaller version of Jud Simpson.

"A real rogues gallery," Harry observed.

"Yeah. And the rogues look friendly. Doesn't look like Weisse's play is hostile, after all. There's something going on here I just don't understand," Suds said.

The men shook hands all around. Weisse climbed into a Mercedes sports car and Ames and Sampson took places in the front passenger's side and back seats of the Navigator, respectively. Rudy drove. Suds and Harry slumped down as the Navigator crawled past them and out of the parking lot.

"Think they saw us?" Harry asked.

"Nah. They were too concerned about clipping one of the cars in the lot. Parking's tight here."

"So what was that all about?"

"Wild-assed guess. Weisse and Franklin are exploring ways to launder even more money by investing in a craft brewery closer to Weisse's home base and using Franklin's expertise to get things humming."

"Might be a good guess. Those guys were thicker than thieves."

"How thick is a thief?"

"I hate it when you deconstruct my clichés," Harry said. "Where to now?"

"Drive while I check on airline reservations. I need to beat the boys back to Hershey.

"So back to Rent a Wreck and then on to the airport?"

Suds nodded. "That's right ke-mo sah-be."

"Ug," Harry said as he turned on the engine and slipped the van into gear. "Who do you think killed Graham and Gerry Smith?"

"I'm guessing the Smiths decided to cooperate with the FBI and Weisse silenced them. but that's for Jarrod Fisher to decipher. My Walther might well be the murder weapon and I need to get the both of us out of town."

LINDA FONTAINE STEPS
TO THE PLATE

Rave Pachel wanted nothing to do with the police. The owner of the Buy Mart on the edge of Franklin Ames's exclusive neighborhood eyed Linda Fontaine with a suspicion normally reserved for Amway salesmen.

"How long do you keep footage from the security camera trained on the gas pumps?" Linda asked.

"The video uploads to the cloud and software deletes it after 21 days unless I tell it otherwise. But I won't give it to you. Not without a warrant."

Linda did the math. In four days, footage from the night of Jasmine Cox's murder would be obliterated. It could take longer than that to get a search warrant. She would have to rely on charm alone.

She switched gears. "What's your biggest security concern here?"

"Shoplifting," Pachel said, without hesitation. "Particularly right after school lets out."

"So around 3:30?"

Pachel nodded. "Say 3:15 to 4:30. They come here in bunches and even with the security cams I can't keep track of them all. I lose a lot of inventory on school days. Candy, chips, sodas and such."

"Would an increased police presence at about that time on random days during the school week tamp down that problem?"

Pachel narrowed his eyes. "I suppose there's a pro quo to go with that quid?"

Fontaine laughed. "Sharp man. You can copy outside camera footage from the night of Saturday, July 21, to a DVD, right?"

"Yes."

"Do that and I'll make sure a black and white swings by here at least twice a week for the next month to scare off the riffraff."

Pachel considered. "Hey Johnny," he said, addressing the generation x-er manning the cash register. "Keep your eyes open and buzz the office if you start getting your head kicked in."

To Linda, he added. "Follow me."

They went through a door in the back of the store marked "Employees Only." Linda followed Rachel down a narrow corridor past the employee bathroom to a tiny office where a computer tower, monitor, and keyboard were arrayed on a cheap Staples' desk.

Pachel sat down behind the computer. "Sorry I don't have an extra chair. You'll have to stand."

Linda grunted in acknowledgement.

"July 21st, huh. For how many hours?"

"Let's say from 6 P.M. to midnight."

Pachel sniffed. OK. Might take a couple of disks. You willing to pay?"

"How much?"

"Let's say $10 bucks a disk."

Fontaine extracted her wallet from her back pocket and inventoried her cash. She could afford five disks' worth. She hoped that was enough. She was pretty sure Evie Pinson wouldn't balk at her recovering the money on her expense account.

"Go ahead," she said.

Pachel busied himself about the computer, sucking his teeth in annoying fashion as he accessed the cloud, and began copying footage onto first one DVD and then another and another.

"You know the police in Pakistan are not as pretty as you," he said. His lilting speech carried smarmy overtones that made Linda's skin crawl. But she couldn't let her disgust show. She smiled her way through clumsy repartee.

"In America, police are encouraged to maintain a professional demeanor at all times when they are on the job," she replied," but I'm not always on the job." Her ears hurt at the sound of her own innuendo. She felt guilty for leading the little man on.

Hope kept him copying. And hope led him to say: "That's OK. No charge," when the copying was done. "What's your phone number?"

She rattled off the Derry Township Police's office line, reminding herself to tell the receptionist to vet all calls from Rave Pachel.

She left the Buy Mart with three DVDs, climbed into her patrol unit and drove toward police headquarters to savor the fruits of her deceit.

SUDS TOUCHES DOWN
IN HERSHEY

Wednesday, August 8, 2018

Eschewing a hug and a kiss because the squad room was full at change-of-shift, Suds Ferguson eased into Evie Pinson's visitor's chair. "I have news."

"Me, too, but you first."

"I found my Walther. In Charleston."

"Where in Charleston?"

"At another murder scene."

Evie's face went slack as she processed his words.

He filled the dead air. "Graham and Gerry Smith are dead. Staged to look like a murder/suicide. Harry and I were first at the scene. I picked up my piece and beat feet. Harry colluded."

"You reported the crime?"

"That's right."

"You realize the ballistics on your piece are in the system now for Jasmine's murder."

"I know. I know. I'm in deep shit."

"We are in deep shit," Evie corrected.

Suds sighed. "Sorry to have gotten you into all of this."

"The person I really feel sorry for is Alex Smith," Evie said.

Suds's face softened. "Wow! In the middle of this shit storm your first thought is of that sick little boy who just lost both of his parents."

Evie teared up. "It just . . . it's so similar to Rufus."

Tears burned the corners of Suds's eyes as well. He reached across Evie's desk. She clasped his hand and smiled into his soul.

Suds leaned into the moment. Held her hand without speaking. He took a deep breath. Let go of her hand. "You said you had news, too?"

"That's right. Zeke Morrow."

"What about him?"

"Linda sweated him about out-of-town talent who may have been around at the time of Jasmine's murder."

"He told me to pound sand. What stick did she use?"

"Linda searched Dunkel's apartment, where she found evidence of his abrupt beating of feet, a busted front door, and a .38 slug in the wall. The land-lord was pissed. Said it was about time someone took his crime report seriously. Showed Linda security cam footage of Zeke Morrow kicking in Dunkel's door."

"Go on."

"Linda tracked down Zeke to one of his haunts—Harry's Tavern, as it turns out."

"Talk about your coincidences."

Evie frowned at the interruption. "Anyway. Linda confronted Zeke with the security cam evidence. Asked if he carried a .38. Said she was of a mind to frisk him on the spot. He said, he'd enjoy that. He tried to shoulder past her. She kneed him in the balls. Grabbed his piece. Not the one he wanted her to grab. It was a .38 all right."

"Bet Harry was pissed that Zeke was packing in his joint."

"You bet he was. That's how she got away with it. When Zeke was finished dry heaving, he revealed . . ."

She paused for dramatic effect.

"Don't tease me, woman. Out with it."

"That he got outmuscled by a dude named Sampson who made the not-so-polite suggestion that Zeke 'lay the fuck off fucking with Franklin Ames.'"

"Sampson? Really?"

"Yep. As in Delilah," Evie said,

"You mean as in Reeves."

"Huh?"

"Sampson Reeves is a big, black ex-con who works for Franklin Ames."

"Which means he works for you, too," Evie said.

"Sampson was with Franklin Ames on his recent trip to Charleston."

"Interesting."

"Isn't though? I thought Franklin musta decided he needed to double up on the muscle when he confronted Mike Weisse. But as it turns out I was wrong."

"Why?"

"Because Franklin and Mike Weisse are thicker than thieves."

"Had to trot out that old cliché, did ya?"

"Actually, it's Harry Ford's cliché. He used it first. That's my story and I'm sticking to it."

Evie groaned. "Not another one!"

Suds smiled and explained about Palmetto State Craft Brewhaus and his surveillance of a meeting among Weisse, Ames, Sampson, Rudy and Ralph Simpson.

"Who's Ralph Simpson?" Evie asked.

"Proprietor of the brewery. I'm thinking Weisse and Frank are in cahoots now. Looking for ways to clean even more dirty money with beer."

They were interrupted by a knock on Evie's office door. Turning, Suds saw Linda Fontaine at the door.

"If you say nice knocker, I want a divorce," Evie said.

"We're already divorced," Suds replied.

"For the time being."

"You're holding all the aces," Suds said. "I fold."

"Smart man," Evie whispered. Raising her voice, she said, "Come in Linda, we're not doing anything we're ashamed of."

Suds was choking on his own spit as Linda Fontaine opened Evie's office door and crossed the threshold into the inner sanctum. Linda's face was stone. "Evie. Suds," she said, nodding.

Evie bit off a laugh. "It's OK Linda. Suds has been gelded. He's just one of the girls now. We can talk among ourselves without sharpening the axes."

Linda's face composed. She allowed herself a tentative smile, which escalated into a shit-eating grin. "Nice to see the two of you aren't at each other's throats. There's been a breakthrough in the Jasmine Cox-Ames murder case."

She waved a memory stick in the air triumphantly.

"What's that?" Evie asked.

"Surveillance footage from the Buy Mart near Franklin Ames's house."

"And?"

"Your computer warmed up?"

"It is," Evie said.

"Plug this into your USB port."

Evie moved the mouse, awakening her computer, and inserted the memory stick. Suds, Evie and Linda huddled around her monitor. Evie surrendered the mouse to Linda who clicked through a couple of menus and launched the video.

"I downloaded this from a DVD from Buy Mart's security cam. I've edited it to show five minutes of pertinent footage starting at 21:40 hours on the evening of Jasmine Cox's murder. This is from the outside camera centered on the gas pumps to record drive-aways, but it shows the street in front of the store as well."

Linda double clicked file on the flash card's index and the video loaded. A spinning circle resolved itself into a video. The area right around the pumps was illuminated by the store's outside lights and by a street light on the other side of the road.

Several cars passed. It was possible to discern the make and model. Sometimes the license plates were visible. More often they were lost in luminescent reflections off parked cares, the asphalt of the street and the metal of the gas pumps. The drivers could not be seen, protected by darkened windows and the poor resolution of the video camera.

A dark Crown Vic flashed by. Evie and Suds started. Linda was oblivious. "Look!" She said. "The Forester right behind the Crown Vic. Right there. The windshield is shattered. You can only catch a couple digits of the license plate, but they're consistent with the numbers on Franklin Ames's vehicle. He swears he was passed out at a motel at the time of the murder. This is proof that he, or at least his car, was on the road near his home near the time of his wife's murder!"

"You can't make out the driver and you've got an incomplete plate, but yeah. I'd say we have a pretty solid clue here," Evie said. "Don't you agree Suds?"

Suds said nothing, consumed by the certainty that the Crown Vic just ahead of the Forester was his. He knew it. Evie knew it. Linda didn't. But the revelation suggested an unpleasant scenario. Just maybe Franklin Ames had followed Suds to the murder scene on the night of the murder. That might explain how Suds's Walther fired the shot that killed Jasmine Cox. Could Suds have done it? The thought paralyzed him.

Suds had no recollection of his activities on the night of the murder. Unwittingly, Linda Fontaine had just turned up even more evidence that Suds had been involved.

Both women were staring at him, wondering at his silence. "I think it's time to subpoena the data records on Franklin's Forester," Suds said.

Evie was all business. "I agree. Can you take care of the paper work for that and to secure the original security cam footage? I don't want any chain of evidence issues."

Linda nodded. "I'm on it."

"Good work!" Evie said.

Linda smiled and hustled off on her appointed task.

REPORTING TO THE MAN UPSTAIRS

Thursday, August 9, 2018

Suds Ferguson had no more settled into his chair in his office at Hop Central when the house line buzzed. Suds picked it up. "In my office. ASAP!" Franklin Ames barked.

Franklin didn't often bark. Suds hoped he wasn't about to bite. Apprehension gripped him as he climbed to his feet. The vultures were circling the corpse of Jasmine Cox and they were looking for fresher meat. Suds was on the menu. "Stay calm," he told himself, wondering if Weisse or Jud Simpson had let the cat out of the bag and told Franklin of Suds's visit to Charleston.

He made his way to the third floor, passed by the phalanx of desks and cubicles, and knocked on the beer baron's door.

"Come!" Franklin said.

Suds tiptoed tentatively across Franklin's plush carpeted inner sanctum and eased himself into the boss's visitor's chair.

"Report!"

"I twisted Zeke Morrow's arm. No evidence of any outside talent coming to town before your wife's . . .

"Murder. Don't be namby pamby."

"Your wife's murder," Suds agreed. "Zeke, however, was aware of some strong-arming by home-grown talent, a big black guy named Sampson. Sounds like our Sampson."

Franklin confirmed it. "I turned Sampson loose on Johnny Lewis and Zeke Morrow. Wanted to see if I could decipher the Weisse/Lewis connection."

"Which was among the reasons you went to Charleston."

"That and to explore some business opportunities south of the border."

"Such as."

"Palmetto State Craft Brewhaus. They got a good product and are positioned for growth, with an infusion of cash."

"We got extra cash? I thought you were planning to invest considerable capital here."

Franklin's eyes narrowed. "I smell a man who's been sniffing around," he said.

Suds laughed, trying to defuse the tension. "I'm a professional bloodhound. You told me to sniff. So I've been sniffing."

"Not sure you're sniffing the right asshole, but I'll let it go because I like to encourage initiative. Any developments on my wife's murder case?"

Suds decided to go fishing.

"Evie has subpoenaed security video for the night of the murder from the Buy Mart near your house. The owner is being pissy. Won't release it without a court order. And the clock is ticking. Video will be automatically erased from the cloud on Saturday, without a court order stopping it."

"What are you thinking the video will show?"

Suds set the trap. "License plates of suspects that might have been in the area immediately prior to the murder."

"Let me know how that turns out. In the meantime, are you getting a handle on the business side of the business?"

"Think so. Numbers aren't my game, but the one's I've been looking at seem pretty good to me. With an infusion of outside cash, we should be sitting even prettier. What sort of opportunity do you see in Charleston?"

"Weisse's involved. I'm still sorting out who is backing his play. But Palmetto State Craft Brewhaus makes good beer."

Suds couldn't let on that he agreed with the boss 100 percent on the quality of the beer. "Anything else, or should I get back to it?"

"Go. But keep me apprised on the security camera issue."

Suds nodded. As he prepared to leave, he said: "Any news from Charleston about Alex?"

"He's still in the hospital. He'll clear isolation in a couple of days. All his numbers look good. And . . ."

"And what?"

"Might as well tell you. You'll find out anyway."

"Tell me what?"

"Graham and Gerry Smith are dead. Murdered. Chest wound for Graham. Impact headshot for Gerry. Halmarks of a murder/suicide but no firearm found of the scene."

Suds's pulse raced. He fought to maintain self-control. Decided to play it like a cop.

"Who discovered the bodies?"

"Can't shake that loose from the police."

"Want me to call my buddy in Charleston?"

"Harrison Ford? You mentioned him before."

"That's right."

"Sure. Reach out to him."

"What will become of Alex?"

"I've asked Les Benson to intervene in the matter of his custody. Graham Smith's parents are infirm and Gerry does not have any survivors. I'd like to take custody of the boy. He is, after all, my son."

"That very generous of you," Suds said. "Let me know if there is anything I can do to help."

"You can help by reading the prospectus for Palmetto State Craft Brewhaus. It's attached to an email in your inbox."

Ames waved a hand in dismissal.

FRANKLIN AMES WORKS THE PHONE

Franklin Ames watched Suds's departure making sure he was well out of earshot before picking up his cell phone. He scrolled to Sampson Reeves's number in his phone book and punched the listing with his index finger.

"Yo. Boss."

"Got a job for you."

"What's that?"

Franklin told him.

"I'm on it already," Sampson said.

"Good man."

Franklin disconnected and scrolled to Les Benson's number in his phone book. "Couple of things to discuss with you," he said when Benson picked up.

"Shoot."

"You certain that my will provides for Miles Karfan to take over as executor and custodian should Sidney Ferguson be unavailable?" Franklin asked.

"Yes. Who is Miles Karfan, by the way?"

"A second cousin. A lawyer. Figured he'd be able to settle my estate if Suds isn't up to it. I want to ensure that Karfan also will be empowered to vote my shares, take over the management of the brewery and assume custodial rights to my offspring in the event Suds is unavailable."

"That's right. The will is very clear and precise on both of those points," Benson said. "Why do you ask?"

"It just occurred to me that we had discussed those points rather peripherally, and I'm a careful man."

"Anything else, Mr. Ames?"

"No. That just about covers it."

Benson's "good bye" was delivered to dead air. Franklin was on to his next phone call.

"Hey Todd," Ames said when Rudy picked up.

"Yeah."

"It's time to execute plan B."

"Already? We're rushing the timeline quite a bit aren't we?"

"Got to do it. The hounds are loose. We need to rub red pepper up their noses."

"Ok boss. I'll set the ball rolling."

"Perfect."

"One more thing, boss."

"What's that Todd?"

"You're far too young to die."

Franklin laughed. "Careful Todd, you'll have me wiping a tear from the corner of my eye."

LINDA FONTAINE FOLLOWS
A CLUE

Friday, August 10, 2018

Linda Fontaine took the call as a courtesy to the weary warriors who were getting ready to go off shift at 8 A.M. She was an early bird, arriving on the job 45 minutes ahead of time, not because she coveted worms, but because sleep so often eluded her.

"Yo. D'is da po-lice?"

"It is. How can I help you?"

"You don't sound like no po-lice."

"Why because I'm a woman?"

"No cause you sound sexy. Never been rousted by no sexy po-lice."

"Give me one reason I shouldn't hang up right now," Linda said.

"Cause I know somthin' that might get your juices goin'."

Linda sighed. Decided to ride it out. "I'm listening."

"I hear maybe Jasmine Cox's doer is an ex-cop."

Linda's pulse quickened. "Who is this?" she demanded.

"Someone in da know. That' all I'm sayin'. Run the ballistics on the bullet that offed Jasmine past Charleston PD see if you get a hit."

238

'Which Charleston?"

The man laughed. "Yo da po-lice go po-lice."

And then he hung up.

Linda launched Google on her desktop computer. As it turned out more than 20 towns in the U.S. were named Charleston. The ones in South Carolina and West Virginia were the most prominent. Was it worth emailing those PDs? Bet your ass it was. Probably a crank call but it could be a feather in her cap if she were to mine a clue that could bust open the Jasmine Cox/Ernest Flowers murder.

She opened the department's email program and wrote a note. In it, she explained that she was investigating an apparent murder/suicide that had occurred on July 21. She said that the investigation had taken a hard left turn after ballistics on the murder bullet didn't match the weapon left at the crime scene. She said that she was following up on a long shot phoned in by an anonymous tipster that Charleston PD was investigating a similar case. Before sending off her email, she attached the ballistics report on the .380 bullet that had killed Jasmine Cox.

She sent her email just as the hubbub of shift change overtook the squad room and she was swept up in the business of bidding adieu to one set of colleagues and greeting a new set. The rhythm of her day had been derailed by the anonymous phone call. She'd missed the opportunity to make the morning's first pot of coffee. Sergeant Fuller had seen to that task as she busied herself with the email. Now she'd have to endure his terrible coffee.

She drew a cup. Flavored it with sugar and French vanilla Coffeemate. Took a sip and winced. She would make certain her duties took her past a Starbucks by mid-morning. Her office line buzzed. She picked up. Evie said: "I've got the court order for Rave Pachel. Can you deliver it first thing this morning? We've got to establish the chain of custody on the video. Your copy may be inadmissible."

"I'll execute it right away," Linda said and hung up.

She passed a Starbucks on the way to the Buy Mart. The allure was inescapable. Regular blend with a squeeze of honey and a dollop of half-and-half. She took a sip, sighed in satisfaction and nestled the cup into the holder in the center console. As she arrived at the Buy Mart, a black Ford F250 with oversized tires was backing from a space. The driver's side widow of the pickup was open. She noted that the driver was a large black man with a shaved dome and a large earring. He scowled at her as she snugged the cruiser into an empty space.

He shifted into drive and left the parking lot as she opened the front door of the Buy Mart. Her cop reflexes compelled her to commit his license plate number to memory. Something about him was off. She'd run the plate if for no other reason than to scratch that cop itch.

Bells above the door jangled and Rave Pachel stepped through the employee-only portal to tend to his customer. His right eye was swollen and he walked with a limp.

"What the hell happened to you?" Linda asked.

"Slipped getting out of the shower this morning and banged my head on the edge of the tub," Pachel said. He tried on a smile but it didn't fit.

Linda waved the court order at him like she was flagging a personal foul.

"What's that?"

"A court order to preserve the surveillance video," she said.

"Come on back," he said, waggling a thumb over his shoulder at the office door.

She followed him to his office, noticing a ding in a wall beside the door. She toed a pile of pulverized wallboard on the floor. "Doing some office renovation?"

"Nah. Pushed the door open too hard carrying a heavy box and the nob slammed into the wall."

"Where's the box?"

"Unloaded it. Took it to the Dumpster."

Linda jingled pocket change as she waited while he awakened his computer. He scanned the screen for a minute. Double clicked on the appropriate icon and said: "Sorry about that. You're too late. The video has been deleted. Must have had the time sequencing wrong."

"What?"

"I don't know what happened, but see for yourself."

He stepped from behind his desk and waved Linda into his office chair. She double clicked on the video. A dialog box popped up. "File no longer exists."

"Shit! You must have deleted the file. Why?"

"I did no such thing."

Her mind flashed to the image of the big, angry black man who had just pulled from the Buy Mart lot.

"You didn't happen to block a fist with your eye and a knee with your testicles? I'm betting forensic guys could establish that the video was deleted not more than five minutes ago."

Pachel didn't have enough stomach to stop his face from falling all the way to the floor. "Come on Officer Fontaine. Give me a break. Dude was big, and black, and scary, and said he'd come back and break both my legs if I didn't play dumb when you asked about the video. Right now I'm feeling about as dumb as they come. Things aren't so different here than they are in Pakistan."

"What do you mean by that?"

"Authorities won't protect you, unless it's in their best interests," he said.

Linda pulled her wallet from the back pocket of her uniform pants. She thumbed out a business card and handed it to Pachel. "The number on the card rings my cell. I answer it day or night. Keep your mouth shut and stay calm. Lock down your office. I'll have forensics stop by to take a look at your computer. Maybe they can recover the original files. They'll be discreet. No marked cars or sirens."

Pachel licked his lips nervously. "You sure?"

Linda laid a comforting hand on his forearm. "In this case our best interests intertwine. I have your back, Rave. You can count on it."

THE EVIDENCE AGAINST SUDS
BECOMES ARRESTING

The phone call buzzed and fretted in her head like a bottle fly trying to escape through plate glass. She replayed it over and again.

"Hey chief?"

"Yes."

"This is Todd Rudy. I work with your husband . . ."

"Ex-husband," she corrected.

"Yeah right. At Hops Central. I also bartend at Murphy's Irish bar."

"I know who you are."

"I'm ready to fill in some details on what happened to Suds on the night of July 21."

""Still listening."

"I slipped Suds the mickey."

"He told me as much."

"What I didn't tell him is who paid me to do it."

"Thought that was Jasmine Cox."

"I lied. Mr. Ames told me to do it."

Her pulse quickened. "You willing to say that on the record."

"Not so fast. Suds isn't lily white in all of this, you know."

"What do you mean by that?"

"He left the bar on his own free will, with Jasmine and Ernie. I didn't slip him the mickey until later that night. At Mr. Ames's house."

Evie's knuckles whitened on the phone handset. "You're saying that Suds was at the house on the night of the murder?"

"I'm saying more than that. I'm saying Suds helped with the murder. Lugged Ernie's body to the beer spa and plopped him in."

"You have proof of that?"

"Video. Yeah. I'm willing to hand it over if you meet me at the brewery at 11:30 tonight. Come to the door next to the loading dock. I'll buzz you in."

"Wait a minute . . ."

She was talking to dead air.

"Fuck!" The profanity could not excise the bottle fly buzzing in her head.

She was interrupted by a knock at the door. Looking up, she saw Linda Fontaine. She motioned her inside.

"Got some bad news and some worse news. Which you want first?" Linda said.

Evie motioned her to her visitor's chair. "Sit."

Linda said, straightening the creases on her uniform pants and adjusting her gun belt so the butt of her service weapon didn't pinch her waist.

"Why don't you give me the bad news first."

"We may have lost chain of custody on the Buy Mart surveillance video. It's already gone from the server. Rave Pachel erased it before I had the chance to execute the court order."

"Shit. He might be clear of charges because the chicken came before the egg."

Linda fielded the allusion. "That's right, but we can always call him to testify about the physical assault and terroristic threats that preceded his erasing the tape."

"Huh?"

Linda explained: "Saw a big black guy in a pickup truck leave as I arrived. When I got inside, Pachel had a black eye and was limping. He took me back to his office, logged onto his computer and told me the video had been erased from the cloud server. I put two and two together and he fessed up to having been threatened with bodily harm by the guy I saw leaving his parking lot."

"You didn't happen to record the plate on the truck?"

Linda smiled. "As a matter of fact, I did. Truck belongs to Sampson Reeves. Black, six foot six, with a record just as tall as he is. Assault. Battery. Criminal conspiracy."

"I am familiar with Sampson. Or at least Suds is. Bring him in."

"Who Suds or Sampson?"

"That's too close to the bone to be funny."

Linda grimaced. "I'll get right on it. I'll have hold hands with the witness first. Rav Pachel, the Buy Mart proprietor, is apt to be ginky."

"I'll leave the details to you. Was that the bad news, or the worse news?"

"The bad news. The worse news is I got a ballistics hit from a double murder in Charleston, South Carolina." Linda deadpanned the denouement. "Both sets of bullets are from Suds's Walther."

Evie realized she had been holding her breath. She exhaled explosively. "God damn it, I'm sorry for keeping you in the dark. Suds followed Franklin Ames to Charleston because he smelled a rat. He and his buddy Harrison Ford stumbled on the crime scene. Rev's gun was next to woman's body, staged to make it look like a suicide. Suds's initials are on the butt plate, so he pocketed the Walther and called Charleston PD to report the crime."

"How the fuck did Suds's piece wind up in Charleston?"

"I'm guessing Franklin Ames set him up?"

"Why?"

"To be determined."

"Suds have an alibi?" Linda asked.

"Watertight. He was on a plane when the murder occurred. Ford met Suds at the airport and drove him to the crime scene."

"Still be tough to explain how Suds's personal weapon turned up at a crime scene 800 miles from Hershey."

"There is that, which is why I'm not going to tell anyone. There is nothing in the ballistics database to link Suds with the murder weapon and I intend to keep it that way because I know he's innocent."

"I know it, too," Linda replied. "I've got your backs on this. One hundred percent. I'll be circumspect in my report to Charleston PD."

"Somehow the word 'thanks' doesn't mean nearly enough."

"Doesn't have to. You're welcome," Linda said.

Linda arose, turned and headed for the door, saying "I'm going to roust Sampson and arrange a lineup for my pal Rav Pachel."

When she had left, Evie picked up her cell phone. Dialed Suds who answered on the third ring.

"Get your ass over here," she said.

"Where's here?"

"My office. The shit has hit the fan and we need to talk."

"Maybe our house is a better place. Quieter."

"Yeah. You're right. Meet you there . . . Evie checked her watch "in forty minutes."

"Can you give me a hint?"

"Too dangerous. The cell towers might have ears."

Suds sighed. "See you soon." And hung up.

SUDS AND EVIE CHEW THE FAT

"Should I have left my weapon at the scene in Charleston? There's no connection between it and me."

"Wooda, cooda shooda. Hell I don't know. Probably."

"My fingerprints may have been on the piece. Whoever is behind this could have used gloves when they handled my weapon."

"I often did," Evie said.

"Ha. Ha."

"Your prints are on file with the military and with the PD here and elsewhere. So yeah. You probably did the right thing picking the piece up."

Suds nodded. "You comfortable with the meeting tonight at the brewery?"

"No way to avoid it. I'm pretty sure it's a trap, but as long as you have your Walther and I have my Glock, we should be safe in the short run."

"How about back up?"

"Linda is locked and loaded."

"You sure we can trust her?"

"She's a straight shooter, for an adulteress, I mean."

"And I'm a straight shooter for an adulterer?"

"An absolved adulterer."

"Are you really that . . . magnanimous?"

"No. I'm really that guilty. I was a bitch. I had my reasons, but I was a bitch. I drove you to her. I can't give you a pass on being weak. Her either. But Rufus binds us. He was a monument to our commitment to each other . . . to the future."

"And I burned it down."

"No. He did. By dying. One of the most horrible things I had to deal with after he died was my own guilt."

"Guilt? Guilt for what?"

"For hating Rufus because he caused us so much pain. It was almost a relief to hate you even more. No guilt there. My rage was, I don't know. Somehow sanctified."

Suds nodded. "I get that. Will you marry me, again?"

Evie bent forward over their kitchen table. She kissed Suds lightly on the lips. "Maybe. But first we have to get through this."

"This being proving that I was not a drug-crazed murderer who drowned a lawyer in a bathtub full a beer before murdering the lawyer's mistress with my handgun. This also being that I didn't then abscond to Charleston where I murdered Gerry and Graham Smith."

Evie smiled. "Yes. This being that times two."

"I just can't figure out Franklin's agenda. Four murders. For what purpose?" Suds said.

"I don't think you can pin it all on one motive and I'm not sure the same person killed all four of them. Not to mention Chuck Dubbel and Boyd Porter. That makes six. Murders, I mean. How does all of that fit into the big picture?"

"There's a clear cause and effect there," Suds said. "Dubbel was trying to silence a blackmailer, although I will admit that nothing we've learned about Dubbel would indicate he was the sort of self-reflective guy who'd be remorseful enough to take his own life."

"Maybe his death was a legit accident, not a suicide."

"Maybe. But who else benefitted from it?" Suds said. "And why would Lisa and Julie present a suicide note, unless it was legit. They have nothing to gain from Dubbel's death being declared a suicide. And a lot to lose."

Evie considered. "They coughed up the note when I accused Lisa of murder. Julie is the beneficiary of his life-insurance policy and is likely to claim some sort of payday from a wrongful death lawsuit against the brewery."

"And by extension so will Lisa and her child to be," Suds mused.

"I think we can mark the fetus off the list of suspects," Evie said.

Suds acknowledge her wit with a groan. "The suicide note Julie received in the mail was written on a computer?"

"Don't know," Evie said.

"And Julie confirmed his signature?"

"I didn't actually look at the note, but Julie swore the signature was genuine. But, then, any wife worth her salt gets pretty good at faking her husband's signature."

"Have you ever faked mine?" Suds asked.

"I refuse to answer that question on grounds it might incriminate me," Evie replied.

"So if there is a suspect in Dubbel's death, other than himself, of course, it's either Lisa or Julie, and damnably hard to prove either."

Evie nodded.

"Let's close the books on Dubbel and Porter. I think we can agree that they deserved each other. And give Lisa and Julie a pass. If they are guilty maybe they did everyone a favor. Two bad guys off the board with no expense to the taxpayers."

"Not sure that the sort of admission I'd want on my personnel record at the PD, but yeah. I'm right there with ya," Evie said.

"Let's spitball this thing. One murder at a time. Who killed Ernie Flowers?"

"Two suspects. Mike Weisse because Ernie was trying to queer his deal to launder money through the brewery. Or Franklin Ames because Ernie was doing his wife," Evie said.

"Linda did me, but you didn't kill her. I get the sense that maybe Franklin is more dispassionate about that sort of thing than you give him credit for," Suds said.

"So maybe Franklin did it because Ernie betrayed his trust by climbing in bed with Jasmine and by extension the investors she was lining up to sell the brewery out from under him," Evie said.

"But then he turns around and jumps in bed with Mike Weisse who also is angling to steal the brewery for entirely different reasons," Suds said. "I just can't figure Franklin out. And why make me the executor of his will and heir apparent at the brewery?"

"Setting you up as the patsy?"

"That's what Harry says. But how? How does my being the executor of his estate motivate me to kill Jasmine, Ernie, Graham and Gerry? I won't profit by his death. I'd just have to do a lot of paperwork."

"You'd gain control of the brewery with years to plot how to profit from it," Evie observed. "You're focused on your defense. I get that, but we've got to treat this as prosecutors. What profit does Ames have in killing those four people?"

"Preserving his absolute ownership of the brewery is the obvious answer," Suds said. "That's why ceding it to Mike Weisse make such little sense."

"Unless he intends to set Weisse up on the murders of Gerry and Graham Smith."

"Chain of custody puts my Walther in the possession of someone from Hershey. Suspects include Todd, Sampson, Franklin. Hell Zach Dunkel for that matter."

"Didn't Harry tell you that the feds were closing in on Weisse? Maybe the Smiths were thinking turning state's evidence. Maybe Weisse, or one of his goons pulled the trigger and Franklin gave him your Walther."

"About that, why leave my handgun at the scene of the Smith's murders?"

"I don't know. To muddy the waters. To take us off our game. To make us compliant," Evie said.

"So you're saying maybe Franklin set both me and Weisse up on the Smiths' murder rap? There's a whole crime organization standing behind Weisse and, well, you and a whole police department standing behind me. That's a serpent with many heads. Franklin must know that."

"So maybe preserving the brewery isn't Franklin's end game," Evie said.

"What is?"

"That's what we need to find out."

MIDNIGHT AT THE BREWERY

The employee parking lot was vacant. Save for a black Ford 250 with over-sized tires parked beneath a lamppost and a dented-up panel van not unlike the rent-a-wreck Suds had used to surveil Franklin Ames in Charleston.

Evie drove her personal vehicle, a Jeep Cherokee. Suds rode shotgun. She snugged her Jeep into a parking space next to the van. She turned off the engine, cracked the front door and the dome light came on.

"You ready for this?" Suds asked, studying Evie in profile.

She nodded. "Equipment check."

Suds checked his phone. "I've got a full charge on my cell. I'll run the tape recorder ap the whole time we're inside, in case someone says something incriminating."

Evie considered. "You realize a tape recording also could incriminate you, depending on what Todd Rudy brings to the table?"

Suds scratched his chin. "That's a chance we're going to have to take."

"My cell has a full charge, too. I've disabled the sleep function and the passcode. I can press one button to summon Linda."

Suds pulled his Walther from its holster, snugged inside the waistband of his jeans. He jacked a round into the chamber and ejected the clip. Burrowing in his pocket, he pulled out a single .380 hollow point and thumbed it into the clip before reinserting the clip in the butt of his Walther. He made sure the weapon was safetied and returned it to the holster.

"So you've got one in the pipe and seven in the clip. That's not much fire power. I can rip off three times that many rounds without reloading."

"Is this really the time for a game of whose gun is bigger?" Suds said. "I hit what I aim at with my Walther. It's metal, solid and it never jams. I'd much rather carry it into battle than your plastic Glock. Besides, I've got my .38 in an ankle holster for back up."

"That's an argument seven years of marriage never settled. I doubt we'll settle it now."

"We're whistling in the graveyard here, Evie. I don't want to go inside any more than you do." He looked at his watch. "But it's time."

"Think arriving a half hour early will throw Rudy off his game?" Suds asked. "Can't hurt."

They alit from Evie's Cherokee. Nighttime muffled the closing of the Jeep doors but the parking lot and loading dock lights diminished the darkness. Suds led the way up the loading dock stairs past the spot where Boyd Porter had met his demise. He waved his employee ID to activate the electronic door lock.

Evie paused. She fumbled with something in her pocket and stooped to examine the dead bolt on the door.

"What are you doing?"

"Putting duct tape over the deadbolt so the door won't lock when it closes." Suds nodded. "Good play."

Pneumatics whispered the door closed and they made their way up the back staircase past the employee cubicles on the third floor eerily somnolent in the security lighting. Franklin Ames's glass palace was aglow in warm lights. Todd Rudy was seated behind the boss's desk with a laptop computer positioned in front of him. Sampson Reeves stood sentinel next to Rudy's chair. Sampson pledged allegiance with a big 1911 .45 clasped across his chest in his meaty fist.

"You're early," Rudy said. "And you brought back up. Smart. I'm sure you're both carrying. But I won't make you suffer the indignity of a frisking. If you blink wrong, Sampson will kill you and no one will hear because we're not working a third shift right now and Sampson is the night watchman."

Sampson grinned. His diamond-studded tooth gleamed.

Rudy spun the laptop around so the screen faced Evie and Suds. "Have a seat. Punch play and enjoy the show."

Evie and Suds sat down in front of the desk. Evie learned forward, studied the screen, centered the cursor and clicked the enter key. The video launched. The camera was focused on Jasmine Cox's chaise lounge. She lay upon it, with her legs cast over Suds's lap. She was alive. And terrified because Suds Ferguson was pointing a handgun straight at her forehead. Suds had a vacant look on his face. His eyes were out of focus as he stared not at Jasmine but off into space in the direction of whoever was holding the camera. The footage, probably taken on a smart phone, was surprisingly vivid, sharp enough to identify the gun Suds held in his hand—his Walther PPK, clearly.

Evie looked at the live version of Suds who shrugged. "I don't remember any of this," he said.

"Nor will you. That's the beauty of Rohypnol," Rudy said. "Keep watching."

Suds and Evie returned their attention to the computer screen. An off-camera voice clearly that of Franklin Ames said: "OK Suds. Hand me your gun, slide out from under the slut's feet. Jasmine shut the fuck up and stay put unless you want to die right now."

The video refocused on the floor where Ernie Flowers lay supine, snoring with his mouth agape and eyes closed. The audio continued off camera.

There was a meaty slap. The sort of sound an open hand makes when it collides violently with a woman's cheek. Jasmine gasped. "You bastard! You won't shoot me. You're a gutless fag. You haven't the balls!"

Her voice was defiant. "Dickie will hear and come running."

"Another reason to keep your mouth shut, slut. You don't want me to kill Dickie, too. Do ya?"

In real time, Suds glanced at Evie. She winked as she fumbled with something in the pocket of her jacket.'

"Hands on the desktop!" Sampson shouted.

Evie complied.

The video resumed and focused on Suds's back as he bent over Flowers. Suds straightened his legs, grunting with the effort and lifted the body from the floor. The camera re-centered, this time showing Flowers from the front, moving wobbly legged across the carpet with Suds marching along zombie like behind him.

"That's right. Walk him into the bathroom. The spa's filled and ready to go," said a voice off camera. The frame froze and the video faded, restarting with a camera angle that showed Suds in profile lowering Flowers into the tub, with beer splashing over the sides and into Suds's shoes.

And there, the video ended.

Evie closed the lid of the laptop. "So what do you want?"

Rudy laughed. "This isn't a negotiation. It's an execution."

"An execution of what?" Suds asked, willing himself to keep his voice steady.

"You carrying?" Sampson asked, speaking for the first time.

His voice was gravelly and low, and the words came out with a reptilian sibilance as if he had swallowed a snake.

Suds made no progress in staring Sampson down. He gave up. Looked at Evie, who was maintaining a stiff upper lip with a resolve that Suds found admirable. He took courage from her demeanor. He patted his waist. "Right here."

Sampson aimed the business end of his 1911 .45 at the narrow space between Evie and Suds. A flick of the wrist and one, then the other of them, would be dead. Precision shooting would not be required at this distance. A .45 slug would disable and probably kill even if it hit an extremity.

"Stand up!" Sampson said.

Suds stood, moving subtly to his left to put more of his body between Sampson's .45 and Evie. Sampson saluted the chivalry with an evil grin. His diamond tooth sparkled. "Now raise your right hand in the air and pull out your piece with your left hand. Place it on the desktop with the barrel pointed toward you."

Suds raised his right hand as instructed and grabbed the butt of his Walther with his left. He eased the Walther out of its holster and dropped it, feigning clumsiness, to the carpeted floor.

"Oops!"

"Pick it up asshole."

Suds licked his lips, nodded and bent slowly at the waist, keeping his eyes elevated so he could keep track of Sampson. When he presented the smallest possible target he dropped to the ground in a ball, ignored the Walther lying on the carpeted floor, rolled away from Sampson and yanked the .38 police special from the ankle holster.

Instinctively, Sampson tracked the .45 toward Suds. The .45 roared loud and bass, shattering eardrums. Two staccato explosions in baritone followed in quick succession. Evie weighing in with her Glock. Blood blossomed on Sampson's chest as he staggered into the back wall of Franklin Ames's glass palace and collapsed onto the floor, legs akimbo.

Recognizing that Sampson was out of commission, Suds arose to his knees. He centered the barrel of his .38 on Rudy who had arisen from his desk chair and was reaching for something in the top drawer of the desk. Suds figured it was a gun and in a split second decided not to wait and see. He squeezed of two rounds. He didn't miss. Rudy careened backward holding a .9mm in his twitching hand. His gun fired futilely into the ceiling as he collapsed into the chair, which rocked back violently, spilling him onto the office floor and onto the body of the late Sampson Reeves.

Evie had arisen from her chair. She aimed her Glock at the two tangled bodies on the floor as Suds arose from his knees and kicked their guns out of reach with the toe of his right shoe.

As they stood there observing the carnage they were startled by the sound of someone laughing. "Bravo! You've eliminated my co-conspirators," a voice said, adding, quickly, "Don't turn around! If you do I'll shoot you and you'll die not knowing who done it and why."

Suds said: "I already know who done it."

"But you don't know why. Now drop your guns on the floor, both of you and turn around slowly. The crime scene will be easier to stage if you don't make me shoot you in the back."

Suds cast his eyes toward Evie and shrugged. She shrugged right back. They were out of plays between the two of them. The time had come to face the reaper. Their guns bounced on the carpeted floor as they turned. The man, who centered the barrel of an AR-15 in the narrow space between them, was not who they expected him to be.

"Surprise," he said.

"Who the hell are you?" Evie asked.

"Zachary Dunkel, esquire. At your service. Kick your weapons toward me. I can read the newspaper report already. Headline: Death by beer. Police chief and her ex-husband killed in a brewery shootout."

He was so intent on developing the shoot-out scenario that he didn't sense movement from behind. But Evie and Suds did. Something in their suddenly relaxed demeanor made Dunkel turn his head.

"Think you're going to have to re-write that story," said a voice from behind. Drop the rifle and turn around slowly."

"About time you showed up," Evie said.

"Thanks for leaving the door open for me," Linda Fontaine replied.

MOPPING UP

Evie called in the state police. Her department was too close to the crime scene to do an impartial job on the forensics, with two active officers and one former officer present at the time of the shootout. Captain Joseph Farley, the commanding officer of Troop H, Harrisburg, took charge of the investigation personally. He knew Evie well. Suds, too, for that matter.

It was Farley who noticed the camera, hidden in the fixture of a ceiling light. Evie, Suds, and Linda all had been too shell-shocked to fine-tooth-comb the crime scene the way Farley did at a glance.

The forensics team soon confirmed what Farley suspected. The camera was broadcasting a live stream to a remote location. Someone out there had an indelible record of what had just transpired. The geeks got busy trying to back-track the signal while Farley pulled Linda, Evie and Suds aside in the brewery's conference room.

"As a professional courtesy. I'll let you file reports on what happened to-night," Farley said. "I won't break out the rubber gloves for a prostate exam, but if I catch one thing I don't like in your reports well, then, it's time to bend over. And remember, it's at least possible that we'll be able to track down a video record of what happened."

Suds looked at Evie. She shrugged. He pulled his iPhone from his pocket. "I recorded the whole thing on audio as well. You should be able to hear everything that happened as you reconstruct the crime scene," Suds said. He handed his phone over. "Code's is 972009," he said.

"Our wedding date?" Evie said.

Farley grinned. "You old romantic you."

"You'll hear mention of another video on Suds's tape," Evie said. "If you check out the laptop on the desk in the office you'll see what we were reacting to."

"What will I see?"

Suds grabbed the ball and ran with it. "You'll see me sitting on a chaise lounge with Jasmine Cox's feet across my lap. I'm pointing my personal weapon a Walther PPK. The ballistics will match up with the bullet the ME pulled from Jasmine's brain pan."

Evie interrupted. "I keep ballistics on all of our officers' personal weapons on file, in house. It's a policy Suds started when he was chief. I've been sitting on that information because of extenuating circumstances."

"Such as."

"The fact that Suds was doped senseless on the night of the murders. We found him incoherent in his apartment the next day. I was concerned. I had seen that kind of hangover before in rohypnol cases."

Farley started. "The date rape drug? Suds was raped?"

"All of my orifices are virginal, as far as I know," Suds said. "The late Todd Rudy, one of the corpses in Ames's office, also is a bartender at Murphy's Irish Bar. He slipped me a mickey on the night of the murder. My guess at the bequest of Ames or someone who was working for him."

"Why?"

"To put me at the scene at the time of the crime and to use my personal weapon to implicate me in a double homicide if the murder/suicide scenario collapsed."

Evie took a hand off. "Murder/suicide was my first impression. But two things jumped out."

"What's that?"

"Number one. Jasmine Cox is left-handed, but she was shot in the right temple."

Farley was a quick study. "Got it. And number two?"

Evie nodded. "Jasmine's body was found with a 9mm Ruger—at the fingertips of her right hand, incidentally. But ballistics confirmed that she was killed by a .380. She had bought the 9 a week or two earlier at a gun shop in Elizabethtown."

"So Suds was set up to be the fall-back patsy if the murder/suicide scenario faltered?"

Suds nodded. "That's right. The video you'll find on the laptop on Ames's desk neither proves nor disproves that I shot Jasmine. But it does show me lowering Ernest Flowers into a tubful of beer in Cox's master bathroom where he was found drowned to death."

Suds clawed through his hair with stiff fingers. "I don't know whether I'm culpable in either crime. But the video puts me at the scene. And it gets worse."

"How could it . . . possibly?" Farley asked.

Suds continued. "The weapon was out of my possession from July 21 until yesterday afternoon when I found it at a crime scene in Charleston, South Carolina. An almost identical scenario. An apparent murder/suicide staged with the bodies of Graham and Gerry Smith."

Linda Fontaine, who had been watching the exchange with the rapt attention of a spectator at center court of a tennis match, found her voice. "Sorry Evie. Haven't had a chance to tell you. Charleston PD checked in. The bullets are a match."

"Jesus," Joe Farley said. "You are afloat in a sea of shit, aren't ya?"

"Yeah. It's pretty shitty being me right now," Suds admitted.

"The lawyer we have in custody, Zach Dunkel. What's his role in all of this?"

Linda's smart phone dinged. She looked at the display and cleared her throat. "Think I can throw another monkey wrench in the murder scenario."

"What's that?"

"We just fingerprinted Zach Dunkel and I ran his prints. They match an unidentified set on the Ruger found at Jasmine's fingertips."

Suds shook his head. "Jesus. Don't know what to make of that."

"We'll ask Dunkel to explain that one," Farley said.

"I'm still processing why Dunkel was ready to kill us both," Evie said.

"He said something about staging the crime scene to suggest all four of us had died in a shootout," Suds said.

"What do we know about Dunkel?"

"We know that he was Jasmine Cox's attorney. We know that he had served Franklin Ames with divorce papers on her behalf."

"Well I guess it's time to sweat Zach Dunkel," Farley said.

He arose from his chair in the brewery conference room and led them back to Ames's office, where Farley conferred with one of the state troopers pawing over the crime scene.

Suds overheard snatches of the conversation. "Dunkel is en route to Dauphin County prison," the trooper said.

"Good, put him in an interrogation room and keep him there until I arrive. I'm going to conduct the interview personally."

The trooper nodded and activated the radio link clipped to a shoulder lanyard.

Meanwhile, Evie and Linda were conferring in an aside.

"You stay here and assist state police with processing the crime scene. This happened in our jurisdiction, so I want you to be our eyes and ears."

Linda nodded, turned, elbowed her way into a gaggle of state police who were conferring over the laptop on Franklin Ames's big desk.

"Hey Joe!" Evie called out. "OK if we sit in on the Zach Dunkel interview?"

Farley broke free of the gathering about the computer and joined them in the office doorway. "Few things to clear up here first, but sure. I'll meet you at Dauphin County Prison . . ." He looked at his wristwatch. "In an hour. Won't be a bad thing to let Dunkel sweat for a while. I'll tell the troopers patrolling the perimeter to let you pass. Why don't you grab a cup of coffee? Looks like you could use it."

Evie and Suds descended the back stairs from Franklin's office to the factory floor and exited the building through the same door they had entered. As they climbed into Evie's SUV, Suds noticed something.

"What happened to the white van?" he asked.

"Whoever was driving it musta left before the state police set up their cordon," Evie said.

"Curious."

She started the engine and waved at the state trooper who removed the sawhorse barrier blocking the employee parking lot. "There's a Denny's just down the road. It's open 24 hours. I could use some bacon and eggs," Evie said.

"I could use a stiff drink," Suds said.

"There's a bottle of Jim Beam in the pouch behind your front seat," Evie said.

"Isn't against the law to have an open bottle in car?"

"Ain't open yet and besides, I know the chief of police," Evie said.

Suds laughed. "So do I and in the Biblical sense."

ZACH DUNKEL IS IN THE WIND

With bacon, hash browns, and two eggs over easy in his belly, Suds was feeling more optimistic as they left the parking lot of the Denny's with Evie at the wheel of her Jeep.

"So we lost track of Zach Dunkel two days after the murder," Suds said.

"Yep. Linda found him on a passenger list out of HIA, final destination Grand Cayman. He was peripheral to the case so we let it go, figuring he'd come back eventually and we'd interview him."

"Looks like he made it back," Suds said.

"That's one of the things I love about you."

"What's that?"

"Your genius for stating the obvious."

"It's a gift. So do you think Joe Farley is going to clap me in irons when we arrive at Dauphin County Prison."

"That would be ironic," Evie said.

"How so?"

"A cop turning himself in at the prison on a murder rap."

"Hah. Hah. Sort of like a mortician driving himself to his own funeral."

"A grave undertaking, that," Evie agreed.

"We've got to take this act on the road," Suds said.

"We will. Just as soon as you get out of prison."

Suds took a deep breath. "You know this helps to deal with the aftershock."

He kissed his index finger and dotted Evie's nose as she drove.

"Gallows humor?"

"Maybe. But more than that. It's a connection. An affirmation that, you know, we aren't in this alone."

Evie teared up. "Yeah. I missed that . . . after you left. The conversation, I mean. Silence is one of the stages of grief but damn it gets lonely after a while."

"Me too. About Joe Farley."

"What about him?"

"He seemed too eager to give me a pass."

"You caught that did you?"

"What?"

"The tension between the two of us, me and Joe, I mean."

"My radar is particularly sensitive where you are involved."

"That's because Joe and I were involved, briefly, after you moved out."

"You mean after you threw me out."

"Whatever. I'm not trying to start a fight here. Just trying to explain."

Suds sucked it up. "I get it. 'Nough said."

The tension drained from Evie's shoulders. She always held it there. Tension drew her shoulders to her ears. It was not an attractive look. Made her neck disappear, which was a shame. She had a lovely neck.

"Joe was going through a rough patch in his marriage and I was dealing with Rufus . . . and you. We found some solace in each other for a while, a short while."

"Like I said, enough said."

Evie squeezed Suds's wrist. "Thanks."

"No thank you. For taking me back."

Evie squeezed a second time. "It was the right thing to do."

"For the both of us," Suds agreed.

"Sampson . . . and Rudy? How are you processing that?"

"I'm sorry we had to kill them, but I'm not sorry they are dead," Suds said

"Explain."

"If they weren't dead. We would be."

"What makes our lives more valuable?"

"We're the good guys."

"And who decided that?"

"Fate, I suppose. Nah. That's too glib. My life has been blessed with good luck. I have food. I have clothes. I have shelter. I have beer. I found you. I lost you. You forgave me. You took me back. I don't know, things for me just seem to turn out the way they should."

"What about Rufus?"

Tears stung Suds, eyes. His throat thickened. "There is that. But in a strange way his passing has brought us back together. We had drifted apart. Both of us more involved in being parents than in loving each other."

"Lemonade from lemons?"

"Really sour lemons." Suds took Evie's hand, the one she wasn't driving with. He squeezed. "And really sweet lemonade."

Evie pulled into the lot at Dauphin County Prison. She killed the engine. They alit and went inside. The corrections officer manning the front desk looked up from paperwork arrayed before him. "You Pinson and Ferguson?"

"That's right," Evie said.

"Capt. Farley said I should show you to the warden's office." The officer arose and ushered them through the door at his back, down a corridor to an open office door. Inside two men were conferring. One of them was Farley.

Farley turned as the CO knocked on the doorframe.

"Suds. Evie. Come on in," he said. "This is Mark Clemens. The assistant warden. He's letting me use his office. The shit has hit the fan."

They gathered in a huddle as if to discuss the next play.

"Zup?" Suds asked.

"Zach Dunkel escaped en route."

"How?" Evie asked.

"Trooper Foster came across an accident scene. An ancient Ford Econoline plowed into a road barrier on Route 322 with a man slumped over the wheel. Foster stopped to render assistance. Called it in on the radio. Approached the man in the van who, to make a long story short, tased him."

"Any description on the man?"

"Actually he tased him three or four times for good measure. Trooper Foster isn't making much sense right now. Whoever it was, apparently fled on foot taking Dunkel with him. The van was undriveable and the cruiser was left at the scene with Foster handcuffed to the steering wheel."

"You check with the cab services and Uber too see if there were any calls in that area?" Evie asked.

"Checking right now. We'll get a more thorough briefing once Foster clears his medical exam at the Harrisburg Hospital. He's pretty shook up right now."

"APB out on Dunkel?" Suds asked.

"Already done," Farley said.

"So now we wait," Evie said.

"I'd check the bus and train station and HIA while we wait," Suds said.

"On it already," Farley said.

"So now we wait," Suds agreed. "Could I have my iPhone back?" Suds asked.

Farley considered. Patted his pockets. Pulled out Suds's phone. "Tech guys have cloned it. You have no secrets."

Suds pocketed the phone. "Thanks."

"Can we do anything to help?" Evie asked.

"Nah. We've got it covered. Why don't the two of you go home. Get some rest. Come into PSP headquarters mid-morning for a thorough debriefing. And Suds . . ."

"Is this the part where you tell me not to leave town?"

Farley laughed. "You've been watching too many movies. This is the part where I tell you, you have a great woman there. You don't deserve her."

"You got that right," Suds said. He took Evie's hand, claiming ownership and submitting to it at the same time.

———

Evie stretched the shoulder belt across her chest and clicked it in place. Suds sat still staring in rapt attention at his iPhone.

"Aren't you going to buckle up?" Evie asked.

"In a sec."

"Come on Suds. Let me in on the secret."

"What secret?"

"The one that has you chuckling to yourself."

"I don't chuckle."

"Perhaps not. But you've the look of a Cheshire cat."

"Everything has disappeared except my mouth? I'd have my vision checked if I were you."

"You know what I mean."

"I bugged Franklin's car. Not the Subaru. The company car he's been driving while the Forester is out of commission."

"Bugged it?"

"Yeah. A tracking device. Placed under the rear fender. 'Bout a week ago."

"Whatever for?"

"Didn't like his demeanor. Thought I could trust him, but he'd turned, I don't know, ginky."

"If that's a police term, I'm unfamiliar with it."

"Just got this vibe. Like he wasn't what he seemed to be."

"What's your gut telling you now?"

"Other than I put too much hot sauce on Denny's hash browns, it's telling me we ought to drive to the Raddison next to the HIA."

"The airport hotel?"

"Yep. That's where Franklin's car is right now. It's a red Ford Fusion."

Evie sighed. "I get the sense that maybe we're about to surveil."

"Yeah. So."

Evie undid her shoulder belt. Opened her car door.

"Where are you going?"

"Inside to pee. I never surveil on a full bladder."

Suds opened his door to. "Good point," he said. "I could get rid of some of Denny's coffee."

Suds finished before Evie did and returned to her Jeep in the parking lot. He was scrolling through menus on his iPhone when Evie returned.

"Whatcha doin'?"

"Checking on flights out of HIA. There's one leaving tomorrow morning at 7 A.M. bound for Charlotte, which is a hub for the Caribbean, specifically Grand Cayman."

"You planning to take me along?"

"Ha. Ha. I was just thinking that maybe since Zach Dunkel absconded to Grand Cayman once, he'd do it again."

"Want me to have Linda check to see if Zach Dunkel is on a passenger list?"

"Sure. Couldn't hurt."

"What airline?"

"American."

Evie wrestled her phone out of her purse. Called Linda. Told her to check American flights out of HIA with connections to Grand Cayman. Listened for a while. Hung up and announced Linda's on it."

"Anything new from the crime scene?"

"Yeah. Linda says it looks like the video of you with Jasmine and Ernie was doctored."

"Doctored? How so?"

"I don't. Edited. Photoshopped. Whatever you call it. Bottom line is things may not be as they seem."

"That's good. Right?"

"Yes that's good."

"Well let's get going then. To the Raddison."

Evie buckled up. Started the engine and rammed the Jeep into gear. "Want to stop for doughnuts?"

"Don't be such a cliché."

They found the red Fusion in the flyaway lot behind the Raddison. Evie badged the night desk clerk. Found that no one by the name of Franklin Ames or Zach Dunkel had checked in.

"What do you think, Suds?" She asked.

"Can you check the license numbers of vehicles in your fly-away lot against your registration list?" Suds asked the clerk.

"Sure."

Evie consulted the notebook she always carried in her back pocket. Rattled off the PA registration. It took the clerk a couple of minutes. "License plate matches up with a fly-away reservation for Miles Karfan," he said.

"Odd name," Evie observed. Then she looked at Suds.

"Someone just walk over your grave?" she asked. "Your face. You look like you just kissed your sister on the mouth by accident."

"I don't have a sister. And I don't make mistakes," Suds said. "What room is Miles Karfan in?"

"One-twenty-one," the clerk replied.

Suds and Evie returned to her Jeep. "Is this the part where we surveil?"

"Would you prefer knocking on the door and getting a shotgun greeting."

"Might be a blast."

"Stop it."

"Just trying to lighten the mood."

Evie deposited her Jeep in a parking space with a clear view of Room 121. They took a chance. Walked the perimeter, satisfying themselves that the only way out of the room was through the front door. A midget couldn't escape through the bathroom window to the rear. So Evie and Suds settled into her Jeep to wait and watch.

"Miles Karfan. I could tell it struck a bell," Evie said.

"It did," Suds admitted.

"Care to enlighten me?"

"Prepare to be enlightened."

"Asshole."

"Miles Karfan is the alternate executor of Franklin Ames's last will and testament."

"The one that makes you CEO in the event of his death?"

"That's the one. It also makes me the guardian of Alex, in the event of the deaths of Graham and Gerry Smith and Franklin Ames."

"So Miles Karfan is a pseudonym for . . ."

"Not a pseudonym. An anagram."

"What's an anagram?" Evie asked.

"'Bout six pounds."

"Huh?"

"Nothing. Old joke."

"You're an old guy."

"Thanks. Rearrange the letters for Miles Karfan and you get . . ."

Evie furrowed her brow. "I give up."

Suds did the math for her. "Franklin Ames," he said.

She frowned. Working it out. "OK. So?"

"So I think Franklin Ames aimed to make me the fall guy in four murders, kill me, fake his own death and leave his estate and life insurance policy . . ."

"To himself!"

"Eureka!"

FINISHING WITH A BANG!

Following the rules of stakeout etiquette, Suds and Evie relieved each other while relieving themselves. Suds glanced at his wristwatch as he returned toward the Jeep after his second pee—5:39 A.M. The clerk told him the shuttle left for the airport at 6. He was cutting it thin, but a full bladder has no conscience.

As he reached for the handle on the passenger side door he noticed that Evie was not behind the wheel, and he heard movement from behind. The sounds of shoe soles scuffing on gravel. Before he could turn, he felt something cold and hard press into the back of his neck.

"Don't move!"

Cold hands groped at this waist and yanked the Walther from its holster.

"Evie is waiting for you inside."

"Why?"

"That's the ten million question. I guess you're due an answer. Before you die. The both of you."

Suds walked stiff legged, with the barrel of a gun pressing hard in the small of his back, toward Room 121.

"Push the door open. It isn't locked."

Suds complied. Stepped inside the room. Evie was trussed up like a calf at a rodeo, prone on one of two queen-sized beds in the Raddison flyaway. Couple of turns of duct tape secured her ankles and wrists. Her purse was propped against the pillows.

"Sit on the edge of the bed next to your wife."

Suds turned and sat, giving him the opportunity to observe his assailant. Franklin Ames.

Suds wasn't particularly surprised. "Where's Zach?"

"Off on a mission that doesn't involve you."

"Care to explain?"

Franklin dug into his pants pocket with his left hand. Extracted a pocket-knife, which he tossed to Suds. The abrupt gesture caught Suds off guard. He fumbled the catch and the pocketknife tumbled onto the bed beside him.

"Cut your wife free," Franklin said.

Suds picked up the pocketknife. Opened the blade with thick fingers. He turned, knelt beside Evie and sawed through the duct tape on first her ankles and then her wrists. He grabbed Evie's right arm and helped her to a seated position on the bed with her feet on the floor facing Franklin.

"Sorry Suds. Son of a bitch got the drop on me. Musta dozed off for a minute or two and woke up with a gun jammed in my ear," Evie said.

Suds put his arm around her shoulders. "It's OK. He did the same thing to me. Careless."

He looked at Franklin. "Ball's in your court."

"And the score is 40-love," Franklin said, building on the allusion.

"What gives?" Suds said.

"Zach's my lover. Soon to be my husband and Alex will be our son."

Suds shook his head like a boxer trying to see his way clear of a right cross. "Mr. and Mr. Miles Karfan, I presume."

Franklin Ames studied Suds's face, looking, Suds' supposed, for signs of pity or disgust. Suds refused to react and Franklin moved on.

"That's right. Zach and I had something in common other than we both fucked Jasmine. So did Boyd Porter. The slut. Bullet to the brain was too good for her."

"So you're gay," Evie said. "What's the big deal?"

"Bi-sexual, actually. But it would be a big deal in the Navy reserve and on the brewery floor. We're not all that far removed from don't ask don't tell.

Particularly with that asshole in the Oval Office now. And queer beer? That's what they'd call it. I couldn't stand that, no way."

"So what's the end game?" Suds asked.

"Wouldn't want you to go unenlightened to your great reward, whatever that might be."

"So tell me."

Ames glanced at his wristwatch. "I'll give you a few more minutes. Here's what's going to happen. The bodies of two men are going to be found in my burned-out Forester on a remote road in Perry County. It will look like they died in a horrific, fiery, alcohol-involved collision with a big oak tree. But once investigators get around to a closer look they'll determine they died of gunshot wounds. The bullets will match your handgun."

"So who are to two poor stiffs in your burned out Forester?" Suds asked, chocking back his fear, eager to keep the conversation going for as long as possible as the clock ran out on his life, Evie's too.

"Two patsies I picked up at Stallions," Franklin said, referring to Harrisburg's notorious gay bar. "I've had them on ice for a couple of weeks in a cooler at the brewery."

"The accident site is near my cabin in the woods," Franklin continued. "The locals know both of us because it was our sanctuary. The bodies will carry papers identifying the dead men as Zach Dunkel and Franklin Ames. Your body will be found here in the bathroom. Evie's on the bed. Staged as a classic murder/suicide."

Franklin patted the waistband of his trousers where Suds's Walther now resided. "I'll use the Walther. Suds's suicide note will express your deep regret at killing me and Zach."

"How many times can you go to that well?"

"So far it has served me well."

"And with me out of the picture, you will become the executor and custodian of your own estate and you, Zach and Alex will live happily ever after on Grand Cayman as the Miles Karfan family."

"That's the gist of it, although we may move around," Franklin agreed.

"Mike Weisse?" Suds asked.

"A last-minute wrinkle, facilitated by Zach. Weisse's alliance with Johnny Lewis and my late wife muddled my plans. But in the end, he turned out to be useful, call it a confluence of interests. We both wanted Graham and Gerry Smith dead, but for entirely different reasons. I was more than happy to pretend I welcomed his presence in my business, so he'd take care of some other business."

"Murdering the Smiths so you could claim custody of your son," Evie interjected.

Franklin smiled. "Actually I did that deed myself, but Weisse is a handy scapegoat."

Franklin laid his .38 down on a dresser, as he drew Suds's Walther from the waistband of his trousers.

Suds could see the resolve build in Franklin's eyes.

"You might want to rethink things," Evie said.

"Why?"

"I figured out the Miles Karfan anagram a couple of days ago, included it in a summary of the Derry Twp. Police Department's investigation into the deaths of Jasmine and Ernie. There's hard copy in my purse and it's backed up on my work and home computers. If we turn up dead, I'm sure Linda Fontaine will share the file with the Charleston PD."

Franklin licked his lips. "You're bluffing."

"One way to find out. Let me open my purse."

"So you can pull out your back-up piece and shoot me? I don't think so. Toss your purse over here, I'll see for myself."

With Franklin's attention centered on Evie as she picked up her purse, Suds made his move. Lowering his shoulder he sprang toward Franklin who reacted by steeping back and sticking out his foot. Suds tripped and careened face down onto the second king-sized bed. Franklin swiveled and pointed Suds's Walther at the center of Suds's back. "On your feet!"

As Suds regained his feet, Evie's hand darted into her purse and she withdrew her hide-away piece, a neat .22 caliber automatic. Anticipating that development, Franklin retreated behind Suds, using him as a shield. "What we have here is a Mexican standoff," he said.

Suds could guess what was coming next. He went limp. Dropped dead weight to the floor. Franklin yanked the trigger as Suds fell. Bang! Suds felt a searing burn across his right shoulder.

Evie's little .22 made a lesser noise.

Bang!

Bang!

Bang!

Bang!

Suds couldn't imagine how Evie could have missed, but Franklin somehow stayed on his feet. A .22 kills slowly. Not much stopping power. The bullets rattle around, the wounded bleed out. Franklin brought his .38 around, intending to shoot Evie before she could shoot him, again.

Suds interceded. He kicked Franklin's feet out from under him. He toppled to the ground.

Cat quick Evie, leapt from the bed. Kicked the .38 from Franklin's grasp. Suds regained his feet, bleeding from a graze wound to the shoulder. Evie joined him at his side, threw her arm around his waist for mutual support as the two of them watched Franklin Ames die.

CHILD'S PLAY

Alex Smith was scared. "I want Mommy," he told the duty nurse, Laura Fisher.

Laura's eyes stung. She had been Alex's go-to nurse for two weeks now and had developed an attachment to the little boy. The shift supervisor had shared the news. Gerri Smith was dead. So was her husband, Graham. Administrators were still arguing over who would break the news and who would pay the bills.

Alex was better. Much better. The bone marrow transplant worked. His numbers were normal, or the next thing to it. Laura could tell the little boy felt better. His eyes were clear. He was engaged with the medical staff. Less likely to cling and less likely to take whatever they said to him at face value. Trudging had been replaced by sprinting. You needed a net to corral the little guy.

Alex was perched on the edge of his hospital bed, wearing distressed jeans with slits at the knees and a long-sleeved Ninja turtle T, featuring Donatello. New Balance sneakers in blue completed his ensemble. The outfit bespoke the affluence of his parents. But death does dead people no favors. Graham and Gerry Smith were as impoverished as the lowliest riffraff in the county morgue.

Turmoil roiled Laura Fisher's soul. The kindest thing to do punched the legally correct thing to do smack in the nose. Should she serve Alex's interests or her own? And just tell the little boy in the kindest of terms that his parents were dead. Or should she keep quiet until instructed otherwise? The demarcation between those two points was clear. Laura couldn't lie. So she evaded.

"How are you feeling, sweetie?"

"Wanna go home," Alex said. "Wanna see Mommy."

"The doctor needs to check you out, first. Make sure you're ready."

"I'm ready. Right now! Where's Mommy?"

Laura told the truth. "She's not here."

There was a commotion at the door. Shoes squeaked on freshly waxed tile. Janette Engle, the hospital administrator swept in the room, followed by a suave man in a gray, pinstriped business suit wearing tasseled loafers. A faux handkerchief was tucked in the front pocket of his jacket.

Janette prided herself on remembering the names of staff without looking at their nametags. "Hey Lauren," she said as she entered the room.

Discretion dictated Laura's response. She opted not to correct her boss.

"Hey Mrs. Engle, I was just about to check Alex's vitals, but I already can tell he's doing much better."

"That's good. That's good," Engle said, all business. "This is Zach Karfan. He's a lawyer representing Alex's biological father. Mr. Karfan has a court order releasing Alex to his care."

Karfan nodded somberly at Laura and approached Alex's bed with the stealth of a cat at a bird feeder. There was something feline about Karfan. He rubbed Laura the wrong way even though she liked cats.

"Hey Alex. Your father has asked me to collect you. We're going to ride on an airplane. What do you think about that?"

"Which father? The one who art in heaven?"

Laura could tell that the question put Zach Karfan on his ear. He didn't know what to say.

"Alex has spent a lot of time in church," Laura said. "His mother says that a lot and he's a little magpie."

"What's a magpie, Miss Laura?" Alex asked.

"A smart little bird that repeats things that it hears," Laura said.

"I'm not a bird," Alex said, kicking his feet against the side of the bed.

Karfan sat down beside Alex on the bed. "Does he know yet?"

Jeanette Engle fielded the question. "We've been discussing who should tell him."

Karfan took a deep breath. "Guess I should handle this one. Hey buddy. I don't know how to tell you this, but your Mommy and Daddy are both with the angels now."

"What's that mean?"

Laura Fisher stepped into the breach. She knelt before the little boy. Took both of his hands in hers. "There is no easy way to say this, Sweetie, but both your parents are dead."

Alex knew about death. He'd be fighting it for months now. The little boy studied Laura's face. Saw the sadness there and began to cry. Mostly because Laura had started to cry. He hopped off the bed and wrapped his arms around Laura's neck. "Can I come to live with you?"

That made Laura cry even louder.

Zach Karfan snatched a couple of tissues from the box on Alex's roll away tray. He shoved the tissues into Laura Fisher's hands. "See to yourself, nurse. I'll see to my son."

"Your son?" Laura snuffed.

"That's what the court order says.

ZACH DUNKEL MISSES HIS FLIGHT

Harrison Ford studied Zach Dunkel's picture. Longish hair, expertly coiffed, deep tan, an aquiline nose. Chocolate eyes.

Harry slid the picture back into his jacket pocket. His ticket for Flight 279 to Dulles was his pass to the departure concourse. He'd expense it to Suds Ferguson. Suds would bitch about it, but he'd pay up, eventually.

Charleston PD Lieutenant Jarrod Fisher was stationed on Harry's six. Fisher had badged his way past the TSA. Fisher elbowed Harry in the ribs.

"What?"

"Flight's due to board in 15 minutes. I haven't seen a suave man holding a little boy's hand, have you?"

Zach and Alex Karfan were ticketed passengers on Flight 279, Charleston to Dulles. Linda Fontaine had ferreted out their itinerary. Plan was they'd join Miles Karfan for Flight 662, Dulles to Grand Cayman that afternoon.

Harry and Fisher aimed to spoil that plan.

"Be patient," Harry said. "If I were on the lam, I wouldn't show up early. I'd hang back, scope the crowd. Plane at the last possible minute."

"You sure Dunkel has no idea that Franklin Ames is dead?"

274

"Police have thrown a blanket over it. But, no. I'm not sure. They could have had some fail-safe in place. A confirming phone call or text. That sort of thing."

"So we wait?"

"Don't know what else to do."

Down the concourse an airline attendant, a pretty young woman in a crisp uniform, pleated trousers, walking shoes and United Airlines blouse, pushed a wheelchair along at a brisk pace. Trailing behind her was a pale young boy, five or so years old.

In the wheelchair slumped an old man wrapped in blankets. One encircled his lower legs and torso. Another shrouded his neck and shoulders. The young boy made Harry pay attention. "You watching this?" he asked Fisher, nodding toward the procession moving toward them.

"Yeah. We'll hover if they wheel into the departure lounge."

As they neared, Harry heard the attendant say: "Don't you worry Mr. DeBrunner, I'll get you to your flight on time. The crew is ready. You'll get priority seating." Over her shoulder to the little boy, she said: "Come on sweetie. Your plane is waiting."

They steamed right past the Flight 279 departure lounge and continued along the concourse at a brisk pace. The little boy struggled to keep up.

"Does that look like Alex Smith?"

"Who. The boy? Dunno. Only saw him once and just for a moment. One little kid looks pretty much like another at that age."

"Still worth checking out, don't you think? Divide and conquer?" Fisher asked.

"Not a bad idea. I'll go. You stay."

Harry hurried after the old man in the wheelchair. It took a half jog to catch up 100 yards or so down the concourse. The attendant wheeled the chair into the departure lounge for Flight 794, service to Charlotte. Harry lingered in the concourse outside the departure lounge as the old man handed his boarding pass to a female attendant behind the desk.

Harry drew close enough to eavesdrop. "How are you feeling Mr. DeBrunner?"

"As well as can be expected," the old man said. His voice was breathy as if every syllable was an ordeal.

"We will board you in a minute or two. You can wait next to the gate."

She handed the boarding passes back to the old man and his attended wheeled him to the gate. "Do you want me to wait with you, Mr. DeBrunner?" she asked.

"I think I can handle it from here. Thanks Jeannie," the old man said.

Jeannie smiled and squeaked away on rubber-soled shoes.

Harry approached the man and the boy from behind. "Hey Alex," he called out.

The little boy wheeled around.

"You feeling better since your operation?" Harry asked.

The little boy studied his shoes. Obviously schooled in stranger danger. But in a tiny voice, he followed his manners. "Yes. Thank you," he said.

A that moment a flight attendant emerged from the flyaway. "We're ready to board you, Mr. DeBrunner," he said.

Harry was already on his phone. "Hey Jarrod, shake a leg. Flight 794 to Charlotte. It's them. Shake a leg!"

To the flight attendant, he said. "Not so fast, please. This man is flying under a false name. He's a wanted fugitive, escaped police custody in Harrisburg, Pennsylvania."

"This is preposterous!" the old man said. His voice was strong now. No evidence of wheeze. "This man has presented no credentials. I am a ticketed passenger. I demand that you seat me and my grandson, Jameson, immediately."

"Mr. DeBrunner is right," the attendant said.

Jarrod Fisher arrived in a rush. He badged the flight attendant and knelt on one knee next to the little boy. "What's your name son?" he asked.

"Alex Smith," the little boy repeated.

"Gotcha!" Harry exulted.

"Fuck!" Zach Dunkel said, arising effortlessly from his wheelchair. "I take it you've arrested Franklin."

Harry didn't sugar coat. "Franklin Ames is dead. Killed in the commission of a crime."

Dunkel flopped back down in the wheelchair and wept.

ZACH DUNKEL COMES CLEAN

Wednesday, September 26, 2018

Zach Dunkel didn't look at all suave in prison orange. He'd been behind bars for less than a month, but his Grand Cayman tan already had retreated to an unhealthy sallow under harsh prison florescence. His formerly razor-cut hair was shaggy and his eyes sunken as he settled into a folding chair on the far side of six inches of bulletproof glass in the visitors' room at Dauphin County Prison.

The correction officer, who had escorted Dunkel from his cell, nodded at Suds and Evie. "Take as much time as you want. The warden is OK with it," the CO said, his voice muffled in crystalline armor. He closed the door behind him.

Suds and Evie huddled on the other side of the glass stuffed shoulder to shoulder twixt the privacy walls of the cubicle.

"I'm talking to you because the judge says I have to," Dunkel said. "It's part of my plea deal. One charge, felony three, of conspiracy to commit a capital crime, three to five years, but only if I elocute, first to you and then in open court. What do you want to know?"

"Did I kill anyone?" Suds asked.

Dunkel's smile was ironic. "You mean other than Sampson and Todd. Not to mention Franklin, you sons of bitches?"

"Self defense. Don't expect us to feel guilty about that," Suds said.

"Actually, I do feel guilty. I always do when I have to put my life ahead of another," Evie said.

"Wow! A police officer who understands nuance."

"Sarcasm forgiven," Evie said, aiming at establishing rapport. And succeeding.

"Touché.

"So what's the answer? Did I kill either Jasmine or Ernie?" Suds said.

"Sort of," Dunkel said.

"What's that mean?"

"This is hearsay, mind you, second-hand through Franklin."

Dunkel's eyes teared up. "You must think he was a monster. Franklin did it for me. He did it for Alex."

"You sure he didn't do it to avoid being outed and to protect his own self-interests? I have a hard time seeing Franklin Ames as a martyr," Suds said. "He framed me for murder and he was complicit in orphaning an innocent little boy. Don't ask me to shed tears over Franklin Ames."

Vitriol cleared Dunkel's tears. "You're a sexual racist just like all the rest. Afraid to countenance alternate lifestyles. That's why Franklin and I stayed closeted. It's just easier that way."

Suds half rose. "My concern is for the boy. I don't care who you stick your dick into as long as it's not him."

Evie laid a calming hand on Suds's forearm. He sat back down. "Easy boys. Play nice," she said.

Dunkel snuffed snot and wiped tears. Crocodile tears in Suds's estimation. "We're bi-sexual. Not pederasts. You asshole. I'll play ball cause I have to, but I won't play nice. You're a bastard, but not a murderer by Franklin's account. He told me that you put Flowers in the beer spa, but Rudy held his head under until he drowned."

"And Jasmine?" Evie asked.

"Franklin told me that he did the deed himself. His rationale? She shot first and missed. He didn't miss."

"Nor would he at point-blank range," Suds said, dismissively.

"How did three men escape the house in the time it took Dickie Cox to make it down the hall to his mother's bedroom?" Evie wanted to know.

"Good question. I never asked. My guess is that Rudy muscled Suds down the back stairs and out through the garage well before Franklin shot Jasmine."

"So Ames was alone with his wife and sprinted down the back stairs before Dickie arrived on the scene," Evie said.

"As good a guess as any," Dunkel agreed. "Like I said. I wasn't there."

"So why use my gun to kill Jasmine and leave hers on the floor beside her?" Suds asked.

"Franklin's idea. He wanted leverage to keep you off-balance. If the murder/suicide scenario didn't hold together, he wanted to leave a bread trail leading to you."

"And scenario failed because Jasmine is left-handed and was shot in the right temple and who the hell commits suicide by drowning themselves in a bathtub full of beer?" Evie said.

"Yeah. Franklin missed the left-handed thing. We both knew it, but in the heat of the moment. He forgot. And the beer bath? It was his ultimate fuck you to his disloyal subject."

"Death by beer. Pretty extreme. Tell me what Flowers did to deserve that," Suds said.

Dunkel took a deep breath. "Ernie had a hard-on for Jasmine from day one. They met for the first time when he drafted their pre-nup. It was his idea for Franklin to give Jasmine the 200 shares of stock as a wedding gift. It gave Franklin pause, but he relented when Ernie promised to insert a fidelity clause in the pre-nup, requiring Jasmine to surrender her shares for moral turpitude should the two divorce."

Dunkel paused. Laughed. "Ernie never inserted the clause. Told Franklin he would and just plain didn't. Jasmine had him wrapped up tight. Franklin didn't read the pre-nup carefully enough. Trusted Ernie and signed it."

Evie cleared her throat. "How did you and Ames . . ."

Dunkel saw her discomfort. Made it easy for her. "Hook up?"

Evie nodded.

Dunkels eyed glowed. "I bat both ways. Jasmine was a good fuck from either side of the plate. She came to me six months ago. Had me review her pre-nup and asked me to prepare divorce papers. She asked how she could sell her 200 shares of Hop Central. My ears perked up at that because I also represent Johnny Lewis and I knew he was looking at ways to force the sale of the brewery so he could cash in on his investment."

"So you went running to Lewis and the two of you lined up enough stock-holders to sell the brewery without Ames's consent."

Dunkel nodded. "That's right. And with Jasmine's enthusiastic consent."

"You didn't answer the question. Franklin Ames. How did you . . ." Evie hesitated and came up with the vernacular, "hook up with him?"

"I'm getting to that. Franklin didn't trust Boyd Porter."

"And with good reason," Suds interjected.

Dunkel frowned at the interruption. "Franklin was certain that Porter was lying. That Jasmine was cheating on him. So he followed Porter . . . to my apartment and interrupted a ménage a trios among the three of us."

"What three?" Suds asked.

Dunkel sighed in exasperation. "Come on Suds, concentrate! Don't make me spell it all out."

"Spell it out," Evie said. "I'm lost, too."

"OK for you slow learners. Franklin broke into my bedroom unannounced and caught Boyd fucking Jasmine while I was fucking Boyd. Franklin tried to play the part of the outraged cuckold, but his heart wasn't in it. And I could tell he was aroused, more by the man-on-man than man-on-woman. He stormed out demanding a divorce. I called him the next day to apologize and to discuss the terms of the divorce. We met for lunch and . . ."

"One thing led to another?" Jasmine said, eager to avoid further detail.

"That's right."

"So, you became a double agent, ostensibly working for Lewis, Jasmine . . ."

"And don't forget Ernie. He had already approached Lewis about forcing the sale of Hop Central," Dunkel said.

"So you ratted out Ernie and Franklin killed him and Jasmine, too."

Flowers nodded.

"What about Mike Weisse and the Smiths?"

"A happy confluence of interests. Weisse wanted the Smiths dead because they were about to give him up to the feds and Ernie wanted them dead so he could get Alex."

"So Weisse killed the Smiths?"

"Don't know. Hell Franklin could have done it himself, for that matter. When I asked him he told me 'some things are better left unsaid.'"

"About that," Suds said. "Why leave my gun at the Smiths' murder scene?"

"Another way to ball you up in the conspiracy. Franklin figured you'd be so confused that you'd lose sight of his real purpose."

"Which was to live happily ever after with you and Alex on Grand Cayman while managing his brewery interest from afar?"

"Something like that," Dunkel agreed.

"Would that have satisfied you?" Evie asked.

Dunkel's eyes softened. "How very nice of you to show some empathy. I don't know if I am cut out for domestic bliss, but I was willing to try. For Franklin's sake."

"For goodness sake, I'm glad you won't live happily ever after," Suds said.

EPILOGUE

WIDE SMILES ALL AROUND

Suds still was not feeling entirely comfortable, sitting behind the late Franklin Ames's desk with the brewery workers scurrying about their appointed tasks below. Everything seemed back to normal. Only it wasn't. Jan Murphy buzzed him on the intercom. "Harrison Ford is here to see you."

Suds had kept Jan on as his personal secretary. She knew where all the bodies were buried. And she had gone to bat for him at the inquest. Testified that she had suspected for years that Franklin Ames was gay but closeted tightly because life had taught him that gays guys finish last. No queer beer for him. It wouldn't look good on the label.

"Send him in."

Harry didn't bother knocking. Suds smiled and waved him to a chair. He punched the intercom button. "Hey Jan. Have Sammie send us up two flights of our scratch beers. I want to wow a Bud man."

"Will do, boss."

"I can tell the boss thing gets your rocks off," Harry said, settling into a chair.

"Only Evie gets my rocks off."

"I've heard that said," Harry agreed.

"So. Mike Weisse?"

"Protesting wildly to the murder wrap. But Johnny Lewis ratted him out. Said Franklin Ames and Mike Weisse had colluded on the Smith murders."

"Why?"

"Gerry Smith had contacted the FBI, said she was willing to testify that her husband was complicit in a money laundering scheme through the church. She was ready to name names."

"So she had Weisse's balls in a vise."

Ford nodded. "Their deaths silenced an FBI witness against Weisse."

"And?"

"And facilitated Ames's claiming guardianship of his son."

"So. Ames made me the executor of his will . . ."

"To set you up on a murder charge and facilitate his leaving his estate to himself."

"So I fell into a pile of shit and . . .

Ford sniffed. "Came up smelling like beer."

The intercom buzzed. Mrs. Ferguson is here to see you."

Evie came into the office. She was holding the hand of a small boy.

"Harry. I'd like you to meet our son. Alex Pinson Ferguson."

Evie's smile was a mile wide.

So was Suds's heart.

ABOUT THE AUTHOR

Wade Fowler is a retired journalist with more than 40 years of experience as a reporter and editor with *The Patriot-News* (Harrisburg) and *The News-Sun* (Newport, PA), *Duncannon Record* (Duncannon PA) and *Perry County Times* (New Bloomfield, PA). He has won numerous Keystone Press Awards and served one term as president of the Pennsylvania Society of Newspaper Editors. His novels include: *The Compass Island Incident, The Honey Trap*, and *Rising Sun Descending* (Sunbury Press all).